The White House
Pantry Murder

Also by Elliott Roosevelt:

Murder and the First Lady
The Hyde Park Murder
Murder at Hobcaw Barony

The White House Pantry Murder

Elliott Roosevelt

St. Martin's Press
New York

Library of Congress Cataloging-in-Publication Data

Roosevelt, Elliott, 1910–
    The White House pantry murder.

    1. Roosevelt, Eleanor, 1884–1962—Fiction.
I. Title.
PS3535.0549W5   1987   813'.54   86-26249
ISBN 0-312-00202-5

First Edition
10 9 8 7 6 5 4 3 2 1

As always and forever,
to Patty

I would like to express my thanks to my friend the novelist William Harrington who has been my mentor in the craft of mystery writing and has given me invaluable assistance with the First Lady mysteries.

—*Elliott Roosevelt*

The White House
Pantry Murder

1

Later—ten and fifteen years later—Mrs. Roosevelt would find it difficult to reconstruct those weeks, much less to believe events had occurred that she could never recount, except to that very small group in whom she trusted without reservation. In twelve years in the White House, she was privy to many secrets. From history, she believed, one should keep very few secrets; but some things she would never tell, even to people who thought they knew all she had to tell. Other secrets she would confide, charily, to a select few.

The White House. The public has never understood this, but the White House is appreciated by its tenants, if it is appreciated at all, for the honor of living there, not for its luxury. The handsome rooms on the first floor—the ones the public sees on tours—are *public* rooms: show-case rooms for state occasions, otherwise a museum. Well and good. But the public, if it could see the private apartments on the second floor, might be dismayed to discover that the First Family lives in a suite of awkwardly connected rooms furnished chiefly with what they have brought from home. Only half a dozen rooms are really private, and the family sitting room is actually a part of the west hallway.

None of this counted much with Mrs. Roosevelt—or with the President, for that matter. They were content with the White House. After all, as the President might have said, no one condemned them to live there. All he ever complained of was the food, and that was not a function of the mansion itself but of the housekeeper Mrs. Roosevelt employed to command the kitchen. The White House was not an unpleasant place to live, and the Roosevelts had made a home of it. They'd had time enough.

Until December of 1941. That was when everything changed.

As Mrs. Roosevelt contemplated Christmas 1941, she was depressed as she had never before been in her White House years. The war news was alarmingly bad. Hundreds of thousands—in time it would be millions—of young men were being processed hurriedly into the armed forces, and there could be no question but that many of them would die in their country's service. Her own sons were going to war; and, simply as a matter of statistics, she had to anticipate that at least one might be killed or injured. How could all the good things this presidency had achieved—and for which she had hoped it would be remembered—possibly survive the ordeal the nation now faced?

She would always remember that December as a time of darkness—real darkness, that is, not just darkness of mood. The days were the shortest of the year, the nights longest. The weather was cold and gray. What was gloomier, the White House had been enveloped in grim wartime security. The windows were fitted with blackout curtains. Anti-aircraft guns were mounted on the roof and on the grounds. Soldiers patrolled the fence. (It was only because the President had specifically forbidden it that army tanks did not guard the gates.) Gas masks in khaki canvas bags hung from their straps on the furniture everywhere in the house. They were urged to carry them about, though no one did. Her independence of movement was circumscribed. She had been accustomed to shaking off her Secret Service escort and traveling as she wished. No more. Now the agents insisted she must have their protection—and in this the President concurred.

The First Lady could not look forward to Christmas, knowing that none of her children could come home. For Franklin it would be a difficult time for yet another reason—his mother had died in September, and this would be his first Christmas without her. (He still wore a black crepe armband on his left arm, the sign of his formal mourning.) Distressing as holidays with her formidable mother-in-law had sometimes been, she had been able nevertheless to look forward to having the family together at Hyde Park, with a fire burning in the great fireplace, stockings hung, a tree . . . This year, even Christmas would not bring relief from gloom and tension.

She hid her feelings and showed a face of resolute self-confidence. She was no less energetic; indeed, she reached out for new responsibilities, as if she possessed reserves of energy that had never yet been tapped. As the President shouldered the heavy new burdens of wartime leadership, she searched for ways to do her share, and she found them.

In private, though, for a time, her optimism failed her. More than once during those weeks, she shut herself for a little while in her room; and there, in small moments of privacy, Mrs. Roosevelt wept.

Monday evening, December 22—

"Tonight?" exclaimed Mrs. Roosevelt. "But they were not due until tomorrow."

The President nodded. He had sucked in his cheeks,

and the corners of his mouth turned down slightly. He shrugged and pulled smoke through his holder, into his mouth and deep into his body. Then he nodded again and let a faint smile replace the expression of mild annoyance with which he had made his announcement.

"They've been at sea ten days, you remember." He shrugged again. "They decided to leave the battleship at Hampton Roads and are flying into Washington."

"Then they will be here for dinner!"

"Something very informal," he said.

"For how many?"

"Oh, I should think fifteen. Maybe twenty."

"I don't see how Mrs. Nesbitt can be ready."

The President's smile broadened. "Tell her she'll have to be ready," he said. "Tell her she'll just have to set her schedule ahead a few hours."

"But *Churchill!* He requires . . ."

"Brandy. Cigars. (I trust he'll have brought those with him.) A hearty meal. None of Henrietta's tuna sandwiches. And tell her to send people upstairs to be sure his rooms are ready."

Mrs. Roosevelt sighed. "Yes, of course."

The President glanced at his watch. "I'll be leaving for the airport soon. Will you join me, Babs?"

"With dinner for fifteen to prepare, on an hour's notice? Really!"

"That's what you pay Henrietta for. Give her her marching orders and come along to greet the Prime Minister."

She shook her head. "I shall greet him here. I have a feeling that this is not the first time he will completely abandon his schedule and impose a new one on us at a moment's notice."

The President laughed. "According to Elliott, who visited him at Chequers, you recall, Winston is more royal

than the King. Let Henrietta remember that. I won't
have the Grand Alliance broken up over some household
idiosyncrasy."

She recognized him, of course, as soon as he stepped
through the door. He was unmistakable: short, rotund
(cherubic, some said), florid, the sandy-red hair almost
gone from the top of his solid head, jaunty little bow tie
a bit askew, heavy watch chain draped over his ample
belly, fat cigar clamped between two fingers of his left
hand—not an especially prepossessing figure at an instant's glance, yet a man whose calm, confident power
required but a moment to make itself evident even to a
casual observer.

"I believe I have the honor of addressing Mrs. Roosevelt," he said before anyone could introduce them.

"Mr. Churchill," she said. "Welcome to America. Welcome to the White House."

"Thank you. And please allow me to present my col-
league Lord Beaverbrook, our Minister of Supply."

She smiled and greeted Beaverbrook—the Canadian
millionaire who had transplanted himself to London,
there to occupy the center of British journalism and political life. For all the years he had spent in England, Beaverbrook somehow retained the look of a North
American: something indefinable in his style, in his
bland, uncommunicative face, that set him apart from
the archetypal Englishman who had introduced him.

"Admiral Pound," said Churchill. "And Field Marshal
Dill."

He did not see fit to introduce the others who stood
behind him, and she took them for staff: his personal
valet probably, a secretary or two, perhaps a security
officer or two.

"The Prime Minister," said the President, "has told me

he will not require more than a few minutes in his rooms before he is ready for a pre-dinner drink. Shall we say cocktails in the Green Room in fifteen minutes, dinner in an hour?"

"That arrangement," said the Prime Minister, "would be most agreeable."

Mrs. Roosevelt found Winston Churchill an engaging and yet infuriating man. He had, as Elliott had warned, a regal air about him; though the Prime Minister was cordial and friendly and faithfully attentive to the small niceties of courtesy, he kept between himself and everyone around him a measured distance that was not to be crossed. He was witty. He was entertaining. Yet his conversation was heavy; he tended to pontificate, and when he did, he expected his pronouncements to be heard and pondered. She was surprised to discover that this most famous of parliamentary orators had a speech impediment. He spoke with a slight lisp. She suspected he had worked to correct it only up to a point and beyond that point had kept it as an element of his unique style.

"We must not," she overheard him tell the President and Harry Hopkins, "forget *Jean Bart* and *Richelieu*."

He was talking about two French battleships that remained in North African ports. It was important they not fall into the hands of the Germans. It was serious talk, but she could not help but smile at the way he tried to impart a French accent to his pronunciation of the names of the two ships. The French language, she concluded, was not powerful enough to overcome the Churchillian accent.

He partook thirstily of the brandy the President offered him, so much that Mrs. Roosevelt guessed he was tired and tense and would want to retire immediately after dinner. Although there had been talk of assembling a first conference, she guessed it had been postponed. When she heard the President and the Prime Minister agreeing on an agenda for the evening, she was surprised.

As they took their drinks and chatted, Secretary of State Cordell Hull arrived, followed by Sumner Welles and General George Marshall. Lord Halifax, the British ambassador, appeared soon after.

A few minutes before they were to go in to dinner, Mrs. Roosevelt noticed a tall young man in the uniform of the British Navy standing uneasily to one side of the room, without a drink, conspicuously ill at ease. It was not in her nature to allow anyone to remain so—she had suffered too many awkward hours herself, many years ago, when the company of crowds of people she did not know was painfully uncomfortable to her. She stepped over to the young man and spoke to him.

"Oh!" he said. "Mrs. Rose-vult. It is an honor to meet you, ma'am."

"And you are?"

"Excuse me. I am Lieutenant-Commander George Leach, of His Majesty's Ship *Duke of York.*"

He was tall, more than three inches above six feet, she judged. His face was lean and bony, the pale skin of his cheeks oddly shiny, as if newly and delicately scraped with a sharp razor. His disciplined dark-brown hair lay smoothly combed. He looked down at her with an expression of grave unease, which she decided might not be of the circumstances in which he found himself but a constant of his personality.

"Allow me introduce you to the President," she said.

He followed her across the room to where the President sat in his wood-and-steel wheelchair, his cigarette holder atilt in the famous Rooseveltian gesture, his second martini in his hand.

"Let me present Lieutenant-Commander Leach," said Mrs. Roosevelt, interrupting a dialogue between the President and the Prime Minister.

"I am pleased to meet you, Lieutenant-Commander," said the President. "Has no one offered you anything to drink?"

"Well, I . . ."

"Arthur!" The President called for Arthur Prettyman. "Isn't there a bit more of this glorious nectar in the shaker?" he asked, raising his martini glass. "Pour some for Lieutenant-Commander Leach. Let's introduce him to an American vice."

"George is serving in *Duke of York*," said Churchill. "His father is Member for Wapping Old Field and a friend of mine since George was undreamt of. When I found George aboard ship, I invited him to come along as a personal aide, give him an introduction to America and something to remember during all the hard days he's going to have to endure."

"The *Duke of York* is a new battleship, I believe," said the President to the young officer.

"Indeed, sir," said Lieutenant-Commander Leach. "She was only recently commissioned. Bringing the Prime Minister here is something of a shakedown cruise for her."

"You've been comfortably accommodated, I hope," said the President.

"Yes, sir."

"George will be setting up my situation room," said Churchill. "In what I believe you call the Monroe Room. I look forward to receiving you there in the morning, Mr. President. We will have all the latest information, on progress on every front, shown on maps. Libya. Malaya. Russia. All of it. Constantly kept up to date. I urge you to establish such a room here in the White House. It is invaluable for keeping yourself current."

"I will be interested," said the President. "Perhaps Lieutenant-Commander Leach can show one of my people how you have it arranged."

"I will be more than pleased to, Mr. President," said the young officer.

Mrs. Roosevelt, herself never taking more than a single glass of sherry before dinner, was a close observer of people and their drinking habits. She found it difficult to approve her husband's long-time habit of drinking two martini cocktails every evening—although she had never seen any ill effect on his personality or on his ability to cope with whatever the next hour might bring. The President's personal assistant Harry Hopkins, on the other hand, did not handle it so well; he sometimes came down to dinner in a state approaching inebriation. (He lived in the White House, in the Lincoln rooms in the East Wing of the second floor, so he might be available to the President at a moment's notice and at any hour; and when he did not join the President for his evening cocktails, he ordered up ice from Mrs. Nesbitt and held his own cocktail hour, sometimes bringing in friends from outside.) She observed that these Britishers tossed off whiskies and brandies as if they were lemonade.

Winston Churchill, she knew, had something of a reputation for his intemperate consumption of spirits: whiskey and brandy. There were even jokes about it. (Lady: "Mr. Churchill, *you are drunk!*" Churchill: "I am, madame. But consider—in the morning *I* shall be sober, and *you* will still be ugly.") It was amusing to watch him clutch both his cigar and his glass of brandy in one hand. With practiced facility, he put first one and then the other to his mouth, never ceasing to talk and gesticulate, as if he were unconscious of smoking and drinking. The brandy had no visible impact on him. He drank what Mrs. Roosevelt considered a rather large amount of it, but his voice remained biting and his carriage firm.

"My grandfather," she overheard him say, "was American, you know. Leonard Jerome, my mother's father. A fascinating man. Captain of industry. Did you know that Minnie Hawk, the world-famous operatic soprano, was my mother's illegitimate half-sister?" He nodded. "The resemblance between her and my mother was remarkable. And she was not his only illegitimate child. He founded the Jockey Club in New York, you know. Made and lost several fortunes. He once sailed a small boat across the Atlantic on a bet. A far more interesting man than the seventh Duke of Marlborough." (This referred to his paternal grandfather.) "I should like to think I manifest some of the qualities of Leonard Jerome."

"Which ones?" asked the President in mock innocence.

Churchill chuckled appreciatively. "Take your choice," he said.

Mrs. Roosevelt's next surprise occurred at the dinner table. She should not have been surprised—as she realized when she thought about it. All the English visitors, including Lieutenant-Commander Leach, ate with hungry enthusiasm, expressing their appreciation of the fresh vegetables and fruits on the White House table. It had not occurred to Mrs. Roosevelt that even the Prime Minister did not have access, in London, to fresh food and plenty of it. She made a mental note to tell Mrs. Nesbitt to serve as many fresh vegetables and fruits as she could.

The company did not linger over the meal. Although Churchill allowed his wineglass to be refilled twice, as the hour passed, instead of growing drowsy, he seemed to become more animated and more anxious to open the conference. He asked her, in fact, if she would mind if the conferees were served their coffee in the Oval Office, rather than at the dinner table, to which of course she readily consented. It was with an undiminished sense of surprise that she watched the President and the Prime Minister, with their chief assistants and advisers, troop off toward the Oval Office to open an immensely important conference in the middle of the evening.

For herself, she went up to the third floor to look in on Missy. Missy LeHand, who had served the President faithfully through so many years, was ill now and kept largely to her room, her speech impaired, her left hand partially paralyzed. She continued her valiant effort to bear her share of the President's burdens, but she was too weak to be what she had been. She spent lonely hours in her little suite on the third floor, and Mrs. Roosevelt made a point of going up to visit as often as she could.

Coming down to the second floor after a quarter of an hour with Missy, she encountered Lieutenant-Commander Leach crossing the stair hall from the Prime Minister's suite to the Monroe Room. He carried a red wooden box.

"Ah, Mrs. Roosevelt," he said. "Our situation room is almost ready. Would you care to see it?"

She accompanied him into the Monroe Room, where huge maps now hung from the walls or stood on easels, each one brightly lighted with floodlamps. Another naval officer was at work sticking flagged pins into a map of the North Atlantic—showing apparently the location of British ships and perhaps the location of U-boat sightings. Another officer at a desk listened intently to the telephone, frowned, and made notes.

"Situation in Malaya is deteriorating, I'm afraid," said Lieutenant-Commander Leach. "Defense of Singapore is going to be a rum go."

"What news from Russia?" she asked.

He pointed at the map. "Reasonably stable for the moment," he said. "This"—he touched a pin—"is the deepest penetration by Army Group Center, which is the one that most worried the Prime Minister. Field Marshal Bock seems to be stalled."

The only place name that immediately impressed itself on Mrs. Roosevelt was Moscow, and it seemed to be half surrounded, if she read the flagged pins correctly.

"I suppose you mean the Russians *claim* they've stalled him," she said.

Lieutenant-Commander Leach smiled. "The Prime Minister pays no attention to Russian communiqués," he said. "Our information is from Jerry. We monitor his radio traffic."

"But isn't it coded?" she asked.

He smiled again. "I'm sure it is. But our chaps have their ways."

She stepped closer to the map and studied the pins showing the location of German army divisions.

"George . . . Oh, I beg your pardon."

"Quite all right, Sir Alan. Come in. Allow me to introduce you to Mrs. Roosevelt. Ma'am, let me introduce Sir Alan Burton of Scotland Yard."

"Sir Alan Burton!" she exclaimed.

"Quite so, madame," said the tall, sepulchral English civilian. "And I don't look a thing like Archibald Adkins, do I?"

Mrs. Roosevelt laughed. "No, Sir Alan, you do not."

He was the Scotland Yard inspector who had been impersonated by the criminal Archibald Adkins during the investigation of the poisoning of Philip Garber, more than two years ago. Adkins had succeeded in convincing the British Embassy as well as Mrs. Roosevelt, J. Edgar Hoover, and everyone else concerned that he was Sir Alan Burton, the man who now stood smiling at her.

"Do I owe you an apology, Sir Alan?" she asked.

"Oh, not a-*tawl*, dear lady. Not a-tawl. Archie was a smooth one. He might have convinced *me* he was I."

"Not if you looked in the mirror, Sir Alan," she said.

Sir Alan Burton was a thin man, with a long, hollow-cheeked face and very mobile, thin and gleaming red lips which seemed to extend halfway to his ear lobes. He was perhaps fifty years old. His complexion was gray, his eyes watery blue. His graying yellow hair was stuck in place with dressing.

"To what do we owe the honor?" asked Mrs. Roosevelt.

"My current assignment is to attempt to prevent Winston from getting himself assassinated," said Sir Alan. "I've spent the evening with your Secret Service chaps. Decent fellows. I think we shall have no problem. Who, after all, would want to harm so marvelous an old boy as Winston?"

2

She did not know how late the conference continued. Her bedroom and sitting room were at the southwest corner of the house, and she did not hear the President returning to his bedroom to retire. Tuesday morning, out of her room at her usual early hour, she was surprised to see how busy the Britishers were. Looking in on their situation room, she found the Prime Minister already there, fully dressed, already smoking, already on the telephone, stabbing a short finger at one of the maps and saying something emphatic to someone on the other end of the line.

He looked up and saluted her silently, obviously continuing to listen to some response over the wire.

Mrs. Roosevelt smiled and returned to the elevator in the west hall. She descended to the ground floor. Her first meeting of the day had to be with her chief housekeeper, Mrs. Nesbitt.

Ordinarily, Mrs. Nesbitt came to the second floor to meet with Mrs. Roosevelt and discuss the day's meal requirements and other housekeeping problems. Today Mrs. Roosevelt wanted to start earlier, since she knew Mrs. Nesbitt would spend much of the day shopping in Washington food markets to find, at reasonable prices, the kind of food she hoped to serve the Englishmen.

Mrs. Henrietta Nesbitt was a neighbor from a town near Hyde Park, New York. She was a stolid, unimaginative German woman who had never allowed herself to be shaken by the President's or anyone else's complaints and jokes about her kitchen. She knew nothing of haute cuisine, cared less, and set herself to serve solid, nourishing food out of the restricted budget imposed on her. Mrs. Roosevelt liked and respected her.

What was more the woman was bearing up well. Last night's dinner had won praise from the Prime Minister, and even the President had complimented it. Even so, it was doubtful that either Mrs. Roosevelt or Mrs. Nesbitt had anticipated the kind of visit this was turning out to be, and meeting the expectations of the regal Mr. Churchill was going to prove trying.

The main kitchen of the White House was a spacious wood-paneled room, equipped with the heavy old cast-iron ranges and sinks of the last century. Mrs. Nesbitt complained little, but she had complained of the battered utensils with which her staff was expected to prepare the White House food. The household budget had been strained to buy a few new pots and pans. Congress did not appropriate funds to reequip the kitchen. It was a make-do kind of place, in which the staff struggled to prepare everything from sandwich lunches to state dinners.

Mrs. Nesbitt was primly—some would have said grimly—dressed in gray, with her graying hair tied back tightly, her rimless spectacles set firmly astride her nose. "Ach. I was on my way up," she said, glancing at the kitchen clock to see if she had somehow lost track of the time and omitted to keep her morning appointment with Mrs. Roosevelt.

"We have lots to talk about, and I thought we might get an early start," said Mrs. Roosevelt. "Have you had any problems?"

"Not really. Only that Mr. Churchill sent his valet down last evening to pick up half a dozen cakes of bath soap. Half a dozen! He said Mr. Churchill would want them all around him as he soaks in his bath."

"Indeed. Half a dozen! And what else?"

"About a gallon of coffee, at five-thirty this morning. I am told he soaks in his bath before dawn, surrounded by soap, drinking coffee and smoking cigars."

"Temporarily," said Mrs. Roosevelt, "we seem to have become an outpost of the British Empire. If he asks for a Negro to fan him with an ostrich plume, tell him we can't accommodate him."

Mrs. Nesbitt was not often seen to smile. Doubtless she did, but doubtless also she considered it an unseemly expression to be displayed in public. Now, however, she allowed herself the luxury of a small, pinched-lip smile—one that might actually have turned into a grin if she had allowed it.

"They have not had fresh vegetables, fresh fruit," said Mrs. Roosevelt. "Buy as much as you can. Serve as much as you can. They can't get fresh produce in wartime London."

"Will the Congress appropriate something for the extra expense?" asked Mrs. Nesbitt.

"Yes," said Mrs. Roosevelt. "For Mr. Churchill's table, they might even appropriate money for brandy and cigars. Anyway, we'll take the chance. Spend what you have to."

"Ach," said Mrs. Nesbitt. "I'm told he's brought his own brandy: several gallons of it. And enough cigars to fill the house with smoke."

"But *fresh* things," said Mrs. Roosevelt. "Fresh meat, fresh bread."

"I quite understand."

"We . . . *What?* Oh, my *dear!*"

A maid had stumbled into the middle of the kitchen: ashen, mouth agape, eyes wide and vacant. She gurgled, unable to find words.

"Joyce!" exclaimed Mrs. Nesbitt. "What in the name of heaven—?"

The young woman choked on her words and pointed to the door of the walk-in refrigerator. "Aaghh! *Aaghh!*"

Mrs. Roosevelt and Mrs. Nesbitt rushed to the refrigerator door. Mrs. Nesbitt shrieked and staggered back. Mrs. Roosevelt stood and stared.

Lying face up, on the floor of the refrigerator, was the body of a man. His blue eyes were open, as if he were staring; but an instant's attention to them showed they were as lifeless as the eyes of a fish on ice. His lips were parted, his pallid face fixed in his final paroxysm of surprise. He seemed about to speak, yet it was plain he would never speak again.

Mrs. Roosevelt stepped back from the door. "Call . . ." she whispered.

Mrs. Nesbitt had the telephone in one trembling hand already. Nodding, she spoke to the White House operator and asked for the duty officer, Secret Service.

Mrs. Roosevelt steeled herself and stepped into the refrigerator. She forced herself to kneel and touch the forehead of the dead man. It was cold—unnaturally cold, since he lay on the floor of a room kept at something like thirty-eight degrees Farenheit. It was difficult to believe his eyes would not turn and follow her hand as she reached out tentatively and touched his clammy flesh, but of course they did not move; in the grotesque paralysis of death they remained in a stare fixed forever. Shuddering, she rose and left the refrigerator.

"Mr. Baines will be here in a moment," said Mrs. Nesbitt.

And he was. Gerald Baines, Special Agent, Secret Service, Department of the Treasury, chief agent on duty that early morning of December 23, 1941, had only a short distance to trot to respond to Mrs. Nesbitt's anguished call. He entered the kitchen within the minute, followed immediately by a second agent.

Joyce Carter, the uniformed maid who had discovered the body, sat on a straight, wooden chair, her face covered by her hands, weeping quietly. She was a young black woman who had worked in the White House for six years and who had impressed Mrs. Roosevelt with her quiet and faithful attendance to duty.

"Joyce," said Baines softly. "You slip across the hall to the doctor's office. We don't need you here."

"Don't need no doctah." Joyce wept.

"But you can be comfortable there," he said. "Just lie down and be comfortable. If we need to ask you anything, I'll come over."

Joyce nodded and slipped out of the room.

"I think I need not inconvenience you, Mrs. Roosevelt," said Baines. "I'm sure Mrs. Nesbitt has any information I need. If I need any from you, I can call."

"With your consent, Mr. Baines, I will stay," said Mrs. Roosevelt in a crisp, forceful voice. "In all the circumstances—the presence of Mr. Churchill and his people in the house, and all the rest of it—we may find some special considerations prevail. I am especially concerned that no unfortunate publicity attend this matter. We cannot imagine, for this moment, what consequences might follow a public announcement that a mysterious corpse has been found in a White House refrigerator. I speak of diplomatic consequences, et cetera."

"Of course, ma'am," said Baines deferentially. "I didn't mean to dismiss you, only to suggest you might *rather* leave."

"I think I should rather stay, Mr. Baines." She sighed.

"Unfortunately, this gentleman is not the first human corpse I have seen."

Baines nodded. He was a florid fifty-year-old man, his bald head flecked with liver spots, his modestly rotund belly shoving out the vest of his gray wool suit. In ordinary circumstances, Jerry Baines was a bright, cheery man, ready with a quip, a smile fixed on his shiny face. Right now, he was sober-faced; but Mrs. Roosevelt judged that even confronted with an unidentified corpse in a White House refrigerator, Jerry Baines would rather smile.

The second agent squatted beside the body in the refrigerator. Mrs. Roosevelt did not know his name and quietly asked Baines who he was.

"Dom Deconcini," said Baines quietly. "A good man."

Deconcini ("Dee-con-CHEE-nee," Baines had pronounced it) was an exceptionally handsome young man: features sharp and fine, complexion swarthy, eyes dark and penetrating, a noncomittal, non-communicating smile fixed on his face. He was going through the dead man's pockets.

"Odd, this," he said, looking up at Baines.

"What?"

"His pockets are empty. There's nothing to identify him. No wallet. No keys. No money. Not even a nickel. Not even a trolley token."

"What killed him?" asked Baines. "That's what *I* want to know."

Deconcini shook his head. "Not a mark that I can find so far. No blood. I don't see a bruise. There might be one—"

"Check the label in his suit," said Baines.

Deconcini pulled the man's suit jacket open. It was true there was no blood to be seen, not a stain on the white shirt. The agent squinted at the label inside the suit.

"Sears, Roebuck," he said. "Could have been bought anywhere for $17.95."

"That makes him an American, anyway," said Baines.

"Not necessarily," said Mrs. Roosevelt.

"No, of course not," Baines agreed. "I meant to say he's probably American, probably not one of our British guests."

"It's really odd," said Deconcini, continuing to search through the clothes on the corpse. "No money. No keys. Somebody went through his pockets and took everything off him before they dumped him in the refrigerator."

"What evidence is there that he was 'dumped' in there?" asked Mrs. Roosevelt. "Maybe he died right where we see him."

"What would have been the last hour when anyone entered this refrigerator?" Baines asked Mrs. Nesbitt.

She shrugged. "I can't imagine anyone having any proper purpose in it after, say, midnight," she said. "You can see what's stored in it: meat, vegetables . . . Someone may have called for ice after midnight, but ice would have come out of one of the smaller refrigerators. Oysters—"

"Oysters? *After midnight?*" Mrs. Roosevelt asked.

Mrs. Nesbitt lifted her chin. "Mr. Hopkins calls for oysters at *all* hours," she said. "He eats oysters and drinks whiskey. At any hour."

"Indeed," said Mrs. Roosevelt thoughtfully. "Well . . . Anyway. We don't know who this man is or when he died. We don't know why. So we have on our hands a very difficult problem, have we not, Mr. Baines?"

"We certainly do, ma'am," said Baines dolefully. "Of course, the autopsy . . ."

Mrs. Roosevelt cleared her throat and Baines took it for a signal to be silent and let her speak (though in fact such was not her intention at all).

"The circumstances," she said, "create an unusually

delicate situation. Will you permit me to offer some
suggestions?"

"Why, certainly."

"First, I am afraid that we have no choice but to allow
the agents in charge of the Prime Minister's security to
participate in the investigation. It would be most awkward, would it not, Mr. Baines, Mr. Deconcini, if we kept
the matter from them, only to discover, say, a week from
now, that the dead man is one of their party or that they
know who he is? We are fortunate in that Sir Alan Burton
of Scotland Yard has come to America with Mr. Churchill. I am told he is a most experienced, shrewd, and circumspect investigator. I suggest we take him into our
confidence."

Baines nodded. "Very well. I'll ask him to come down
before we move the body."

Mrs. Roosevelt nodded at Baines. "I think that is a wise
course," she said. "Now. Second. I think we will all understand the absolute necessity of keeping this matter entirely confidential. It simply *must not* become a matter of
public record until the English party has returned to
London. We have enough reporters beating on our doors
as is—what with the Prime Minister and his party here
—without attracting the police reporters from every
newspaper in the nation."

"I entirely agree," said Baines. He glanced at the body
lying on the floor of the refrigerator. "God knows what
the significance . . ."

"Joyce can be trusted," said Mrs. Nesbitt. "Other than
Joyce Carter, no one knows about this but . . . but this
group here, the four of us."

"Of course," said Deconcini as he rose from kneeling by
the corpse, "we mustn't forget the one who killed him.
That makes five at the least."

"For once," said Mrs. Roosevelt, "there may be something positive in wartime secrecy. Let's see to it that no one who is not possessed of the highest security clearance is given the information."

"What about the President?" asked Mrs. Nesbitt. "Surely you'll have to tell him."

"I'd rather not," said Mrs. Roosevelt. "But, yes, I suppose I will have to tell the President. And I suppose Sir Alan Burton will insist on telling the Prime Minister. But please. Please allow me to take responsibility for that."

"Will you act as coordinator between us and the British?" asked Gerald Baines.

Mrs. Roosevelt nodded. "Let's not call it anything all so official as 'coordinator,' " she said. "Let's say that I will speak with the President and with Sir Alan Burton. If necessary, I will speak with Mr. Churchill."

Baines frowned at the staring corpse. "I hope we find he is just a young man who went in to steal a bit of steak and slipped and banged his head. I'm afraid, though, it won't be so simple."

Sir Alan Burton—the real Sir Alan Burton, not the impostor who had visited the White House in 1939—came to the kitchen a few minutes after he was called. He was occupying a room on the third floor, as were Lieutenant-Commander Leach and others of the British party.

"You see," said Baines. "We haven't moved him."

Sir Alan lifted his chin and looked down over his cheekbones at the corpse that still lay on its back on the refrigerator floor. "Ah," he said. "Quite dead, I imagine. If not dead from other causes, then likely frozen. What possibility he was thrown in here unconscious but alive and then did, indeed, freeze to death overnight?"

"Well, the autopsy will answer that question," said Baines. "Short of that, I think the fact that his eyes are open is pretty clear evidence that he was dead when he was deposited here."

"Not necessarily, dear chap," said Sir Alan. "I am reminded of the case of the late Marchioness of Windmore, who was found eyes-open just like that—in 1928, I believe it was—and proved to have died of her own carelessness, having elected to lie down for a nap on her lawn on a wintry night—"

"In a White House refrigerator, Sir Alan?" interrupted Mrs. Roosevelt. "Few, I should think, would lie down for a nap in there."

"Be certain the blood-alcohol level is checked," said Sir Alan. He squatted beside the corpse. "Not one of our chaps, let me assure you. Do you mind if I pull up his clothes?"

Baines shook his head, and the English detective proceeded to pull up the shirt and undershirt, exposing pale skin. The chest and stomach were unmarked.

"Odd," said Sir Alan. "Damned odd. Shall we turn him over?"

Dominic Deconcini squatted beside Sir Alan, and the two of them rolled the corpse. The back was similarly unmarked.

"Not strangled, not shot, not stabbed," said Sir Alan. "Not bludgeoned. And he has not the appearance of someone who has been poisoned. Damned odd."

"Perhaps," said Mrs. Roosevelt, "Mrs. Nesbitt and I should retire to her office, that you may make a more complete examination."

"Yes," said Sir Alan. "If you don't mind."

The kitchen staff was busy preparing breakfasts, so the three men remained shivering inside the refrigerator as they undertook the awkward business of pulling the clothes off the corpse.

Sir Alan turned out the trouser pockets. "Damned, damned odd," he repeated. "Look, there's not even any lint in these pockets. It's as if he'd run a vacuum in them."

"Maybe the suit is new," suggested Deconcini.

"A better theory," said Sir Alan.

The corpse lay naked now, once again on its back. It was the body of a young man, some six feet tall, slender and tautly muscled. In fact, the musculature was so well developed as to suggest that the young man might have been an athlete. He was blond, his body virtually hairless. His hair was close-cropped. His lips were full and, though bluish now, had probably been red.

They rolled him on his belly once more.

"Here you are," said Deconcini.

"What?"

The younger agent pointed to a tiny hole on the back of the neck, just at the base of the skull. The wound had bled little and was almost hidden in bristly blond hair.

"A sharp instrument has entered here," said Deconcini. "An ice pick maybe."

"Yes," said Sir Alan Burton. "When the depth of that is measured, I wager it will go all the way into the brain. A man would die instantly of that. No struggle. Not much blood—particularly if he were dragged into this cold room with the instrument still stuck in him."

"A silent, efficient way to kill," said Baines soberly.

"Professional, one might guess," said Sir Alan.

"Well . . ." Gerald Baines sighed. "Let's get out of the cold. Our next problem—perhaps the most difficult one—is going to be to identify the man. We'll never discover who killed him, or why, until we know who he is."

3

Mrs. Roosevelt was able to stop Harry Hopkins for a moment as he hurried toward the President's study. He told her the meeting the previous night had gone on to 1:30 A.M. The decision had been made that the Allies would mount an invasion of northwest Africa at the earliest possible opportunity. Also during that first formal meeting, the President had suggested to the Prime Minister that three or four divisions of American troops would be sent to Northern Ireland (where a German landing was feared), so that the British garrison there could be shipped to the battlefronts. Churchill had gratefully accepted that idea.

The President was most pleased, Hopkins said, with the way the discussions had gone so far. So, he thought, was the Prime Minister.

"The conference has reassembled already," Mrs. Roosevelt told Mrs. Nesbitt when she came up to the First Lady's office in mid-morning to resume their discussion that had been interrupted by the discovery of the body in the refrigerator. "The President had barely had his breakfast when Mr. Churchill came booming in and reopened the discussions. Where such a fat little man finds all the energy, I should like to know."

"When he sleeps, he sleeps," said Mrs. Nesbitt. "The maid who cleaned his bathroom found a bottle of sleeping pills."

"That is the kind of information we must keep *entirely* confidential," said Mrs. Roosevelt.

"Do you know what they've done with that corpse?" asked Mrs. Nesbitt. "It's in the refrigerator again. After the doctor finished examining it, they brought it back, wrapped in a sheet, and put it on the floor, not far from where it was found. Most of our people will not go in there. Anyway, can it be sanitary to keep meat and vegetables in the same place where . . . ?"

Mrs. Roosevelt's face turned red, and she could not suppress a chuckle. "I understand their reasoning," she said. "They don't want to remove the body from the White House yet. Obviously, once it is taken to a morgue or to an undertaker, the secret is out. But I shall speak to Mr. Baines about removing it to a hospital somewhere."

"I hope you do," said Mrs. Nesbitt indignantly. "I must say, it gives me the willies."

Mrs. Nesbitt glanced at the slip of paper on which she had made notes of the several questions she wanted to raise with Mrs. Roosevelt. "Are our people to attend to Mr. Churchill's room?" she asked. "Or are his people to do it? He seems to read two dozen newspapers, and he throws them on the floor all over the room. Do you suppose he's got them sorted out in some order, or does he want them carried away?"

"Let his valet take care of that," said Mrs. Roosevelt. "Our staff can take care of the linens and—"

"Honestly, I don't know when," said Mrs. Nesbitt. "He was still awake and drinking coffee at two this morning, and at six he was in his bath, again drinking coffee, scattering cigar ash, tossing newspapers . . ." She shook her head. "King George and Queen Elizabeth were such *orderly* people!"

"Carry on as best you can," said Mrs. Roosevelt. "I warned you nine years ago that working in the White House would present its difficulties."

"I've made Lieutenant-Commander Leach a party to our secret," said Sir Alan Burton to Mrs. Roosevelt about noon. (He of course pronounced the rank "lff-tenant co-mahnder.") "He has done intelligence work for the navy and knows his way around investigative procedures. My own varied duties may interfere with my giving the investigation my full attention, so I thought it well to have an assistant."

"I am sure Lieutenant-Commander Leach will make an important contribution," said Mrs. Roosevelt.

"He is at the moment, I believe, assisting Mr. Deconcini in the interrogation of some of the White House personnel."

Lieutenant-Commander Leach was in fact at that moment in the library on the ground floor of the East Wing, listening to Dominic Deconcini interrogate a young woman who had been on duty late last night.

"The first thing we need to know," said Deconcini, "is who the man was. Then we must find out how he got into the White House."

Bonny Battersby nodded and remained silent. She was an exceptionally attractive twenty-seven-year-old woman. Lieutenant-Commander Leach stared at her as if mesmerized: at her golden-blond hair, her round blue eyes, her smooth complexion and regular features, and—maybe a little more than propriety would have allowed—at her prominent breasts. Deconcini either did not notice any of this or, more likely, pretended not to.

"According to the sign-out sheet, you left the White

House a little after two this morning," said Deconcini.
"You must have been one of the very few people here on
the ground floor at that hour."

"Yes," she said. "There were Secret Service agents on
duty and I think someone still in the kitchen. But I—"

"What kept you here so late?"

"Mr. Hopkins left a huge amount of dictation for me to
transcribe," she said. "He uses a Dictaphone, you know;
and he kept bringing me cylinders to transcribe: all about
the meetings, you know. I was still working at eleven, and
he came down with more—his notes on the discussions—
and he wanted it all on paper before the meetings opened
again this morning."

"You worked until two A.M.?"

"If you have any doubt, ask Mr. Hopkins. He was very
grateful."

"I should think he would be," remarked Deconcini.
"No, I'm not suggesting I have any doubt. But you were
working here when a man was killed. No. Let me amend
that. You were working here when the body of a man was
dumped in the refrigerator room. If you could give me *any*
idea—"

"I was working hard, Mr. Deconcini. I was tired. A
typewriter makes a certain amount of noise. I heard nothing. I saw nothing. I'm sorry."

"Were you in this room *all the time?*" asked Deconcini.

"Yes. I was very busy. Mr. Hopkins was very anxious
to have his transcript. I didn't even have time to go to the
pantry for a cup of coffee."

"Why were you working *down here,* incidentally?"
asked Deconcini. "In the old trophy room?"

"Since Mr. Hopkins moved into the White House to be
near the President," she said, "a number of . . . arrangements have had to be made. To be frank with you, Mr.
Deconcini—and in all modesty—Mr. Hopkins would like

for me to *live* in the White House, so his work can be done when he wants it, at any hour. Until the war came, I refused to live here. Now . . . it seems as if I may have to take a room on the third floor. I mean, with our country at war, I can hardly refuse. Can I?"

"Mr. Hopkins must value you," said Deconcini.

"I shouldn't wonder," interjected Lieutenant-Commander Leach. "Miss Battersby worked here until past two. Now we find her again on duty. If it is not too forward of me, I should like to suggest, Miss Battersby, that we slip out and have a proper breakfast—you beyond the reach of Mr. Hopkins, I beyond the reach of Mr. Churchill."

Bonny Battersby looked up into the calm, handsome face of Lieutenant-Commander Leach. She was unable to conceal her surprise—or that the suggestion intrigued and pleased her. "Uh, the kitchen can—" she began to say.

"Ah, but Washington on a December morning," said Lieutenant-Commander Leach. "And, you understand, I have never been in the States before last night. Could we walk a few squares and find one of those marvelous American cafés where, as we hear in London, great numbers of eggs are fried in bacon grease and coffee is served in half-gallon mugs, endlessly refilled?"

Bonny Battersby grinned. "If I am not under arrest," she said, lifting a defiant chin toward Agent Deconcini.

"Of course not," said Deconcini. "And enjoy the morning. The town is decorated for Christmas, Leach. We didn't know, when we began putting up pine roping and lights, that we would be at war on Christmas."

"Can you forgive me, Mr. Deconcini, Miss Battersby, for saying that I can't help but be pleased that you are? We had gone about as far as we could go, alone."

"Understood, sir," said Deconcini.

"Oh, yes," said Bonny Battersby. "It's a fight for civilization. And it's an honor to be here, in the command post."

"We will light the Christmas tree tomorrow evening, as usual," said the President. "I will say a few words to the nation, by radio. It might be appropriate, my friend, if you said a few words, too."

"I should be grateful for the opportunity," intoned the Prime Minister.

It was the Rooseveltian cocktail hour, and the President presided in the west hallway as usual that Tuesday evening. Seated about the long, narrow room were the President and Mrs. Roosevelt, the Prime Minister, Hopkins, Beaverbrook, General Marshall, Sir Charles Wilson (the Prime Minister's physician), Sir Alan Burton, and—at the President's special request—his ailing friend, his long-time secretary, Missy LeHand.

The President was happy with the company. He was in good form, beaming, joking, taking the opportunity to enjoy the hour. Churchill was the same, competitive indeed of the company's attention. For the moment, the concerns of the war were put aside. The President told tales of his visit to Paris after World War I—of the calvados everyone imbibed, of the exuberant atmosphere of a city already entering its brilliant between-the-wars insouciance, trying to forget the tragic losses of 1914–1918. Churchill spoke of polo he had played in India at the turn of the century, of the difficulties he had experienced as a noble but impecunious young man, keeping a string of ponies and paying his dues at the officers' mess and wondering when his checks would bounce. The company laughed.

"This company, I assume," said Mrs. Roosevelt, "is

aware that a dead man was discovered in the refrigerator this morning."

"Ah, Babs," said the President. "Need we go into that now?"

She smiled. "I can think of nothing," she said, "more stimulating to the intellect than a mystery. We have been unable so far even to identify the deceased. It is a worthy puzzle, is it not?"

"Sir Alan," rumbled Churchill, "has outlined the essentials of this puzzle to me. While we cannot give the death of one man much thought when we are pondering global strategy, I am intrigued by the matter, as I am by the crossword puzzles published in *The Times*. It is, as you suggest, dear Mrs. Roosevelt, a stimulating conundrum. As Sir Alan has described the matter to me, you have not as yet so much as identified the corpse."

Sir Alan Burton spoke. "At this hour, Prime Minister, we have not discovered who the young man may be."

"And how, sir, did he die?" asked the Prime Minister.

"By the intrusion into the brain," said Sir Alan gravely, "of some sort of implement: an ice pick most likely—and indeed several ice picks were discovered in the White House kitchen. It was driven with some force into the base of the skull and upwards for a distance of some eight inches. The result was sudden death. The poor fellow hardly knew what hit him. The murder took place not too far from the place where the body was discovered —a refrigerator adjacent to the White House kitchen."

"Fingerprints—" said the President.

"Taken," said Sir Alan. "Delivered to the files maintained by your FBI, where they matched none but the staff's. That line of inquiry has proved, I am afraid, a dead end."

"The pun is forgiven," said Churchill.

"It reminds me," said the now-fragile Missy LeHand, "of the murder of Philip Garber." She smiled weakly at Sir Alan Burton. "As it must remind you, Sir Alan."

"Indeed," said Sir Alan, nodding politely at her.

"Let me see," said Churchill, frowning, thrusting out his lower lip and beginning to tick off points on his fingers. "The elements of this little mystery are: first, that you have discovered in a refrigerator here in the White House the body of a young man; that he was killed in a rather effective, one might say professional, way by the stab of a sharp instrument into the base of his skull; and that you have been so far unable to identify him. Did you not say, Sir Alan, that his pockets were empty?"

"Yes, sir. And his clothes are nondescript, could have been purchased anywhere."

"All the staff have seen his picture," said Mrs. Roosevelt. "No one recalls ever having seen him before."

"Then how did he get into the White House?" asked the President, somewhat agitated, a little impatient. "We suffer the indignities of supposedly tight security, yet we find a corpse in, of all places, Mrs. Nesbitt's refrigerator. Obviously the man entered the White House without authorization and under the noses of the hordes of new guards who are supposed to be protecting us here. Ten hours after he was found, we don't even know who the fellow was, much less who killed him. We know nothing but that the man is dead and was brutally murdered by person or persons unknown. It is entirely possible that the killer is at large in the White House. Can we be sure I am not his next target? Or that my friend the Former Naval Person is? It is not a conundrum. It is not an amusing little puzzle. It's a shocking and threatening breach of security!"

Winston Churchill sipped thoughtfully from his snifter of brandy, commenting quietly into its bowl, "I am not frightened, Mr. President. You need not be concerned for *my* security."

"Maybe J. Edgar Hoover should—" began General Marshall.

"I will not have that headline-hunting oaf running amok in the White House," said the President. "No, George. No. It's up to the Secret Service and your soldiers."

"I'll check everything myself," said General Marshall.

"No," said the President gently. "We can't spare you. You have far greater problems. And so have you, Harry. And you, Babs."

"I can at least," said General Marshall, "give orders that everything possible be done."

"As can I," said Hopkins.

The President nodded. "All right. I have confidence in that. Let's try to get on to bigger things."

In the kitchen, Dominic Deconcini and Lieutenant-Commander Leach watched somberly as two khaki-uniformed men wrapped the body of the unknown man in brown-stained but once white canvas and secured the wrapping with leather straps.

"Your newspaper chaps aren't to know, as I understand it," said Leach.

Deconcini nodded. "National security."

"I can't imagine anything more is to be learned from the corpse," said the British officer. He was still wearing the uniform of the Royal Navy and had, apparently, no intention of changing into civilian clothes during his stay in the White House.

"Who knows?" said Deconcini. "They'll open him up, see what's in his stomach, what's in his bowels. If it's not too late to find out, I'd be curious to know how long before his death he had sexual relations. There was no alcohol in the blood sample they took—"

"Sexual relations?" interrupted Lieutenant-Commander Leach. "Why would you want to know that?"

Deconcini shrugged. "Why did he come here? Who let him in? It could have been a girl, you know. They—"

"Are you thinking of Miss Battersby?"

"I'm not thinking of anyone in particular. Are you?"

"I'm thinking of one fact more than any other," said Leach. "That he was wearing a new suit with absolutely nothing in the pockets. Not even cab fare. In a man's pockets you would normally find a few things. Even if you found nothing identifying, you would expect to find . . . oh, say, ticket stubs . . . a few coins at least. Suppose you killed a man and wanted to take everything identifying from his pockets. You'd take . . . Well, what would an American be carrying?"

"Driver's license," said Deconcini. "A draft card, these days."

"And his latchkey," added Leach. "If it were from a hotel, that would tell you something about him. But would you take his every last coin? Perhaps his pocket-knife? His fingernail file? His comb? His handkerchief? It would take time to go through every pocket." He shook his head. "Most curious."

"Does this raise an idea for you?" asked Deconcini.

"It suggests," said Lieutenant-Commander Leach, "that the man entered the White House with pockets already empty. Wearing a new off-the-rack suit from a common store. Carrying nothing that could identify him."

"Why?"

"I don't know why. But not, I should think, just to have an assignation with a female member of the White House staff. If that were his purpose, he would hardly have gone to the trouble. What is more, such a female is unlikely to have been his murderer, since she is unlikely to have gone to a similar trouble."

"You are suggesting," said Deconcini, "that he came here anticipating—"

"Not being murdered, certainly," said Leach.

"But what?"

"Being caught on the premises and not wishing to be identified."

"Which makes him?"

Lieutenant-Commander Leach shook his head. "We should not speculate," he said. "Speculation stands in the way of one's developing objective theories."

The two attendants in uniform grunted as they lifted the wrapped corpse onto a stretcher. "A stiff stiff," one of them grumbled.

"I beg your pardon?" said Lieutenant-Commander Leach.

"American slang," said Deconcini. "Ignore it." He turned to the two attendants. "Now, gentlemen," he said. "You'll remember: it's your ass if word gets loose that you carried this stiff out of here."

They were a buck sergeant and a corporal, United States Army. The corporal shrugged. "If the doorman there doesn't tell, you can be sure we won't," he drawled.

4

"A distressing document," said Mrs. Roosevelt, looking over the hastily typed autopsy report brought from the army hospital at Fort Meade early on Wednesday morning, December 24.

Parts of it read:

> The body is that of a muscular, well-developed Caucasian male, measuring 70 ¾ inches and weighing 159 pounds. The hair is blond and close-cropped, the eyes are blue, pupils measuring approximately 8 mm. in diameter. The ears, nares, and mouth are essentially unremarkable. The teeth are in good repair, without fillings or denture devices.

> The cause of death is a puncture wound, approximately 155 mm. in depth, penetrating between the first vertebra and the occipital bone slightly to the right of the vertical axis, continuing upward and slightly to the left, partially severing the spinal cord, continuing through the brain stem, the pituitary, and hypothalmus. The wound is larger at the entry point than near the point of deepest penetration, suggesting that the instrument used to inflict it was moved laterally and horizontally, probably in a wob-

bling motion. Damage to this area of the brain caused failure of heart and lung functions, resulting in death within a half minute of the infliction of the wound.

Contents of the stomach and intestines of the subject: well masticated beef, potatoes, lettuce, and other vegetables, cow's milk, coffee, all ingested more than four hours before death.

The subject had not experienced a sexual orgasm within the 24 hours immediately preceding death.

Identifying marks and characteristics: None remarkable. The subject has a thin, well-healed scar between the thumb and index finger of the right hand. It is suggestive of the slice of some sort of blade. In the hairline just above the left eyebrow, there is a similar thin, white scar, 45 mm. in length. The subject's appendix has been surgically removed, as above noted, resulting in a normal appendectomy scar. No birthmarks or tattoos.

"It's not very helpful," said Agent Gerald Baines. "Does nothing to help us identify the body."

"Laboratory examination of the clothing?"

"Nothing," said Baines. "Everything he was wearing came from Sears, Roebuck—suit, shirt, shoes, socks, necktie, underwear, all of it—and all of it was new."

"That is suggestive in itself, isn't it?" asked Mrs. Roosevelt.

"I suppose it is," said Baines. "But suggestive of what? That's the problem."

"I can think of a number of possibilities," she said. "Perhaps his usual clothing was a military or naval uniform. A lot of young men around here these days are in uniform."

"Yes," said Barnes. "Or, I suppose, he could have been a man who usually wore work clothes: overalls or something like that."

"Or maybe he was a Westerner who wanted to look like an Easterner, or a foreigner who wanted to look like an American," suggested Mrs. Roosevelt.

"I'd think, though," said Baines, frowning, "that he would have been satisfied with his socks and underwear. This man was dressed in new Sears, Roebuck clothes from the skin out."

"A deliberate attempt to make identification difficult," said Mrs. Roosevelt.

"Which brings us back to why," said Baines.

"To steal, to spy, to kill," said Mrs. Roosevelt grimly.

"Yes."

"Or maybe to *be* killed," she added.

"To *be* killed? Why?"

She sighed, tossed a little shrug. "The thought that comes to me is that someone might want to shake the Prime Minister's confidence in our security arrangements—or perhaps that someone hopes to embarrass our government in the midst of these important meetings and at the outset of America's participation in the war."

Baines's frown deepened. "A somewhat . . . remote pair of possibilities, I'd say."

Mrs. Roosevelt shrugged again. "We must not close our minds," she said.

"Indeed not, ma'am," said Baines. "We'll keep all possibilities in mind—with any others we think of."

"Have you as yet developed any theory as to how he entered the White House? The President is quite concerned about that."

"Dom Deconcini and the British admiral are working on that," he said.

*   *   *

The "British admiral" was Lieutenant-Commander George Leach. He was, as Baines had said, working with Agent Dominic Deconcini on the ground floor.

The day before they had interviewed every man who had been on security duty the night of the murder—a mix of Secret Service agents and officers and men of the army. Each of them had viewed the body—not a photograph, but the body, which was why it had been kept in the refrigerator most of the day. The man's clothes had been put on him once again, so he would look something like the way he had when he entered the White House. Even so, no one recognized him. No one would acknowledge having seen him.

Today they were supervising a group of agents and soldiers who were searching the grounds and examining the doors and windows, to see if they could learn the way the man had entered the house.

"Sherlock Holmes kind of work," grumbled Leach. "Now, if we were Holmes and Watson, Dom, we would come on a lump of cigar ash beneath a window and from our long study of different characteristics of cigar ash we would conclude that the man who entered the White House smoked . . . Well, what do you Americans smoke? A cigar labeled 'Indian Chief' or something like that. And then we would recall that no one in the White House but the arch-fiend Harry Hopkins smokes Indian Chief cigars, and—"

"But it was not Mr. Hopkins who admitted the mysterious stranger into the White House," interrupted Deconcini. "It was his dog, Sport, who also smokes Indian Chief cigars and is in the employ of dog conspirators who plan to overthrow the government. George. It's cold out here. Let's get on with it."

"Quite so," said Lieutenant-Commander Leach. "Let's . . . How do you say?"

They were tramping around the west border of the South Portico, outside the ground-floor oval room from which the President broadcast his fireside chats. The ground just outside the South Portico was paved, and distinguished visitors to the White House were often driven to this entrance and came into the house privately, since this entry was not nearly as public as entry through the North Portico.

Deconcini and Leach moved to the west, to the ground outside the old trophy room just to the west of the ground-floor oval room.

"Oh, so," said Deconcini suddenly, as he opened a window. He lifted a hand. "Good morning, Miss Battersby." He closed the window.

He had opened and closed a window of the room where Bonny Battersby worked temporarily as Harry Hopkins's secretary—where she was working now and where she had worked the night when the as-yet-unidentified man had been murdered.

"He could have entered the White House through this window," said Deconcini.

Lieutenant-Commander Leach shrugged. "Or through any of two dozen other windows and doors."

"No," said Deconcini. "The doors are all guarded."

"Even so," said Leach. "This window. What is so significant about this window?"

"If you come in through this window," said Deconcini, "and go through this room into the hall, you have only a few steps to go to reach the stairs or elevator that take you all the way up to the private quarters of the President. If you came out of the room reached through this window, you could probably cross the hall and come to the stairs and elevator without being stopped."

"Are you suggesting that this window has been left

outside the observation of the guards around the building?"

"The periphery of the grounds is tightly guarded," said Deconcini. "But once inside the fence and the perimeter of security, you could move about the grounds pretty much at will. Particularly in the dark."

"Still," said Leach, "you have the problem of entering the well-guarded grounds without being stopped by a soldier."

"It can be done," said Deconcini. "I know how to get in. I've warned my chief about a gap in the perimeter, but nothing has been done about it yet, I don't think."

"You know it because—"

"Because I work in the White House all the time. Security is my job."

"Which, of course, suggests a theory as to the identity of our intruder," said Leach.

Deconcini sighed loudly. "You mean that he was an employee here, maybe in the past."

"No," said Leach. "I mean that he was admitted to the White House by someone who knows what you know."

"An accomplice."

"Dom," said Lieutenant-Commander Leach. "Obviously, someone else is involved in this matter. At the very least, one more person is involved."

"The one who killed him."

"Which may be the same one who let him in."

"Ah . . . that doesn't make much sense," said Deconcini.

"There has to be someone," Leach insisted.

"Well, I'm sorry to have to point this out to you, old boy," said Deconcini, "but if our dead man entered the White House by this route, he passed through the room where your new friend Bonny Battersby said she was working all evening."

"He watched her through the window," said Leach. "He waited until she went out to the lady's loo. Then—"

"Sure. And he came in through the only unlatched window on the ground floor. An interesting coincidence."

Lieutenant-Commander Leach turned his eyes away from Deconcini for the moment. He looked away across The Ellipse, toward the Tidal Basin. "Is it really possible," he asked, "to enter the grounds during the night, without being observed?"

"I don't know for sure," said Deconcini. "I think it is."

"We must *know*," said Leach. "I suggest you try it. I suggest you try entering the White House tonight, the way you have suggested. If it works—"

"If it works, we have a suspect," said Deconcini.

"Yes," said Leach, nodding. "I fear you do."

"Will you come with me?" asked Deconcini.

"I?"

"You. I want you to see how it works. I want to settle any doubts you might have."

"Well, that's decent of you, Dom. I will join you. You do assure me, I suppose, that we shall not be shot by an alert guard?"

It was Christmas Eve. The President and the Prime Minister, with their staffs, spent much of the day, nevertheless, discussing the problems they confronted:

—Field Marshal Erwin Rommel was running wild in the Western Desert.

—General Douglas MacArthur was being pressed back through Bataan and onto Corregidor.

—Japanese troops were steadily advancing down the Malay Peninsula, and a siege of Singapore seemed likely to begin shortly.

—Growing evidence that Hitler was accumulating tank-carrying invasion barges in the Channel ports suggested that he might be contemplating an invasion of the British Isles before American help could arrive.

At dusk, even so, a great crowd gathered around the Christmas tree on the lawn just beyond the South Portico —thousands of people admitted to the grounds in spite of the new security. The tree was lighted, as tradition dictated; and as always President Roosevelt stood on the Portico and spoke his Christmas message, to the people there around the tree and to the nation by radio. He called for determination and courage, but it was also a message of hope and optimism. "Our strongest weapon in this war is that conviction of the dignity and brotherhood of man which Christmas Day signifies." At the end, he introduced the Prime Minister.

Winston Churchill spoke briefly, but his little speech was another masterpiece of Churchillian oratory. He reminded his audience that his mother had been an American. He felt like a member of the American family, he said, with perhaps "a right to sit at your fireside and share your Christmas joys." His ending:

> Let the children have their night of fun and laughter. Let the gifts of Father Christmas delight their play. Let us grown-ups share to the full in their unstinted pleasures before we turn again to the stern task and the formidable years that lie before us, resolved that, by sacrifice and daring, these same children shall not be robbed of their inheritance or denied their right to live in a free and decent world.
>
> And so, in God's mercy, a happy Christmas to you all.

When they stepped back inside the Blue Room, the Prime Minister beckoned his physician to his side and asked him to check his pulse. He had been, he said, so moved by the ceremony outside that he had felt heart palpitations. But when the President was again seated in his wheelchair, Churchill stepped behind it, waved off Arthur Prettyman, and indicated he himself would wheel the President to their cocktails and dinner.

They had a formal dinner in the State Dining Room, and later the company sang Christmas carols. Afterward, the President and the Prime Minister, with the principal members of their staffs, returned to work. The President was anxious to obtain agreement on a United Nations Declaration, pledging all the Allies to fight together and sign no separate peace until the war ended with the establishment of a world free of oppression. It was important to the President, and that Christmas Eve he and the Prime Minister worked on the draft.

Lieutenant-Commander George Leach, conspicuously handsome in the uniform of the Royal Navy, had been one of the guests at the dinner in the State Dining Room. He had been seated next to a strange, chattery, motherly little woman who spoke with a peculiar accent and used it to express firm opinions on nearly everything, from global strategy to her distaste for Yorkshire pudding. Her place card bore the name MISS PERKINS, and someone told him she was a member of the President's Cabinet, the Secretary of Labor.

Sir Charles Wilson, the Prime Minister's physician, suggested they share a brandy after dinner; but Leach had an appointment with Dom Deconcini and reluctantly declined.

He went to his modest room on the third floor of the White House and took off his naval uniform. He slipped on instead a pair of dark trousers and a heavy turtleneck sweater, the sort of thing worn by navy men on watch.

Over that he put on his big naval greatcoat, with a white scarf to hide the fact that he was not wearing a necktie at his throat. So dressed, he left the third floor and descended to the ground floor, where Deconcini waited for him in the library.

"We leave through the gates," said Deconcini. "Canonical exit. But we return a different way."

"And exit again by the non-canonical route?" asked Leach.

Deconcini nodded. "By the non-canonical route."

The two of them—Secret Service Agent Dominic Deconcini and Lieutenant-Commander George Leach, Royal Navy—left the White House at 10:31 P.M. by signing out with the duty officers at the door and again at the gate. By now, as both noted, the crowd who had come for the lighting of the tree had cleared the grounds. It was dark and quiet all over.

"We couldn't have picked a better night," said Deconcini. "You can bet they have swept the grounds and are still searching, to get all those people out. Strong, alert security tonight."

"All the better, if we are to prove a point," said Leach.

They left the White House grounds through the northwest gate. Deconcini led the way to G Street, where a car he identified as his was parked at the curb. It was a 1939 Plymouth coupe. Deconcini unlocked the doors and told Leach to leave his greatcoat and naval cap on the seat. He himself left an overcoat on the seat on the driver's side. As they walked away from the car, they were dressed much the same: in dark, serviceable clothes.

From G Street they walked south on 17th, all the way to Constitution Avenue, then east on Constitution to 15th Street and north to E.

Leach was confused and lost, in spite of his officer's training to keep his bearings wherever he went. Washington was not under blackout, as was London, but the big lights on the monuments were out, and his points of reference were obscured. He oriented himself on the White House, but as they walked it was sometimes lost behind the trees, and he became unsure of his place. He was conscious of parkland around him—The Ellipse, the grounds of the Washington Monument, all unfamiliar and unidentifiable to him. In any event, the street names and most of the landmarks would have meant nothing to him. He had never been in Washington until two days ago.

"All right," said Deconcini suddenly.

They had stopped on a street. Leach did not know what street, of course; but he could see the White House, looming now to his left and across an expanse of open land.

"Okay. Look here," said Deconcini.

They were standing above something distinctly American, as Leach saw it: the steel cap to a storm sewer. It was at the street curb, a steel plate some four feet square, with a round hatch in the center. Water could run in through a barred entry at the curb level, and men entered to clean the thing, if cleaning were required, through the round hatch. (The same in London was concreted into the pavement, and to enter it to clean, one would have to crack the pavement. Leach gave an instant's thought to the idea that the Americans had invented something useful.) Leach squinted at the thing in the dim light the city still afforded.

Deconcini also squatted; then, taking a small tool of some kind from his pocket, he pried up the round hatch lid. He lifted it and shoved it aside. The hole gaped.

"Drop through," he said. "It's not more than a four or five-foot drop. You'll land on solid footing, in maybe a few inches of water. I'll pull the lid back on and drop down after you. Move to one side or another, so I don't land on top of you."

Leach squatted beside the round opening, fixed his hands on the steel plate to either side of the hole, lifted himself over the hole, and dropped. As Deconcini had said, he fell only a short distance and stood on a wet, slightly soft surface underground. He moved over, as Deconcini had told him to do, and in a moment Deconcini dropped beside him.

"You understand," said Deconcini. His voice had fallen to a low, conspiratorial level, as if someone down here might be listening. "Storm sewer. Rainwater, off the streets and off the White House grounds, runs through tunnels to the river."

"Understood," said Leach. "And if you know your way, you can traverse these tunnels and emerge—"

"Lots of places," said Deconcini.

Deconcini was carrying a tiny electric torch—what Americans called a flashlight, this one a penlight—and he switched it on and showed that they were at the intersection of four tunnels: each one round and of brick and stone, and some four feet in diameter. They were relatively dry. In winter, no more than six inches of water trickled toward the lower of the four, the one which apparently led downward to the river. The bottoms were covered with mud and with a varied litter of tree twigs, cans and bottles, and some paper trash.

"Now," said Deconcini. "You scooch down"—a new Americanism—"and follow me."

Lieutenant-Commander Leach crouched and followed Deconcini into one of the tunnels. For most of the time, Deconcini kept the electric torch dark, switching it on only occasionally to check the way ahead. They did not need it. The tunnel restricted their movements; where it led, they went, forward into the forbidding darkness, their feet in the gentle flow of water, their heads and shoulders scraping the brick walls of the sewer. Oddly, the air smelled fresh, not at all as Leach had supposed an underground sewer tunnel might. Obviously, no offal was disposed of in this system. It was the system through which the city of Washington sent rainwater drainage to the river.

Leach could not guess the number of yards they traveled. After a while, Deconcini used his torch more often, obviously looking for something. He found an intersection and turned right, into another tunnel identical to the first. They continued.

"Any idea where you are?" Deconcini asked. Again, he spoke in low voice, as if he supposed someone might hear, though Leach could not imagine how anyone could.

"Under the White House, I suppose," said Leach. "Otherwise I am being guided on a most peculiar tour of the city."

"Under the south lawn," said Deconcini. "The runoff has to go somewhere, and it goes into the city's storm-sewer system. It was set up this way in the eighties. These old tunnels are sixty years old."

"Antique," said Leach wryly.

"For Washington," said Deconcini. "Anyway, we are under the south lawn. There are half a dozen openings. When we come up, we are inside the grounds, inside the peripheral security."

"Inside the fence," said Leach.

"Yes. And inside eighty percent of the guards."

"So all we have to do is emerge and effect entry to the house itself," said Leach.

"Exactly," said Deconcini. "There's a bit of danger here. Are you ready to take the risk?"

"My alternative," said Leach, "was to enjoy a spot of

brandy with Sir Charles Wilson. And here I am. Lead on, MacDuff."

Deconcini moved forward along the tunnel, now with his penlight lighted. He reached a shaft leading up to the lawn. Putting the penlight in his pocket, he climbed a set of iron cleats he pointed out to Leach before he started. Leach waited for a moment, then followed, taking purchase on the cleats just below Deconcini's feet. They were but a minute climbing to the surface. Deconcini put the steel hatch aside and the two of them emerged onto the lawn. While Deconcini replaced the hatch cover, Leach oriented himself. They were, as Deconcini had promised, on the lawn beneath the South Portico. The lights of the Christmas tree had already been extinguished, and they crouched in the darkness under the window lights of the White House.

"I pointed this out a month ago," Deconcini whispered. "Maybe tonight's visit will convince them it is dangerous."

"Not by shooting us and discovering who it was they shot, I hope," whispered Leach.

"From now on, no talk," said Deconcini. "They have planted microphones all over the grounds."

Leach nodded and followed Deconcini as he began a half-crawling, half-trotting progress across the lawn toward the house. The wartime security was apparent. In the dim light from the windows, the elevated barrels of anti-aircraft guns were visible. They had been set in trenches to make them inconspicuous from the street. Leach wondered if they had been lowered to horizontal during the visit of the crowd for the lighting of the tree. Low voices spoke everywhere: those of soldiers on duty in the gun emplacements, plus very probably those of others patrolling the grounds. It was as if they were moving through an enemy encampment. For the moment, they *were* moving in an enemy encampment.

Lieutenant-Commander Leach could not help but turn his mind to that night in 1814, when Admiral Cockburn and his men had crossed these same grounds, plundered the White House for souvenirs, and set it afire.

They crouched just south of and beneath the Portico where hours before the President and Prime Minister had stood for the ceremony of lighting the Christmas tree. Deconcini beckoned Leach to follow him to the left, into the shadows of two trees. There they knelt and peered into the dark and listened.

A uniformed policeman stood guard at the center door. The lamps above the doors were not lighted, but he was visible in the light from the interior of the ground floor. A helmeted soldier approached across the grass, walking with his rifle cradled in his arms. He spoke briefly to the policeman and moved on.

A match flared on the first-floor balcony. A Secret Service agent was on duty there, keeping watch over the grounds.

"They have searchlights and floodlights," Deconcini whispered to Leach. "If they think they see or hear anything, it will be as light as daylight all around here."

Leach followed Deconcini in a crouch as they crossed the last few yards from the trees to the house and dropped to their knees at the wall below the west side of the South Portico. For a long moment they crouched there in the shadow of the house, conscious of the sound of their own breathing, waiting for a harsh command, even for a warning shot.

Nothing happened. Two floors above, the President and the Prime Minister met in the third of the oval rooms that faced south. That was the President's study. The next room was his bedroom. The next after that was Mrs.

Roosevelt's bedroom. The Americans, Leach reflected, were not yet accustomed to guarding their President. He wondered if he could approach 10 Downing this way.

Deconcini rose to his feet. They were only a few paces from the window they had found unlatched this morning, a window in the room where Bonny Battersby had sat typing Harry Hopkins's notes while the unidentified man was killed and dumped into the refrigerator. Deconcini looked in. Leach stood, too, and peered through the glass into the dim interior of the old trophy room.

No one was there. Bonny Battersby had not been asked to work on Christmas Eve.

Deconcini glanced around, then he quietly pushed up the sash. Without a word to Leach, he heaved himself upward and squirmed headfirst through the window and into the White House. Leach also glanced around, then he followed.

They closed the window.

"Simple enough, hey?" said Deconcini.

"Your point is made," said Lieutenant-Commander Leach.

"Not yet, it isn't, said Deconcini. "Let's see where we can go."

The door to the west hall was locked, but the lock could be opened from the inside without a key. Deconcini turned the knob cautiously, opened the door a crack, and peered out. Nothing. The long hall that extended the entire length of the ground floor of the White House was lighted but vacant.

This much of the house was already familiar to Leach. Directly across the hall was the elevator vestibule. There, he could take the elevator to the third floor, probably unmolested, and go on to bed. The next door to the left led to the pantry and kitchen. At the west end of the hall was the door into the West Wing, where the famed Oval Office was situated.

Deconcini stepped out into the hall. Leach followed. He pulled the door to the trophy room shut behind him—having been careful to unlock it first. Deconcini walked briskly to the kitchen door. It was open. He hesitated there, looking inside. The first room inside was a pantry, and the kitchen opened off of that. He touched his lips to tell Leach to be quiet, and the two of them stealthily entered the pantry. They slipped around to the door of the kitchen, which was to their right. Inside the kitchen, seated at one of the big tables, a big old black man dozed over a newspaper spread open before him. The telephone was at hand. He was available to respond to whatever orders came down from upstairs, even though it was almost midnight.

Leach and Deconcini returned to the hall and walked east to the elevator vestibule.

"Is no one whatever on duty?" Leach asked.

"Actually, there are a lot of men on duty, all around us," said Deconcini. He pointed to the door that led to the executive wing. "There are men on duty out there in the West Wing," he said. "That's where the Oval Office is, plus Hopkins's office, and Steve Early's, and a bunch of others." He turned and pointed east, toward the door to the ground-floor oval room, the Diplomatic Reception Room. "There's a security desk in there—two men. And there's a man on patrol. He moves. He'll be along."

"But we'll be gone, of course," said Leach. "We proved the point: that someone could have entered the White House and reached the pantry last night. *Two* someones, in fact: the killer and . . . the killed."

"No," said Deconcini. "We've proved that point, but I'm interested in proving another."

"Which is?"

"Why," said Deconcini. "A man did not break into the White House and die here by coincidence. *Why* was he here? I want to see how far he could have gone."

"All right," said Leach. "It's an essential point."

The elevator vestibule opened also onto a flight of stairs —narrow, thin-carpeted stairs that climbed halfway, then turned and led upward in the opposite direction to the elevator lobby on the first floor.

Here they were just outside the ushers' room and at the entry to the great central hall and the state rooms of the White House. This floor was not abandoned, midnight though it might be. They could hear voices and footsteps. Deconcini hurried on up the stairway toward the second floor.

On the second floor it was the same. At the top of the stairs, in the elevator lobby, they were directly across the center hall from the door to the President's bedroom. They were but a few paces from the door to the President's study, where the President and the Prime Minister likely were still conferring. It was plain, distressingly plain, what a desperate man with a gun—or, worse, with a bomb—could do.

Could do at the likely sacrifice of his life—for the center hall was guarded. If Leach did not know who the men he saw by a quick glance through the door were, Deconcini certainly did: they were armed agents of the Secret Service, two of them, and the third man with them was probably one of the Prime Minister's bodyguards, probably also armed. Even so, an assault from the elevator lobby, by two men with the advantage of surprise, willing to shoot, armed maybe with explosives as well as guns . . .

Leach tapped Deconcini's shoulder. The elevator was coming up. The door to the First Lady's office was just behind them. Deconcini seized the knob in his hand,

turned with all his force, and broke the simple lock. He
and Leach backed into the office just as the elevator door
opened and the black butler from the kitchen emerged
with a tray of glasses and a pair of bottles. Deconcini
pulled the door closed, and in the darkness of Mrs. Roosevelt's tiny office he and Leach waited, wondering if the
rumble of the rising elevator had covered the crunch of
the breaking lock.

No one came. Deconcini switched on his flashlight and
by its light wrote a note:

Dear Mrs. Roosevelt,

I broke the lock on your office door tonight. This note will
be evidence of a surprising fact I want to bring to your
attention in the morning.

                              Dominic Deconcini.

They opened the door and peered out. Deconcini ges-
tured to Leach to follow him back down the stairs. They
returned to the ground floor and to the trophy room.

"Now we know," said Deconcini. "At least we know the
possibility. You can get into the White House and you can
get all the way to the family quarters, if you know your
way."

Leach glanced at his wristwatch. "Shall we keep moving?" he asked.

Deconcini nodded. They opened the window again and
dropped lightly to the ground outside. Once more they
had little trouble evading the soldiers on the grounds or
in finding the steel-capped drainage sewer. They pulled
up the hatch cover, descended into the sewer, and pulled
the cover back into place before they lowered themselves
on the cleats to the mud and sand at the bottom.

"On this leg of the expedition, I should be glad for some

light, if you don't mind," said Leach as he stumbled in the dark.

"There's only one way you can go," said Deconcini. "Even so . . . Here, you take the light and lead the way."

Lieutenant-Commander Leach took the small flashlight. He kept its beam aimed down, at the mud and litter and scant pools of dirty water through which they walked in the crouch the tunnel required. The tunnel had branches. From one of them a trickle of water flowed, and after they passed it they walked in ankle-deep running water. The old tunnel was in disrepair. At points the sides had caved in, though not so much as to block it. The stones and bricks were worn smooth by time. Leach looked out for rats, but he saw none. There was nothing edible in the tunnel.

He had begun to feel cold. His feet were wet and . . . He stopped. Deconcini walked into him from behind.

"Dom . . . Look. What's this?"

He fixed the beam of the little electric torch on the object that had caught his attention. Lying in the running water, half covered by silt, was a pistol; a revolver.

"Got something to pick it up with?" Leach asked. "Don't want to put our fingerprints on it."

Deconcini handed him a mechanical pencil, and Leach slipped the pencil through the trigger guard of the revolver and lifted it from the water and mud. It was a .38 Colt, loaded with a cartridge in each chamber.

"No rust," said Leach. "I should judge it has not been here long."

"Since night before last, I imagine," said Deconcini.

5

On Christmas morning the Prime Minister accompanied the President and Mrs. Roosevelt to church. Mr. Churchill seemed especially to enjoy the hymn-singing, though he remarked quietly to Mrs. Roosevelt that "Oh, Little Town of Bethlehem" was a new one to him and he was curious as to where it came from. She was pleased to tell him it was an American Christmas carol, much loved by most Americans; and he nodded and tried to follow in the singing of the second stanza.

Returning to the White House, the President had a crisis to resolve. Henry Stimson, the Secretary of War, had received a report to the effect that the President had, on Christmas Eve, offered to turn over to British command some army divisions supposedly destined for the relief of MacArthur in the Philippines. MacArthur had telephoned Hopkins and announced that if that were true he would resign. When the President returned from church, General Marshall and Hopkins were waiting, both of them excited, Marshall in fact angry and insisting that the matter be settled on the spot.

It was resolved, but not until early afternoon, by agreement between the President and the Prime Minister to create a single combined command for all the Western Pacific, including Malaya and Burma. The commander would be Field Marshal Sir Archibald Wavell. General Marshall was to carry that word with him to the joint military conference, to be attended by senior American and British officers, that afternoon.

Only after lunch did the Prime Minister retreat to his rooms, not this time to take his usual afternoon nap but, rather nervously, to work on the draft of his speech to the Congress, which he was to deliver the next day. It was only then, too, that the President was able to take a little time away from conferences and discussions and to give a bit of his attention to Fala, who had become impatient that his master was taking too little note of how he scampered about with his new rubber toy, his Christmas present. Even during this time, when supposedly he was getting some rest, the President received and read a string of dispatches from the Pacific, plus three telephone calls from Marshall at the military conference.

"Mr. Churchill," remarked Mrs. Roosevelt, "takes a long nap each day, ensures his rest at night by taking sleeping pills, and soaks an hour in a hot tub twice a day. You weren't in bed until almost three last night, and now—"

"I doubt the boys on Wake Island and Guam are getting much sleep," said the President. "Or on Luzon—"

"They're young," she said. "They're soldiers. You are the commander-in-chief, and it is part of your responsibility to remain healthy and alert and strong. You should let Dr. McIntyre—"

The President sighed, revealing more weariness than he had intended to let her see. "All right," he said. "We'll let Ross McIntyre come in tomorrow morning for his usual poke and probe. He'll tell me to stop smoking, stop drinking, and stop being President of the United States."

"And to get your rest," said Mrs. Roosevelt.

"That's what I said—stop being President of the United

States. Particularly in the midst of a world war."

She wanted to write letters to each of her children, and to avoid the stream of interruptions she left the President and went to her office. It was only then that she discovered the note left the night before by Dominic Deconcini. She telephoned the Secret Service office downstairs. Deconcini was on duty and came up.

"The leak is plugged," he said to her after he had described how he and Lieutenant-Commander Leach had entered the White House and penetrated almost to the door of the President's bedroom. "From today on, the stairways will be guarded, and the elevators; and of course a barrier is being installed in the storm sewer."

"Were there fingerprints on the pistol?" she asked.

"No. It had been wiped. But there were fingerprints on the cartridges—the fingerprints of the dead man."

"Oh. How very ominous," said Mrs. Roosevelt.

"Yes. I shudder to think what he intended."

"The implications of his entering through that storm-sewer tunnel are even more ominous," she said. "He couldn't simply have discovered it on his own. He had help—almost certainly someone inside the White House."

"More than one person, I'm thinking," said Deconcini.

"Miss Battersby and—"

"Someone who knew the tunnel. I don't think Bonny Battersby could have known about that."

"And *I* cannot imagine that a young woman could have killed the man by stabbing him in the head with an ice pick," said Mrs. Roosevelt. "That takes a great deal of physical strength, doesn't it?"

"Well, not necessarily," said Deconcini. "Of course it does take a certain amount of—of—"

"Strength of purpose," said Mrs. Roosevelt. "Ruthlessness. Viciousness."

"Something like that," Deconcini agreed.

Mrs. Roosevelt shook her head and frowned. For a moment she was silent in deep thought. "It is not, I suppose, *necessarily* true that Miss Battersby let the man—or men —in. I mean, she could have been out of the room for a few minutes. In fact, are we actually certain that the man was not killed after she left for the night?"

"The autopsy places the time of death at no later than midnight," said Deconcini. "That means the man entered the house sometime before midnight. And let's not forget that someone returned to the tunnel, carrying the pistol, sometime after the murder."

"Are you absolutely convinced that entry was made through the window of the trophy room?"

"Every other window on the ground floor was locked when we checked them yesterday morning," said Deconcini.

"And is it absolutely proven that the man—or men— could not have waited until Miss Battersby left the room, say to go to the bathroom, and then effected entry?"

"If they did, then she lied to us about leaving the room," said Deconcini. "She insisted she could not leave the room all night, even to go to the pantry for a cup of coffee. She was too busy, she said."

"Have you checked to see if she indeed did go to the pantry for a cup of coffee?" asked Mrs. Roosevelt. "Or to the bathroom?"

"She did not go to the pantry," said Deconcini. "We questioned Henry, the night man. As for going to the bathroom . . . Well, she could have done that without being seen."

"The facts then are," said Mrs. Roosevelt, "that Miss Battersby worked without interruption in the trophy room from, say, nine or ten o'clock until after two and that if the dead man entered the White House through the window of that room during those hours she could not but have seen him."

"Or she's lying about not leaving the room—and why would she do that?"

"Why? Yes. I am afraid Miss Battersby has something to explain. Tomorrow we must—"

"We need not wait for tomorrow," said Deconcini. "She reported for work shortly after noon. She is, you understand, Mr. Hopkins's secretary, and he is generating a large volume of notes and memoranda this week. She is hard at work down in the trophy room."

"I shall accompany you downstairs to speak to her," said Mrs. Roosevelt. "She might be more forthcoming with me."

They descended on the elevator to the ground floor and crossed the hall to the trophy room, where they found Bonny Battersby, not hard at work at the desk temporarily established for her there, but enjoying an apparently pleasant conversation with Lieutenant-Commander George Leach.

"Ah, Mrs. Roosevelt!" the girl exclaimed as she rose to her feet. "We . . . we've met, you know."

"Yes, of course," said Mrs. Roosevelt. In fact, she could not remember having been introduced to this slender but busty young woman. Even so, she smiled and pretended she remembered vividly. From her husband and from the late Louis Howe, she had learned a great deal about how people were won, and she practiced what she had learned with a sincerity neither of them were always able to bring to the process. "I am sorry to see you have to work on Christmas."

The young woman smiled. "Thank you," she murmured shyly. "Last night Mr. Churchill said, 'This is a strange Christmas . . .' It is, isn't it? It's a very strange Christmas."

"Good morning, Lieutenant-Commander," said Mrs. Roosevelt. "Mr. Deconcini has told me all about your adventure of last night."

The young naval officer nodded courteously. "Good morning, Mrs. Roosevelt," he said. He pointed toward the window. "That adventure could not be repeated. As you can see."

She looked out. Four workmen were clustered around the storm-sewer hatch in the lawn. One was a welder, in goggles and big gloves, kneeling on the hatch and welding it in place with his acetylene torch.

"I would like to review with you, Miss Battersby, some of what you told Mr. Deconcini and Lieutenant-Commander Leach on Tuesday morning," said Mrs. Roosevelt.

The young woman stiffened with indrawn breath. She frowned. "Very well," she said.

"Did you not leave this room at any time?" asked Mrs. Roosevelt. "Even perhaps to go to the bathroom?"

Bonny Battersby shook her head emphatically. "I was very anxious to finish my work so that I could go home," she said. "To be frank with you, Mrs. Roosevelt, I was a little annoyed at being asked to work so late; and I kept at it, trying to be done with it as quickly as I could. I know that Mr. Deconcini thinks someone came through that window, but I can tell you for a certainty that no one came through it between about ten o'clock and about two o'clock."

Mrs. Roosevelt nodded. "I wish . . . Well, I wish it were otherwise," she said quietly.

"So do I," said the young woman. "As it is, I'm suspected of something—I'm not sure what. Of letting the dead man in, I guess."

"Let's not put it quite so harshly," said Mrs. Roosevelt

sympathetically. "I don't think that 'suspect' is quite the word we should use."

"I'm afraid the word Mr. Deconcini uses is the official word," said Bonny Battersby.

"Mrs. Roosevelt is right," said Deconcini. "I'm not using the word 'suspect.' If I were, you would be under arrest."

The young woman glanced up into the face of Lieutenant-Commander Leach. "I think we'd better not, George," she said.

"In fact, I think we should do exactly as planned," said Leach. He turned to Mrs. Roosevelt. "I've just extended to Miss Battersby an invitation to take dinner with me in some good restaurant." He spoke to Deconcini. "There will be no objection?"

"Of course not," said Deconcini.

"Then," said Leach firmly, "we shall advise Mr. Hopkins that Miss Battersby's services will not be available to him after eighteen hundred hours on Christmas day. Miss Battersby and I intend for one evening to turn our thoughts to something other than war and murder."

"You two," said Gerald Baines. As a senior agent of the Secret Service, he was Deconcini's superior. He was speaking to Deconcini and Leach in his office in the Executive Office Building just west of the White House. "Someone could have shot you."

"I *told* you someone could enter the White House through that tunnel," said Deconcini.

"Easy, Dom," said Baines. "You embarrassed the Service by what you did, but you dramatized a leak in the security that could have resulted in something far worse than embarrassment. Right now you're the President's hero—and the rest of us are in his doghouse. But we are grateful to you just the same. In the future, try to be a little less independent. We could have checked out that tunnel together, and in daylight."

"Wouldn't have proved what we set out to prove," said Leach.

"Maybe so, Admiral," said Baines. "But it would have been embarrassing, too, if one of our guards had shot you last night."

Leach's face hardened. He did not like the "Admiral" quip. But he said nothing.

"Clever of you to spot the revolver lying in the mud," Baines went on. "We've done something further this afternoon. Look."

From his desk drawer he pulled out three grenades, strung on a belt. He laid them on his green desk blotter. Lieutenant-Commander Leach reached for one of them, stopped short, and asked, "Prints?"

"The dead man's. So go ahead."

Leach detached the grenade from the belt, lifted it, and turned it over in his hand. "A Mills Bomb," he said. "Of British manufacture. Standard British military hand grenade. Model 36M, I believe."

"We sent a squad into the storm sewer with a mine detector," said Baines. "They checked the tunnels to both sides of the one you used to move from Executive Avenue to the South Portico. The belt had been tossed back into one of the tunnels."

"It's becoming more and more clear, isn't it?" said Leach. "A pistol and three grenades. He meant to—"

"Yes," Baines interrupted. "An assassination. But who? The President or the Prime Minister?"

"Or both," said Deconcini.

"Let's think of what he had to know," said Leach. "He had to know how to get through the tunnel. He had to know how to get into the White House—that is, that there would be an unlocked window. Then, once inside, he had to know his way about, not only his way from the ground floor to the second but where the guards were likely to be. And finally—and this may be most significant —he had to know where the President and Prime Minister *were*, in what rooms, whether together or apart, and so on."

"I understand exactly what you are suggesting," said Baines. "I've spoken with Sir Alan Burton, and he takes the matter extremely seriously—and for the same reason: that the facts suggest participation by someone intimately acquainted with the White House, with our security measures, and maybe even with the schedule of meetings this week. The significance of this just keeps growing."

Fewer people appeared for the cocktail hour. It was, after all, Christmas day, and everyone who could stayed home, or went home as early as possible, to spend as much of the day as possible with their families. Even so, when the President wheeled himself into the sitting hall and ebulliently declared the hour, the Prime Minister was there, with Beaverbrook and Churchill's physician, Sir Charles Wilson. Mrs. Roosevelt was in her office and came out for a moment to say that she would join the company later. Missy was there, and Hopkins.

The United Nations Declaration was on the President's mind. He had worked on the draft during the afternoon. A sticking point was whether or not the declaration should contain a statement that freedom of religion was among the causes for which the nations were fighting. Freedom of religion had not been mentioned in the Atlantic Charter, and the President was determined it should be mentioned in the United Nations Declaration. The Soviet ambassador, Maxim Litvinov, had said that Marshal Stalin would never agree to any endorsement of freedom of religion.

"I've changed their minds," said the President with a grin of triumph. "I've had word. Marshal Stalin has authorized Litvinov to sign a declaration much like the draft we here have agreed on."

"How did you do that?" Churchill asked.

"I twisted his arm." The President laughed. "Oh, I told him that freedom of religion included the right to have no religion at all, so a Bolshevik and atheist could endorse it with no problem. But I think what really convinced him was a little talk I had with Litvinov about the dangers to his own soul, about the pains of hellfire and so on. He took it very soberly. I think he communicated it all to Stalin. Anyway, they've agreed."

"Mr. President," said Churchill, his pink face glowing with amusement, "if in 1944 you should by some unfortunate chance not be elected to still another term as President of the United States, then I shall recommend to the Cabinet and Crown that you be appointed Archbishop of Canterbury!"

"If appointed, I shall be honored to serve," said the President, bowing from the waist in his chair.

The President and the Prime Minister met after dinner, alone together in the President's study, where they chatted amiably about some minor points in the draft of the Declaration, talked about Churchill's speech to the Congress the next day, and reviewed without staff interruption the major elements of all they had agreed to over the past three days. Churchill poured and drank small glasses of brandy as he smoked his big cigars; and the President allowed himself two more martinis, two more than he usually had on any one day.

Mrs. Roosevelt relaxed in her private sitting room just off her bedroom. She had a few notes to write. Also, she wanted to organize her thoughts about a project she had decided to broach to the President as soon as he could spare a few minutes to think about it. She had decided it would be a good idea to convert the big old house at Hyde Park into a convalescent hospital for some of the wounded soldiers who would soon be returning from the fronts. After all, she had her cottage and Franklin was going to build one of his own; and the ancestral house was too big and expensive for them to maintain. She knew Franklin did not mean to live in it after he retired from the presidency, so why keep it any longer? She was not sure just how to approach him with this idea, and tonight might be a good time to write herself an *aide memoire* on the subject. There was nothing like writing down your ideas to get them in more organized form.

But the telephone rang.

"Mrs. R? Harry here. Jerry Baines and Sir Alan Burton are with me in my suite, having a little snack since they'd had no dinner when they came in; and they've brought me a piece of information you might be interested in. I mean, you are interested in the mystery of the body in the refrigerator. Would you care to join us?"

She walked the length of the long center hall, down the ramp into the east hall, to the entrance to the Lincoln Suite. Harry Hopkins stood at the door, waiting for her; and when she entered the Lincoln Sitting Room, Agent Baines and Sir Alan rose to greet her.

"Would you care for a snack?" Hopkins asked as he drew back a chair for her.

The snack appeared to be several dozen fresh raw oysters, a salad based on avocados, a loaf of French bread with butter, a bottle of white wine, and a bottle of bourbon, with plenty of ice. It was apparent that Hopkins was enjoying the snack as much as his two guests, despite the fact that he had eaten dinner with her and the President and Mr. Churchill only an hour and a half ago. Of long habit, Mrs. Roosevelt mentally estimated the cost of this snack to the White House food budget. Mrs. Nesbitt had complained often lately of Harry Hopkins's expensive tastes in food and liquor—and of the quantity he consumed.

"I can send down for some tea if you don't care for anything else," said Hopkins.

"Thank you, no," she said. "I have dined."

Hopkins smiled. "So have I," he said, and he reached for another oyster.

"You've found something I might like to know about?" she asked.

"Maybe," said Baines. "And maybe not." He wiped his hands on a napkin. "Let me show you what we found in the President's study. This—"

"I should explain," Hopkins interrupted, "that we have not brought anything to the attention of the President as yet. He has asked that security matters be handled—"

Mrs. Roosevelt interrupted him. "And he has more to think about than one man can possibly handle," she said. "I concur with you, Harry, that he should be shielded to the greatest possible extent. Of course, there may come a time when we will have to tell him everything. Until then . . ." She turned up her hands.

Baines reached beneath the table and brought up a telephone. It was an ordinary dial instrument, black, round, with a felt-covered base and the handset sitting in the familiar forked cradle. Attached to it was a length of typical telephone wire: about the thickness of a pencil, covered with woven brown fabric.

"I wonder," said Baines, "if the President noticed that his telephone has been twice replaced in the past several weeks. I suspect he didn't. He said nothing about it. And, of course, there was no reason why he should."

"And this telephone . . . ?"

Baines nodded. "Is different."

He turned it over and pried off the base pad, exposing the tangle of wires and mysterious copper and paper objects inside. She had never seen the inside of a telephone instrument before and saw nothing either usual or unusual.

"This," said Baines, pointing with a pencil at a small oblong object, "is a microphone. This cord"—he pointed at the fabric-covered telephone cord—"has two extra wires in it. It would carry the signal from the microphone out to . . . Well. We're not sure to what. When we discovered this late this afternoon, the wires from the microphone were not attached to anything. But they may have been earlier; say, to a radio transmitter."

"Meaning that conversations between the President and Mr. Churchill—"

"May have been transmitted to a receiver outside the White House," said Baines. "So far we have not found any others, just this one. As you can imagine, every room in the White House is being searched thoroughly."

Mrs. Roosevelt sat silent for a long moment, staring at the upturned telephone with its wicked little electric eavesdropper nested among the complicated works.

"Could be most embarrassing," said Hopkins, popping still another oyster into his mouth and washing it down with a sip of bourbon and water.

"I remember," said Sir Alan Burton, "the remark—was it by Neville Chamberlain?—to the effect that it was dishonorable for Britain to maintain an espionage or counter-espionage service, since gentlemen do not read each other's mail. It has taken our two countries some time to put aside—let us hope temporarily—our long tradition of

decency and to develop, not just a new capacity for dealing in ungentlemanly tricks but a capacity for frustrating
others who adhere to no principles that might discourage
them from such tricks. I fear, Mrs. Roosevelt, that your
government must quickly learn the lessons ours have
learnt most painfully during the past two years."

"I fear so," she said. "The transmitter . . . ?"

"We've not found it yet," said Baines. "Maybe it has not
been brought in yet."

"Perhaps you've nipped the plot in the bud," said Sir
Alan. Raising his brows high, he reached to the platter
and speared an oyster on his fork. Pursing his red lips, he
sucked it into his mouth and visibly savored it before
pushing in after it a morsel of buttered bread and a sip
of wine. "We can hope so, at least."

Mrs. Roosevelt closed her eyes momentarily and
sighed. "The relationship between this and the body in
the refrigerator?" she asked.

"We don't know," said Baines. "Maybe none."

"I should think that's hardly likely," suggested Sir
Alan.

"No, not likely," said Hopkins. "More likely, it's all
interconnected."

"We've got a weasel in the White House," said Baines
grimly. "That's the point. Someone inside switched telephones in the President's study. We're dealing with Nazi
spies, I have no doubt. What bothers me far more, we are
dealing with a traitor inside."

"Does it look like London looks now?" Bonny Battersby
asked Lieutenant-Commander George Leach.

They were in The Palms, the restaurant she had chosen
for their Christmas-night dinner. It was, in her judgment,
the best that was open: round tables with darned floor-
length tablecloths, candles burning in water-filled bowls

on each table, aged, grumpy waiters scurrying between kitchen and tables, strained, solemn men and women in pairs at most of the tables, the men in military or naval uniforms, the women in workday clothes. It was Washington in the third week of America's participation in World War II.

"Actually, no," he said. "Not with that kind of food, in those kinds of quantities." He smiled and touched the flame of his lighter to a cigarette. "And no Blitz, of course—"

"Oh, I'm sorry," she hastened to say. "The Blitz . . . It makes a very big difference."

"I hope you will not have to find out," he said.

"We're so naïve."

"Not really," he said. "Just fortunate."

"In a way, it's more difficult for us," she said. "We're so . . . polyglot. I have German friends, Italian friends."

"I have not," said Leach crisply. "I have traveled through their countries."

"Well, that, of course, very few of us have. We are provincial."

"No one," said Leach, "is more provincial than the self-conscious cosmopolitan."

Bonny Battersby smiled and lifted her glass of bourbon and soda. "Well, anyway, *Left*-tenant-Commander Leach, here's to a better Christmas next year—you free from the *Duke of York* and I from the White House."

His own drink was Scotch, oddly—as he thought—poured over ice, which was melting and diluting the generous measure of whiskey. "Hear, hear," he said quietly.

"And I hope . . . Oh, George, I hope I won't hear again any stories about you crawling around in the Washington sewers." Impulsively she put her hand on his. "I mean . . ." She grinned. "I would just *die* if I heard you had drowned in—"

"Bonny!" he interrupted. "Rainwater. It is only a storm sewer."

She turned her face away from him for a moment, to hide the hot blush that had come to her cheeks. "Well, I wouldn't want to hear you had drowned in rainwater either."

"If I must drown," he said, "I shall endeavor to drown in the North Sea."

"Which God forbid," she said, more solemnly.

He glanced down into his whiskey. "Thank you," he murmured.

"I have assumed you are not married, George," she said frankly.

"No . . . Would it make a difference?"

"It would if you are coming home with me tonight, instead of going back to that bleak little room you have in the White House."

"Oh, my dear!"

She raised her eyes to meet his directly. "That is . . . if you want to."

6

Winston Churchill lay in a tub of scalding, soapy water in his suite in the White House. He was pink, with beads of sweat standing on his forehead, a cigar clenched in his teeth, a mug of scalding coffee within his reach on a stool by the bathtub.

"God!" he grunted. "The Senate and House of Representatives! How will they receive me?"

"With great cordiality and respect, I am sure, Prime Minister," said Harry Hopkins, who sat on the closed toilet and sipped from another mug of the steaming coffee. "You have nothing to fear, sir."

The acrid smoke from Hopkins's cigarette joined the heavy fumes from Churchill's cigar and mixed with the steam from the tub to fill the room with a choking atmosphere that brought tears to the eyes of the young Englishman who was taking dictation.

"How would this go, Harry?" Churchill asked. He settled back in the water, so deep he seemed about to submerge and wet his cigar. " 'I cannot help reflecting that if my father had been American and my mother British, instead of the other way round, I might have got here on my own.' "

"Marvelous," said Hopkins.

"Did you get that, Nigel?" Churchill asked the young man.

"Yes, sir."

"Let me see, Nigel," he said. "Let me see those last sheets. I want to read something to Mr. Hopkins."

The young man had not gotten used to the long-standing Churchillian habit of working with his staff and receiving visitors while he was bathing and dressing—often, as now, stark naked, without so much as a towel draped over his hips. The young man held his gaze on the wall above the tub as he handed the Prime Minister the typed sheets.

"How will they take this, Harry?" asked Churchill. And he began to read: " 'Twice in a single generation the catastrophe of world war has fallen on us. If we had kept together after the last war, if we had taken common measures for our safety, this renewal of the curse need never have fallen upon us. Five or six years ago it would have been easy, without shedding a drop of blood, for the United States and Great Britain to have insisted on fulfillment of the disarmament clauses of the treaties which Germany signed after the Great War . . .' How will the isolationists in Congress like that kind of talk, Harry?"

"They won't like it," said Hopkins. "And God damn them. It's the truth, and they can't deny it now."

Churchill blew a stream of white smoke out over his pink body and through the steam rising from his bathwater. "I think it will be all right," he said. "You don't think the President will be embarrassed?"

"The President will love it," said Hopkins.

Henrietta Nesbitt sat down facing Mrs. Roosevelt in the housekeeper's office. Whenever Mrs. Roosevelt was in the little office, Mrs. Nesbitt could not bring herself to seat herself on her usual queenly chair behind the table she used as a sort of desk. It seemed to her that Mrs. Roosevelt should sit there; and, even though Mrs. Roosevelt never took that chair, Mrs. Nesbitt never sat on it when Mrs. Roosevelt was in the housekeeper's office. Instead, she put herself down uncomfortably on a wooden straight chair and primly adjusted her spectacles.

"A hundred and fifty-five millimeters," she said to Mrs. Roosevelt. "Why can't they use *sensible* measurements? Now, the way I calculate—and I had to look this up and do some figuring—a hundred and fifty-five millimeters is six-and-an-eighth inches. Right? I mean, in *real* measuring terms."

"I'll take your word for it," said Mrs. Roosevelt.

"Okay," said Mrs. Nesbitt. She pushed a wooden-handled ice pick across the table. "Measure that. Six-and-an-eighth inches, point to handle. Hmm?"

"All right. Meaning what, Mrs. Nesbitt?"

"They tell me that fellow was killed by somebody shoving a thin, round blade into the back of his head. A hundred and fifty-five millimeters. Six-and-an-eighth inches. All right. That ice pick is exactly that long, point to handle."

Mrs. Roosevelt smiled. "Well, after all, an ice pick is an ice pick. I suppose—"

Mrs. Nesbitt shook her head firmly. *"Six inches?* Huh-uh. I've got five ice picks in the pantry. This is the only one that's got a six-inch blade. The others—five inches. This is an odd one. Look at that handle. I bet that thing's been around here since the days of Ulysses S. Grant."

"Even so—"

"Oh, but I can tell you more," said Mrs. Nesbitt excitedly. "This ice pick here is one of five, like I said. All but this one are kept in a drawer together in one of the kitchen tables. But this one . . . Well, Ned, he favors this ice pick. He's the one who chips most of the ice—like for champagne, you know, when we have to serve the stuff. He takes this ice pick for *his,* so to speak. He's got a bunch of special tools he thinks are his: a paring knife, a bottle opener, a little silver cup on a chain that he uses to take a taste of every bottle of wine he serves . . . I mean, he's got fancy ideas, Ned has."

"But—"

"The point is," said Mrs. Nesbitt, "that this ice pick wasn't in Ned's drawer where he keeps his special things. It was with the other ice picks, in the big drawer with the cooking forks and such like."

"Coincidence," suggested Mrs. Roosevelt.

Mrs. Nesbitt shook her head. "Nobody else dares touch Ned's things. Even me. He won't yell at me, but he'll sulk for a day, which is worse. He came here in the days of President Wilson, you know, and he has his ways; he's fixed in them. He wouldn't have put *his* ice pick in the big drawer, and if any of the other kitchen staff had used it, they'd have put it back where they found it and hope he wouldn't know they'd ever touched it."

"Have you pointed this out to Mr. Baines?"

"Not yet. It's just this morning I noticed. And I haven't asked Ned about it, either. Anyway, there's something more. Two things more."

"Indeed? Clues, Mrs. Nesbitt?"

"Well, I don't know," said the housekeeper. "All I know is there's two things broken that weren't broken a few days ago. One is the latch handle on the liquor cabinet— you know, the cabinet in the pantry where we keep the whiskey. That's bent, maybe broken inside, like somebody had tried to force it. But there's no bottles missing; I checked. The other thing is that the house telegraph won't work for the West Wing, third floor. You buzz for the butler from up here, he'll hear the buzz but—"

"I'm not sure I know what you—"

"You know," said Mrs. Nesbitt. "The buzzer system. Maybe the President pushes the button in his bedroom. The buzzer goes off in the pantry. Whoever's on duty looks up at the box and can see where the buzz came from, by looking at the little tin arrows that pop up. The White House telegraph system, so to speak. It was installed when Taft was President, they say. Anyhow, the arrow for the third floor, west, is broken and won't pop up."

"And this has some significance?" asked Mrs. Roosevelt.

"Well . . . Henry was the man on duty the night of the murder. He had a buzz from the second floor—from Mrs. Hopkins, it was—and he went up, and when he came back down he looked at the box, as he would always do, to see if anybody had buzzed while he was gone. Sure enough, the arrow was up for third floor, west. So he went up. But nobody had buzzed. He came back down and pushed the lever to reset the arrows, and the little arrow wouldn't go down. It's stuck up, like somebody had *forced* it up."

"Suggesting that someone forced it up to send poor Henry all the way to the third floor—"

"And out of the way," interrupted Mrs. Nesbitt, "so some kind of shenanigans could happen in the pantry or kitchen."

Dominic Deconcini had found most aspects of his White House job exciting, inspiring, fully satisfying. On the other hand, it had its unpleasant elements. Sometimes he had to do things he disliked. He was about to do one of them.

He stood on the street in front of a modest red-brick duplex in Georgetown. Five minutes ago he had once more dialed Bonny Battersby's telephone number; once more the phone had rung ten times in the little house, and no one had answered. According to her personnel file, she rented the south half of the duplex and lived there alone. She was at her desk; he had looked in on her to be sure before he left the White House; but even so he did not want to risk any unpleasant encounter.

The other half of the duplex was rented by a young couple, he a clerk at the Treasury Department, his wife a waitress in the coffee shop at the Mayflower. Deconcini had checked in at the precinct station, and one of the officers had given him that information. There should be no one at home on either side.

He sighed, reached into his overcoat pocket for a ring of skeleton keys, and strode up the short walk. The fourth key turned smoothly in the simple lock. He opened the door and walked in.

She lived modestly. The furniture was probably rented; it was not shabby, but it was well worn—a wine-colored plush davenport and Morris chair with crocheted antimacassars, a Zenith table radio, a tabletop Victrola . . . In the kitchen she had a two-burner gas range with an oven, a small refrigerator, a table with two wooden chairs. The bedroom furniture impressed Deconcini as more likely hers—a double bed with head- and footboard finished in a cheerful pastel green, with birds and flowers painted on the headboard, a matching chest of drawers, and a dressing table. Her alarm clock ticked loudly.

She had not eaten breakfast alone. There were two coffee cups, two plates in the kitchen sink. She had served someone a breakfast of eggs, toast and jelly, and coffee.

Lieutenant-Commander George Leach, he guessed. George had not returned to the White House last night, after his dinner with Miss Battersby.

Deconcini opened the drawer in her nightstand. People often kept personal papers there. She didn't. All he saw was a package of Chesterfields and a book of matches (which was odd, because he did not recall ever having seen her smoke), a little bottle of aspirin tablets, an opened package of Sheik condoms with two missing, and —shoved to the rear and half-hidden under a big white handkerchief—a loaded .38 Colt revolver.

He began to search through her chest of drawers. They were filled with the predictable things: her underwear, stockings, blouses, sweaters . . . Then, under the clothes in the bottom drawer, some things unpredictable: a street map of Bangor, Maine, which, according to her personnel file, was her hometown; a 1935 Bangor telephone directory; an envelope of clippings from the Bangor *Record*, an odd collection of advertisements, together with stories about the openings and closings of local businesses, a downtown fire, sports stories about doings of local high school football and basketball teams.

Deconcini squatted and began to examine the collection. He glanced over the clippings, looking for something in common about them, for some mention perhaps of the Battersby family. Nothing. The clippings had no immediately perceptible significance. All were old, dating from 1934, '35, and '36.

Deconcini checked the telephone directory for the name Battersby. Again, nothing. Which meant nothing. What percentage of the families in Bangor, Maine, had telephones?

He closed the drawer and rose to his feet. There was a closet. He reached for the knob and opened the door. A match fell to the floor. A paper match with the head burned. It had been pinched in the crack between the door and frame, so that it fell when he opened the door. A cautious little trick to tell her someone had opened her closet door in her absence. He would stick it back, but since he could not know exactly where it had been, she would probably know her home had been searched while she was out.

So, what was in here that she was hiding?

Nothing. He checked the pockets of her clothes, then went through the linings and through the shoe boxes on the floor. He lifted the shelf paper and ran his hand over the wood. Nothing.

Why, then, the match? Just as a signal, he decided. If anyone searched her home, whoever did it would of course open the closet. She would know. But if she were hiding something, it was somewhere else. He closed the door and put the match back, feeling it likely she would notice it had been moved.

He returned to the search. Suspicion aroused, he went again to the drawer of her nightstand and pulled it out, to see if anything were taped to the bottom. Nothing. Then he did the same to her bureau drawers. Still nothing.

He entered her bathroom. In the medicine cabinet over her basin he found a Gillette Safety Razor, a soap cup with a brush in it, and another package of Sheiks, this one unopened. It looked as though Bonny either had or anticipated an active social life.

Returning to her living room, and ready to leave, he noticed a black patent-leather purse lying on the table by the door. He picked it up and looked inside. He found a scented handkerchief, a flat tin of aspirin tablets, and a small sheet of paper penciled with what was obviously an old grocery list. She had reminded herself to buy salt, bacon, celery, apple jelly, cheese, Zwieback toast. Zwieback. Interesting . . . She had written the word "Zwieback"—with a slashed Ƶ.

So. This was George's little love den for the rest of his

stay in Washington, until he went back to sea on the *Duke of York.* Deconcini wondered if the lieutenant-commander had noticed anything odd.

Winston Churchill was astounded at the way he was driven from the White House to the Capitol—in a black limousine with a screaming siren and four armed Secret Service agents riding the running boards. He was acutely conscious that he was making history: a British Prime Minister addressing a joint session of the United States Congress. He was nervous and uncomfortable until he stood at the rostrum, behind a dozen microphones, and began to talk; then, like the consummate actor that he was, he gathered his great oratorical forces and played his audience like a master musician.

The Senators and Representatives laughed on cue, applauded on cue, and listened in respectful silence when that was what he expected.

He spoke of the Japanese, of their expectation that the Western democracies would lack the courage and the will to fight them in Asia. *"What sort of people do they think we are?"* he growled, and the Congress rose to its feet and cheered.

He delivered his lecture to the isolationists, and some of the Senators and Representatives turned sullen under the lashing. But they were his again at the end, when he said: "It is not given to us to peer into the mysteries of the future. Still, I avow my hope and faith, sure and inviolate, that in the days to come the British and American peoples will walk together side by side in majesty, in justice, and in peace." The Congress stood and cheered as he walked up the aisle and left the chamber.

Dom Deconcini stood with George Leach at a window and watched as the black limousine and Secret Service cars returned the Prime Minister to the White House.

"It's none of my business, of course," said Deconcini.

"Actually, it is, of course," said Leach.

"Who prints the letter Z with a slash through it?"

"Continentals," said Leach. "French . . . Germans . . ."

"Could be a coincidence, of course," said Deconcini. "A schoolteacher who taught her children to make Zs that way."

"I'll tell you what, old boy," said Leach with a faint smile. "I volunteer to pursue this element of the investigation further. I think perhaps I can encourage her to invite me back to her place tonight. In any event, she cooks an excellent breakfast."

"You know Major Bentz, of course," said Gerald Baines to Mrs. Roosevelt.

"Of course," she said. "Even though he is new to the White House."

Bentz was the grim army officer in command of the uniformed security force that had been placed on the White House grounds. He was a career officer, assigned to Army Intelligence. His boyish face glowed pink. His eyes were pale blue, his blond brows all but invisible, his hair close-cropped. He wore boots and breeches and a Sam Browne belt. She had seen him outside, wearing also a helmet, carrying a riding crop as a swagger stick, and ordering his men peremptorily about. Mrs. Roosevelt was disposed not to like posturing military officers, but she had to admit that Bentz seemed competent and sincere and was probably effective at his work.

"It was Major Bentz who had the idea of going through the storm sewer with the magnetic mine detector, which found the grenades," said Baines. "Now he has been working with me on an additional project. We've found some radio equipment—quite a lot of it, actually."

"You mean the equipment that was transmitting from the President's telephone?" she asked.

"It wasn't working yet, thank God," said Major Bentz. "But it's clever equipment, just the same. When operating, it would have transmitted out of the White House every word the President spoke or heard with his telephone."

"Surely you operate detector equipment that would have intercepted such transmissions and warned us," said Mrs. Roosevelt.

"Yes, of course," said Major Bentz. "But these radios are like nothing the Signal Corps has ever seen before. They transmit on a frequency well outside the bands used by any other radios in the world. We had not supposed it was practicable to use those frequencies. The extra wires on the President's telephone were to have carried his conversations to a tiny transmitter hidden in the telephone box on the wall. Signals from that little transmitter would have been too weak to carry far, so they were to have been relayed by a bigger, more powerful transmitter on the third floor."

"And where did this equipment come from?" she asked.

"It's of German manufacture," said Major Bentz.

"Fortunately," said Baines, "the installation seems to have been incomplete. We found the hidden microphone in the telephone in the President's study but none in his telephone in the Oval Office. We found another microphone in Harry Hopkins's office telephone, plus one in the telephone in his sitting room on the second floor."

"It is quite obvious, is it not," said Mrs. Roosevelt, "that someone hostile has had free access to the White House for some considerable period of time?"

Major Bentz frowned and nodded grimly. "I'm afraid

that's true, ma'am," he said. "We are searching thoroughly."

"For more hidden radios," she said.

"And telephones—"

"And for explosives?" she asked.

"Yes," said Baines. "We are going through every-thing."

Mrs. Roosevelt smiled. "The President remarked this morning that you had searched under his bed."

Bonny Battersby raised herself on tiptoe and kissed Lieutenant-Commander George Leach playfully. "I'm sorry, George," she said. "I really am. But I've got to work tonight, and there's no getting out of it. Mr. Hopkins—"

"Is an unreasonable employer," said Leach. "After all, the sailor home from the sea . . . You know we haven't much time."

She sighed. "How well I know. Whenever duty calls . . ."

"And it could call any time."

"Oh? I thought the Prime Minister was staying on for at least another week."

"He is, so far as I know. But he may not return to England in *Duke of York*. If he decides to fly home, the ship will go on without him."

"Is there a chance of that?"

"I don't know. I really don't know. But tell Mr. Hopkins I am jealous of your evenings."

"Perhaps late tonight, George. Very late. Check with me. Not sooner than midnight, though."

"I'll come down at twelve."

"But not before. I'll be very busy. Not before twelve."

7

"Who is it?" Mrs. Roosevelt called out. Someone was rapping on the door to her sitting room. She had been reading William L. Shirer's *Berlin Diary* and now glanced at her watch. It was ten minutes until eleven.

"Deconcini, Mrs. Roosevelt," said the voice outside the door.

She rose reluctantly from the comfortable chair where she had been absorbed in Shirer's account of his service as a correspondent in Hitler's Germany. She stepped through the little hallway between her bedroom and bathroom, to the door that led to the sitting hall. She opened the door and was surprised by Deconcini's flushed, harried face.

"Whatever . . . ?" she asked.

"A man has been killed downstairs," said Deconcini breathlessly. "Shot. By Jerry Baines. It looks like another attempt to . . . Well, the man was armed with a pistol. Fortunately, Jerry—that is, Agent Baines—was still on duty. He—"

"Have we any idea who the man was?" asked Mrs. Roosevelt.

Deconcini shook his head. "Not yet."

"Another one wearing new Sears, Roebuck clothes and carrying no identification?" she asked.

"Something like that," said Deconcini. "At least, so far that's the way it looks."

Mrs. Roosevelt glanced back at her warmly lighted sitting room, at her chair and book; then she drew a decisive breath. "I shall come down," she said.

"Oh, that's not necessary," said Deconcini. "It's not a pretty sight and—"

"I shall come down, Mr. Deconcini," she said. "Just where did this shooting take place?"

"In the pantry," he said.

A crowd of Secret Service agents, uniformed policemen, army officers, and assorted members of the White House staff separated to make room for Mrs. Roosevelt as she emerged from the elevator, entered the west hall, and walked to the pantry.

The body still lay face down. This man had not been cleanly killed by a sharp instrument driven into the base of the skull. He had been shot, and sticky red blood soaked his clothes and the rug on which he lay. He was oddly dressed: in an olive-drab uniform, consisting of a short jacket, breeches, boots. An olive-drab cap lay beside his head.

"Mrs. Roosevelt!" gasped Baines.

"It appears we are the beneficiaries of another alert service performed by you, Mr. Baines," she said.

Baines's face was deep red, his forehead gleaming with perspiration. "I . . . I wish you didn't have to see this, ma'am," he said.

Mrs. Roosevelt turned her attention to the body. Looking down at it, she asked, "Who is he? Do you know?"

"His identification," said Baines, "may not be as difficult as was that for the other one. This man came in through the door. He was checked in at the Pennsylvania Avenue gate."

"Then who is he?" asked Mrs. Roosevelt.

"I'm afraid there's still a problem, ma'am," said a uniformed police officer. "We have a name, but—"

"I dislike saying this," interrupted Sir Alan Burton, "but I fear you Yanks have still a great deal to learn about how to secure your most important public officers from attempts at assassination."

"The man," said Baines, nodding toward the body, "entered the White House as a Western Union telegraph boy, bringing a telegram. We have reason now to doubt the authenticity of his identification."

"Meaning . . . ?" asked Mrs. Roosevelt.

"Meaning that Western Union never heard of him. So they say. We have called them. They are checking further."

"I should like to hear just how you came upon him, Mr. Baines," said Mrs. Roosevelt. "A full account, please, of exactly what happened."

Baines flushed an even deeper red. "I saw Henry hurry out of the pantry," he said. "On a call upstairs, I suppose. Wasn't that it, Henry?"

The butler, a large black man with a bald head on which the veins traced raised lines, nodded. "Yes, suh," he said. "I was called up to take some coffee to the President's study, where he and Mr. Churchill were meeting. When I came back—"

"It was all over by the time Henry came back," Baines interrupted. "While he was upstairs, I came in the pantry to pour myself a cup of coffee. This man"—he nodded at the body—"was here. He had a gun in his hand. The, uh . . ." Baines pointed at a big automatic pistol lying on Henry's newspaper on the pantry table. "That pistol, there. When he saw me, he fired a shot. You can see where his bullet hit the wall. I dropped. He'd missed me, and I was ducking down; but I guess he thought he'd hit

me and I'd fallen. He turned away from me and I had time
to pull my revolver and fire."

"And fortunately your shot struck the man," said Mrs.
Roosevelt.

"Fortunately, yes," said Baines. "I didn't intend to kill
him, but—"

"But in the circumstances you did not have time to take
very careful aim," said Sir Alan.

Baines nodded. "I'm sorry. I wish we could question
him."

Mrs. Roosevelt frowned deeply. "How did he manage to
carry a loaded pistol into the White House?" she asked.
"Surely our security—amateurish though it may be, Sir
Alan—is better than that."

"The very question we were asking when you arrived,
ma'am," said Baines. He pointed at two uniformed policemen who stood apart and looked miserable. "That's the
very question we were asking."

Mrs. Roosevelt looked at the two men: one a man of
maybe fifty-five years, gray and pale, with his thin white
lips turned downward in a sorry scowl, the other a
younger man with razor-scraped red cheeks.

"This is Sergeant O'Brien," said Baines, nodding toward the elder officer. "And Officer Knopf. Capitol Police.
They were on duty in the gatehouse when the dead man
entered."

"I swear to you, Mrs. Roosevelt," said O'Brien solemnly, with the trace of an Irish accent in his voice.
"That pistol was not on the man's pair-son when he came
through the gate. We sairched him. He could not have hid
somethin' as big as that."

"I know little of weapons," said she, "but I do believe
that is a pistol of German manufacture."

"A nine-millimeter Luger," said Deconcini. "What German officers carry."

"It couldn't have been on him," said Officer Knopf. "I patted him down. I suppose I might miss a little thing, maybe a little automatic, like stuck down in his boot; but he didn't have *that thing* on him when I searched him. I've got no question of it."

"Then where did it come from?" asked Mrs. Roosevelt.

The two officers shook their heads in unison, unhappily.

"I wish to God I knew," said O'Brien.

"He carried good credentials?" asked Mrs. Roosevelt.

"This," said Baines, offering her a yellow card. "It's what any Western Union messenger carries."

"He showed that," said O'Brien. "And the telegram. Said it was a telegram for Mr. Hopkins."

"But didn't you know, Mr. O'Brien, that we receive telegrams in the White House directly, on our own wire? We don't receive them by messenger."

"I know that," affirmed O'Brien. "I do. But the man said this was something special, a radiogram from Switzerland, and couldn't come through on the White House wire. And, after all, a lot of special, different messages have been coming in since the war broke out, especially since the Britishers arrived."

"So he came to the gate, showed this card, and entered the grounds," she said.

"Rode his bicycle up the drive to the door," said Officer Knopf. "I'd looked over the bicycle. That pistol was not anywhere on that bicycle."

"And then . . . ?"

"He was checked again," said Baines. "At the door. Corporal Hagan."

Corporal Hagan was a soldier in khaki: a massive, rawboned man with an unruly cowlick hanging down his forehead and a bulging Adam's apple bobbing at his throat. "He wasn't carryin' no gun when he come by me," he drawled. "I run my hands all over him. I mean, he wasn't carryin' no *nothin'* that he wasn't s'posed to be carryin'."

"Are we to assume, then, Mr. Baines, that the man somehow found a pistol *in* the White House, after he entered?" asked Mrs. Roosevelt.

Baines shook his head. "Inconceivable," he said.

Mrs. Roosevelt glanced at the Western Union identification card. The name printed on it was BILLY DUGAN.

Baines had noticed her glancing at the card. "Tonight's clerks at Western Union say they never heard of Billy Dugan," he said. "Maybe—Maybe we should roust out someone higher up."

"Maybe tomorrow someone will have heard of him," she said. She shook her head. "Though, don't you rather doubt it, Mr. Baines? Anyway, supposing they had, how do we explain how he came through two searches without his pistol being discovered?"

"I have another problem, Mrs. Roosevelt," said Baines. "This man, like the other one, has empty pockets. That identification card seems to be all he was carrying. No money. No keys. Nothing. And, of course, the telegram envelope is empty. If Western Union doesn't know him, and if his fingerprints don't show up in the FBI files, then we have another anonymous corpse."

"And confidentiality, Mr. Baines," she said. "Once again, there is the question of confidentiality."

"No one here will talk," said Baines firmly, looking around at the crowd of maybe a dozen people who hovered in the doorway to the pantry and inside the room. "They understand the importance of confidentiality in the circumstances."

"Well, let me add a word on the subject," said Mrs. Roosevelt. She glanced around. "I am sure you all know how very important are this week's meetings with the

Prime Minister and his staff. If word should reach the press and be circulated throughout the world that our security, here in the White House, is so deficient that we cannot protect the President and Mr. Churchill from ... Well, I am sure that all of you *do* understand. Please think of it as a matter of national security."

There was a general murmuring among the men and women pressing forward to hear Mrs. Roosevelt. Yes, yes, she could hear them murmur. They would keep the secret.

"You may want to stop by the room where Miss Battersby works," Deconcini suggested to Mrs. Roosevelt. "She was typing some reports for Mr. Hopkins and heard the shots."

Bonny Battersby was at her desk, her eyes red and puffy and still wet with tears. Lieutenant-Commander Leach hovered over her.

"Oh, Mrs. Roosevelt!" she whispered shrilly, and she put her hands to her face and shook with sobs.

"Now, now, child," said Mrs. Roosevelt. "It's all over."

Lieutenant-Commander Leach nodded emphatic agreement. "Yes, Bonny," he said softly. "It's over."

Mrs. Roosevelt noticed that the dark-blue sleeves of Leach's uniform jacket were covered with lint from Miss Battersby's light-blue angora sweater. Quite obviously, he had been embracing her, comforting her.

"She heard the shots," said Leach. "She ran out into the hall just as Mr. Baines came out through the pantry door with his pistol still drawn. For an instant, she thought he was going to shoot her. She was terrified."

"I should think so," said Mrs. Roosevelt.

"The dead man," said Deconcini, "had been directed to bring the telegram down here. He was told that Miss Battersby is Mr. Hopkins's secretary and that she would receive the telegram and deliver it to Mr. Hopkins. He was sent down the east stairs and—"

"And somewhere between entering the White House and reaching the pantry on the ground floor, he picked up a weapon," said Mrs. Roosevelt. "May I assume he never entered this room, never spoke to Miss Battersby?"

The young woman uncovered her face. "Oh, God, no!" she exclaimed. "He didn't come in here."

"You were doing some work for Mr. Hopkins?"

Bonny Battersby ran her hand over a pile of handwritten notes. "Transcribing these," she said.

"You keep the door to the hall closed?" asked Mrs. Roosevelt.

Bonny Battersby nodded. "The traffic . . . Too many distractions."

"At what time did you hear the shots?" asked Mrs. Roosevelt.

"I'm not certain," said Bonny Battersby. "Ten-thirty . . ."

"Jerry Baines says ten-thirty," Deconcini confirmed.

Mrs. Roosevelt drew a deep breath and sighed. "I think Mr. Hopkins can spare you for the rest of the evening, Miss Battersby," she said. "At any event, let's say he *must*. Lieutenant-Commander Leach would perhaps not mind escorting you home."

"I believe I can spare the time for that," said Leach.

Bonny Battersby refused to allow George Leach to buy her either dinner or drinks on the way home but insisted they should go directly to her place in Georgetown. She had some hamburger, she said, and they would fry it and eat it on buns with mustard and pickles. She would introduce him to the American hamburger. He did not argue. He was anxious to visit her cozy little home once more.

When the hamburgers were sizzling and coffee was burping in the percolator, Bonny grinned suggestively at Leach and said she would go into her bedroom and change into "something a little more comfortable." Leach did not understand the allusion, but he understood the suggestion. He accepted her instruction to stand at the stove and turn the hamburgers, not to let them scorch.

Bonny was tired. She was anxious to eat and go to bed. She was also a little impatient, and she jerked open her closet door without checking the match she had wedged in the crack between the door and frame before leaving the house in the morning. She saw the match fall to the floor and was satisfied it had served its purpose. She failed to notice that it had not fallen from where she had left it.

Mrs. Roosevelt had decided the President should have his night's sleep without hearing of the new mysterious death in the White House. But upstairs again, she found the President and the Prime Minister alone in the sitting hall, the President in his wheelchair, smoking, a hardly touched glass of wine at his side, the Prime Minister sipping brandy and filling the air with the smoke from another of his immense cigars.

"Well, Sherlock Holmes," said the President, cheerily but with a distinct note of weariness in his voice. "Tell us what new enormity has occurred below stairs."

"You must think us uncivilized, Mr. Churchill," she said to the Prime Minister.

Churchill shook his bulldog head. "Many things of ancient beauty," he said, "lie in ruins on both sides of the Channel, the price we in Europe pay for civilization. To be here and learn nothing more distressing than that two enemy agents—for can we not be certain that was what they were?—have been dispatched . . . Well, that is not particularly distressing."

"Who do I have to bring into the White House," the President asked irritably, "to assure us that we can live and work here in a reasonable degree of security? Need we move out to Shangri La and surround the place with barbed wire?"

"It's not that bad," she said.

"Indeed?" he asked. "I've summoned Morgenthau. If his Treasury Department gumshoes of the Secret Service can't keep gun-toting strangers out of this place, then I propose to turn responsibility for the security of the White House over to some other agency—maybe Army Intelligence. I shouldn't have to tolerate this, Babs."

"Mr. Baines risked his life for us tonight," she said quietly.

"I want a full report," said the President. "I want to know everything that happened, and how, and why. I cannot accept risks to my life and yours and the life of our friend here, the Former Naval Person. I cannot, Babs! We must do whatever we must do."

The investigation into the second death continued. Mrs. Roosevelt received a report of the details the next morning, which she passed along to the President as he demanded. The report established that:

> The deceased was a blue-eyed, brown-haired young man, between the ages of twenty-five and thirty. The body was unscarred, bearing no identifying marks.
>
> He could not be identified. No police agency in the United States had any record of his fingerprints.
>
> He had died of the impact of one .38-caliber bullet, fired at close range, which had struck him in the back, just to the right of his spine, had shattered a rib, torn through his right lung, and exited between

two ribs in front. Cause of death: shock, loss of blood.

The fatal shot had been fired from a .38-caliber Smith & Wesson revolver, identified through ballistics tests as that legitimately carried by Special Agent Gerald Baines.

The dead man was not a messenger for Western Union Telegraph Company, nor had he ever been. The yellow identification card was a forgery.

The apparent Western Union messenger's uniform was an old Boy Scout uniform, from the 1920s. It could have been picked up in any rummage shop.

The rest of his clothes—shirt, underwear, socks, boots—were new, from Sears, Roebuck.

The weapon he had carried and with which he had fired one shot at Special Agent Gerald Baines was a 9 mm. Luger, bearing marks that indicated it was standard German Army issue, manufactured in 1938. It bore no fingerprints but those of the dead man. The bullet dug from the pantry wall had been fired from this Luger.

Intense questioning of the two police guards from the gate and of the army guard at the door produced no clue as to how the weapon had been carried into the White House. It was difficult to believe the man had slipped it past the two searches.

Special Agent Gerald Baines had been justified in firing his service revolver and in killing the deceased.

"Means nothing," the President grumbled when she showed him the typed report. "Let Baines have his commendation—or whatever it is they want to give him. When the time comes to present it, have him up here. I'll present it with a smile. Make sure he's replaced the cartridge he fired. I wouldn't want an agent running around with an empty cartridge in his revolver."

8

"I note an odd fact," said Sir Alan Burton. "The finger-prints on the trigger of the Luger are smudged. Indeed, they are barely clear enough to make an identification. Other fingerprints on the pistol are clear, but these . . . Well, you see? 'Tis an odd circumstance, don't you think?"

Mrs. Roosevelt nodded. "Many things are odd these days, Sir Alan," she said.

The odd circumstance she had in mind at the moment was the fact that it was Saturday morning, two days after Christmas, and business was going on in the White House as if the holiday had never occurred and as if it were not the December weekend between Christmas and New Year's. It could have been a working weekday in February, for all the signs of the holiday in the White House. The few decorations hanging about seemed out of place and awkward. She had never known such a Christmas. Neither, she reflected, had the world.

They were at lunch: she, Sir Alan, Gerald Baines, Dominic Deconcini, Major William Bentz, and Lieutenant-Commander George Leach. There was, at least, a bright winter sun to relieve the gray of a Washington winter.

"What significance do you see in the circumstance, Sir Alan?" asked Baines.

"Oh, perhaps none, my dear chap," said the long-faced Scotland Yard detective. "But wouldn't one think that a trigger just pressed to fire a shot would have distinct prints on it, not a smudged one?"

"I'm afraid one of my boys, with more enthusiasm than good judgment, smudged them when he picked up the Luger," said Baines.

Sir Alan's thoughtful face clouded for an instant. "Perhaps so," he said doubtfully.

She had asked them to join her for this eleven-thirty luncheon so she could review with them all the facts surrounding the two mysterious deaths in the White House in the past few days.

"May I assume no one supposes it is a coincidence that Mr. Baines shot this second man within a few yards of where we found the body of the first?" asked Mrs. Roosevelt.

"For my part," said Sir Alan, "I would not assume anything: either that it is *not* a coincidence or that it *is*. It is an elementary principle of investigation that one does not reason from assumption, only from facts. Of course"—he smiled and nodded at Mrs. Roosevelt—"you have some experience with this sort of thing."

Mrs. Roosevelt smiled around the table. "Sir Alan is reminding me," she said, "of my amateurish meddling in the investigation into the murder of Philip Garber."

" 'Twasn't amateurish a'tawl, dear lady," protested Sir Alan. "Indeed, if not for your shrewd insights, Pamela Rush-Hodgeborn should doubtless have been electrocuted for a murder she did not commit."

"Thank you, Sir Alan. Anyway, I must turn to the fact that the President is most disturbed to know that, not just one, but two anonymous young men have entered the White House with weapons and have met violent deaths here. If we are not safe within the White House—"

"We are doing everything we can," Baines interrupted. "It's not easy."

"I appreciate that, Mr. Baines. But what assurance can we give the President and Mr. Churchill? It is distressing too, that the Prime Minister's safety should also be threatened."

"We must work with the facts we have," said Dominic Deconcini. "Until we have more, we must draw what conclusions we can from those facts and see if they don't lead us to others."

"Very well," said Mrs. Roosevelt. "What facts do we have?"

"Well, I have some new ones," said Deconcini. "I'm afraid, George, they have to do with your friend Miss Battersby."

"The friendship—" Lieutenant-Commander Leach began.

"In the line of duty," Sir Alan interrupted. "I'm sure."

"Actually, no," said the young naval officer. "But what facts, Dom?"

"I telegraphed the police department in Bangor, Maine, yesterday afternoon," said Deconcini. "According to Miss Battersby's personnel file, that is her hometown. The police department, however, says there is no family there named Battersby. In fact, there's none in Pen County, they think. They're checking further, but—"

"Really, Mr. Deconcini, do you suspect Miss Battersby?" interrupted Mrs. Roosevelt. "If so, of what do you suspect her?"

"I suspect her of falsifying at least one major fact on her employment application," said Deconcini. "From that . . . Who knows?"

"Unfortunately, we are in possession of other suggestive facts about Miss Battersby," said Leach. "She keeps a loaded revolver in her bedroom."

"Haw!" Sir Alan Burton laughed. "You've just made a revealing confession, my boy!"

"Dom found it," said Leach. "But I confirmed it last night. She keeps it in a drawer beside her bed."

"Mr. Deconcini," said Mrs. Roosevelt. "Have you searched the young woman's home?"

"I did that yesterday morning," said Deconcini. "Since only one ground-floor window was open the night the first death occurred, and it was hers, I decided to look into—"

"And what else did you find?" asked Mrs. Roosevelt somewhat indignantly.

Deconcini's sharp, dark eyes narrowed and his swarthy complexion colored. He was distressed to see that Mrs. Roosevelt disapproved of a search he had considered routine and necessary. "I wrote some notes," he said, opening a file folder. He handed the notes to her. "Nothing that establishes anything. But curious, don't you think?"

Mrs. Roosevelt read his notes and handed the sheet to Sir Alan. "I agree with your observation that nothing there establishes anything," she said.

"I hope she is not a suspect because she has a pistol in her house," said Major Bentz. "I keep one in *my* bedroom. My wife wouldn't feel safe without it."

"I take it you have not confronted the young woman with any of your facts," said Baines.

"No," said Deconcini. "I thought it better to wait." He smiled faintly. "George volunteered to pursue this line of the investigation."

"And can you say you have learned any facts more important than these, Lieutenant-Commander Leach?" asked Mrs. Roosevelt.

Leach shook his head. "No," he said. "But I shall be having dinner with her again this evening."

"Stick a little more closely to business, George," suggested Sir Alan with a grin.

"Yes, sir."

Mrs. Roosevelt lifted the pitcher and poured more ice water for Gerald Baines. As was her custom, she did not serve wine to her luncheon guests. They were eating tuna-fish sandwiches, celery, and carrot sticks.

"I cannot believe," she said, "that Henry Taylor could have had anything to do with these deaths." She turned to Sir Alan and explained, "He is the Negro butler who was on duty the night of both deaths."

"On the other hand," said Baines, "he *was* in the pantry both nights. And both nights he was conveniently called away—last night just when I encountered the armed man in his pantry, Monday night for long enough for someone to drag a body into the refrigerator."

"Has he been questioned thoroughly?"

"Very thoroughly," said Baines.

"Why are these people coming to the pantry and kitchen?" asked Mrs. Roosevelt. "The two dead men and whoever killed them, which may be one more person or perhaps . . . How thoroughly has the area been searched? Could there be more radio equipment in the pantry or kitchen?"

"We've run magnetic mine detectors over the walls and floors," said Major Bentz.

"When?" she asked.

"This morning."

"I've been wondering," she said, "if last night's man was not in the pantry because his pistol was hidden there. Perhaps, Mr. Baines, you came on him just as he retrieved it from its hiding place."

"I think we may take it as a fact," said Deconcini, "that he did not carry that pistol into the White House last night. If that is so, then he picked it up after he got inside —either from someone who handed it to him or from a hiding place he knew about."

"Then it had been here for some time," said Mrs. Roosevelt.

"God knows what came in through that storm sewer," said Major Bentz. "Or who."

"We left it open too long," said Baines. "I take responsibility for that. Dom warned me."

"It is possible, then," said Mrs. Roosevelt, "that radio equipment and weapons and even explosives were brought into the White House and hidden here."

"Over a period of months, maybe," said Major Bentz. "Before we entered the war and security was tightened."

"Is it possible," she asked, "that no one now in the White House is responsible? Could it be that these men are simply coming in to pick up and use what was hidden here a long time ago?"

"It would be nice to think so," said Baines. "That would mean we have no criminal in the White House. But it doesn't explain why the first man was killed."

"I wish I could shake this feeling that Bonny Battersby let someone climb through her window Monday night," said Deconcini.

"I wish you could, too, Mr. Deconcini," said Mrs. Roosevelt. "I wish that none of us would jump to that conclusion."

The Prime Minister had not gone to bed until four A.M. He was to address the Canadian House of Commons on Tuesday; and, with his full schedule of conferences, he had to prepare his speech at odd hours, especially the hours when others were asleep. His early-morning hours had been productive this day; and when his long conference with the President broke for an afternoon respite, he called Harry Hopkins to his suite.

"You have proved to me, Harry," he said, "that you are

blessed with a sure sense of the political psychology of the American Congress. I wonder if you're as good about the Canadian Parliament."

Hopkins sat down. Churchill lay on his bed, propped up by four or five fat pillows, cigar in hand, a glass of Scotch nearby, the bed littered with newspapers and sheets of paper covered with scribbles.

"I'm not so sure," said Hopkins. "Have they provided any bourbon? Incidentally, when could you find an hour to talk with General Marshall?"

"Oh, shortly, shortly," said Churchill with a dismissing flutter of his hand. "I should be grateful if you would scan some of these notes I've made for the Canadian speech. Some phrases . . . I am uncertain of the Canadian temperament."

Hopkins took half a dozen sheets that the Prime Minister proffered. "People suppose," he said, "that the world-famous Churchillian oratory is extemporaneous, that it just pours forth, as from a fountain."

"They know nothing of speechifying if they think that," said Churchill.

"Oh, this is marvelous!" exclaimed Hopkins with delight.

"What is?"

"What you're saying here about France," he said. "About Vichy." Hopkins grinned and began to read:

> When I warned them that Britain would fight on alone whatever they did, their generals told their Prime Minister and his divided Cabinet, "In three weeks England will have her neck wrung like a chicken."
> *Some chicken!*
> *Some neck!*

Churchill smiled. "Don't tell anyone, Harry, but I fret for weeks over an important speech—and here I've had to make two of them in just a few days, whilst meeting daily with the President."

"Everyone marvels at your stamina," said Hopkins.

"I marvel at the President's," said Churchill. "We're two tough old birds."

"Yes. Yes, you are."

"Tell me something frankly, Harry," said Churchill. "Tell me . . . But first, please pour yourself a drink. I'm sorry I've nothing but Scots whiskey to offer at the moment. I know you're fond of your American bourbon. If I had it, I'd offer you a bit of treacle to mix in your whiskey. That'd make it taste like bourbon." His eyes twinkled and he favored Hopkins with an elfin smile. "But tell me, what of this business of finding dead bodies below stairs? Is the White House invaded? It is unsettling, I must admit, to learn that men armed with pistols and grenades are capering about two floors below my bedroom. And getting themselves killed—though perhaps we're fortunate in that."

"If there were any real danger, we'd move the conferences elsewhere," said Hopkins. "I assure you there is no danger."

"Ah," said Churchill skeptically. "The Nazis would like nothing better than to do us in, you know."

Hopkins opened his mouth to respond, but before he could speak a word he was interrupted by a rap on the door. Sir Charles Wilson, the Prime Minister's physician, entered.

"I regret being so long coming," he said. "Your message came while I was out walking a bit."

"Just wanted you to check my pulse," said Churchill.

"While he does, you'll want some privacy," said Hopkins. "I have some bourbon across the hall and will step across and fetch it."

As soon as Hopkins was out of the room, the Prime Minister pulled off his vest and opened his shirt. "Have a listen, Charles," he said. "I . . . I had a dull pain last night. *Here.* And down my arm. Never had it before. I—"

Churchill fell silent as Sir Charles pressed a stethoscope to his chest and listened. When the physician raised his eyes, he could not conceal his alarm.

"I can't unshoulder the burden right now, Charles," said the Prime Minister quietly. "Don't tell me I have to."

Sir Charles tucked the stethoscope back into his bag. He shook his head. "What can I say? I will say this—you *must* get your rest."

"In a house where German assassins are running about with Lugers in their hands?" hissed the Prime Minister angrily. "We came within an inch of being blown up Monday night, I think. And last night, another one. One of the American security men killed the one last night. But who killed the first one? How can we stay here, Charles? On the other hand, how can we leave?"

Deconcini and Leach sat in the Secret Service office in the Executive Office Building on 17th Street that Saturday afternoon and reviewed the personnel file for Bonny Battersby.

She was twenty-nine years old, according to the information she gave on her application for her job as a secretary to Harry Hopkins. She had been born in Bangor, Maine, the only child of Willard and Emmeline Battersby, whom she listed as still living in Bangor. She had graduated from high school in Bangor in 1930, the application said, and had worked in Bangor, then Boston, then New York, and finally in Washington. She had worked as a waitress and a retail clerk before she got her first secretarial job in New York in 1937. Arriving in Washington in 1939, she had gone to work as a typist at the Department of Justice.

"References," mused Deconcini. "Assistant attorney general. Pastor of the M Street Congregational Church. 'Faithful churchgoer,' he says in his letter. 'A young woman of the highest moral character.' "

"Damn it, I hope she's innocent," said Leach impulsively.

"I'm sorry, George. You're uh . . . how shall we say? Smitten with her. Aren't you?"

Leach frowned. "Well . . . No, I'm not that. After all, she *did* invite me to her bed on very short acquaintance. She's not the sort of girl one would wish to—"

"Never mind," snapped Deconcini.

"In her earthy, innocent way," Leach went on, "she's actually quite appealing."

"The question is, how do you introduce into your conversation this evening something very innocent that will trap her?"

"Well, suppose I, uh, said I have a few free days while the Prime Minister is in Ottawa, would like to see something of the country, and I'd like for her to show me Bangor."

"She'd have to be a fool to believe that," muttered Deconcini.

"Oh."

"But we can come up with something, if we put our minds to it."

"A powerful ship, *Duke of York*," said Bonny. "Isn't it? I mean, George, you serve aboard an important ship, don't you?"

"I suppose it is, actually," said Leach.

"I'm interested," she said. "I read things Mr. Hopkins writes about ships like that, and I don't understand half of what I read."

"Hmm, neither do I," said Leach.

She had changed into something more comfortable again this evening and sat beside him on her living-room sofa, wearing a tea-colored silk negligee that she had allowed to fall open, revealing her lace-trimmed white panties and brassiere. She wore her stockings rolled down to her knees, leaving her thighs bare to the short legs of the panties.

"For example," she continued, "what in the world is a 'gunnery-radar set?'"

"I've never seen one," he lied.

She laughed. "Some kind of secret thing, huh?"

"I s'pose 'tis," he said.

"Well, then I shouldn't mention it. In fact, *I* shouldn't have. Of course . . . You won't tell anyone I did. Mr. Hopkins would be furious if he knew I mentioned anything he writes, even if it's to you and is about the ship you serve aboard."

He grinned. "You can trust me," he said.

"I know," she said softly.

Leach tipped his glass and fortified himself with a sip of the Scotch he had bought on their way home.

"He says awful things about me, doesn't he?" she asked.

"Who?"

"Dominic Deconcini. Because he found that window unlatched, he thinks I opened it and let German spies into the White House." She shrugged. "I'm defenseless against an accusation like that. How can I prove I didn't?"

"You've not been accused," said Leach.

"But he suspects me. Sometimes I think I can see his eyes on me. I mean, when he's not around."

"He's a sincere young man," said Leach.

"An Italian," she said. "Has it ever occurred to anybody that Italy is allied with Hitler and that—"

"I think we shouldn't talk about it," said Leach.

Bonny smiled. "I suppose," she said. "You can understand how I feel."

"Yes, of course."

"Any more word about how long you can stay?" she asked. She reached for the bottle and splashed another swallow of Scotch into her own glass.

"Not as yet."

"Where will you be going?" she asked. "To the Pacific? Will you write me?"

"Of course," he said.

"Please do. Letters coming to the White House will come through without the usual delays."

"If you should not happen to be at the White House any longer, where will you be?" he asked.

"I will be at the White House," she said definitely. "Dominic Deconcini notwithstanding, I will still have my job at the White House."

"Of course," said Leach. "What I meant was, if circumstances should change—I mean some turn in the war—and I wanted to reach you and couldn't find you here in Washington, where would you be, Bonny? There've been people tragically lost from each other in the war, you know. Would you go home to . . . to Maine? How would I address a letter to you there?"

"Oh," she said airily. "In care of my father, Willard Battersby. Address it General Delivery, Bangor, Maine. My parents sold their house recently and are living with my mother's sister. They pick up their mail at the post office. Soon they'll have another address, but for the moment . . . All right?"

"All right," he said as she leaned toward him and offered her mouth for a kiss.

9

"The Prime Minister will be leaving for Ottawa tomorrow," said Harry Hopkins to Gerald Baines. "He'll return on Wednesday. The President wants to tell him on his return that the matter of the two deaths in the White House has been resolved. I'd regard that as something of a deadline if I were you, Mr. Baines."

Baines nodded glumly. "I understand," he said. "Fish or cut bait."

"Something like that."

Deconcini had overheard, and when Hopkins had left the room he shook his head, turned down the corners of his mouth, and sneered, " 'Something of a deadline.' Something of a deadline, indeed. How does he suppose we—"

"I can understand," Baines interrupted. "Times like these demand a whole lot of all of us. The President should not have to divert any of his attention to problems that are ours to solve. He's the commander-in-chief, after all."

"So far as I'm concerned," said Deconcini, "we've got enough on Bonny Battersby to arrest her, lock her up in a cell on one of the army posts, and sweat her a bit. She's not telling the truth."

"If you want to do that," said Baines, "you'll have to

make your case with Mrs. Roosevelt. She won't stand for it unless you have—"

"Since when do we have to clear everything with Mrs. Roosevelt?" asked Deconcini.

"Since she's taken an interest in the investigation," said Baines. "Since she's not just First Lady but the President's personal representative in just about everything that goes on."

"I'm willing to face her on it," said Deconcini. "Are you?"

"No. I'm not convinced."

"Well, you're my superior. I—"

"Go ahead if you want to, Dom," said Baines.

It was Lieutenant-Commander George Leach who joined Deconcini in facing Mrs. Roosevelt in her little office.

"I will not interfere, Mr. Deconcini," she said. "If you think fit to place the young woman under arrest, then do so. Far be it from me to interfere."

Deconcini smiled. "Your words say one thing, Mrs. Roosevelt," he said. "Your voice says another."

"I cannot and will not interfere in your performance of your duties, Mr. Deconcini," she said.

"May I . . . ?" asked Leach deferentially.

She nodded at him. "Why, of course."

"It's a rather simple matter, isn't it, in the end?" Leach suggested. "I couldn't have more sympathy for the young woman, Mrs. Roosevelt, for reasons I suspect you understand. But the unfortunate truth is, she lies. She lied again to me, last night."

"In what regard?" asked Mrs. Roosevelt.

Deconcini picked up the conversation. "She insists her parents live in Bangor, Maine," he said. "She told George he could send mail to her in care of her father at General

Delivery, Bangor. I'm sorry, ma'am, but it simply isn't true. I telephoned the chief of police in Bangor this morning, and at my request he wakened the postmaster. The postmaster went to his office and checked the records, even though today is Sunday. You cannot address mail to a Willard Battersby in Bangor, Maine. You can't. There is no address for him there, and he does not pick up mail there."

"May I ask a question, then?"

"Well, of course. Certainly."

"Have you confronted Miss Battersby with these questions? Have you afforded her an opportunity to explain these inconsistencies?"

"No, ma'am. We have not."

"Then . . ."

She was not in her office. Harry Hopkins was with the President, spending the day in conferences that seemed unlikely ever to break. If there were notes to be transcribed, Bonny Battersby was not there to transcribe them.

"Call her, George," said Deconcini. "It would be better if you did than if I do."

Leach picked up the telephone on her desk and dialed her number in Georgetown. No answer.

"I'm going to search her desk," said Deconcini. "If that troubles you, wait outside."

The young naval officer shrugged. "Search away," he said. "I would be curious to know if she keeps a supply of rubber prophylactics here, too."

"That's been to *your* benefit, I judge," said Deconcini. "If she's innocent—"

"Sorry," said Leach smoothly.

They began to search through the drawers of the battered old yellow-oak desk that had been temporarily placed in the one-time trophy room to turn it into an office for Harry Hopkins's secretary.

The clutter was not suggestive. Apart from pencils, erasers, and paper clips, she had four keys, which turned out to be to four filing cabinets and had been, similarly, moved temporarily into the old trophy room to contain the Hopkins files. The filing cabinets themselves were crammed with onionskin paper in manila files, carbon copies of Hopkins's letters, reports, and memoranda. Deconcini leafed through a few file folders at random. He saw nothing meaningful to the investigation.

"Dom."

Deconcini turned away from the file folders he was flipping through. "Hmm?"

"Something odd here," said Leach.

"What?"

"Cigarettes," said Leach. "A pack here, in the corner of her desk drawer."

"I noticed," said Deconcini.

"But she doesn't smoke," said Leach. "In all the time I've spent with her, she hasn't smoked a single cigarette. What's more, there's something odder than finding the pack here."

"What's that?"

"A butt in the pack," said Leach. "Half smoked and crushed out. In the pack with the rest of the cigarettes. Is it an American custom to put a half-smoked butt back in the pack with the cigarettes?"

"No," said Deconcini. "I don't think I've ever seen anybody do that. What kind of cigarettes are they?"

"Uh . . . Chesterfields," said Leach.

"The same kind that I found in her nightstand. Put them back where you found them. If Harry Hopkins doesn't smoke Chesterfields—"

"Really, Dom! You don't think *he* sleeps in her bedroom?"

"No, I don't. But I'm going to see what kind of cigarettes he smokes."

"Could this mean anything, actually?" Leach asked, looking at the charred, wrinkled butt in the pack of cigarettes.

Deconcini shrugged. "Maybe that someone was in a terrible hurry to put it out, maybe to hide it, and had nowhere else to put it," he suggested. "And maybe it means nothing. Maybe it's just an untidy habit."

Leach returned the cigarette pack to where he had found it in the center drawer of the old desk. "Odd, though," he said. "Since *she* doesn't smoke."

When he returned to the Secret Service office, Deconcini found a message waiting. He was asked to meet with Mrs. Roosevelt in the sitting hall at three o'clock. He stopped at the Prime Minister's map room on his way and suggested to Leach that perhaps he should meet with her, too. When they entered the sitting hall they found Sir Alan Burton with Mrs. Roosevelt.

"Ah, Lieutenant-Commander Leach," she said. "I'm glad you can join us. Be seated, gentlemen. Make yourselves comfortable."

Putting aside a newspaper to make room to sit on the couch that faced Mrs. Roosevelt's chair, Deconcini's eyes fastened on a large chart drawn on a big sheet of white poster board and displayed on an easel.

"It's a chart of the west end of the ground floor," said Mrs. Roosevelt, noticing that both Deconcini and Leach were staring at it. "Simplified a bit, omitting bathrooms and closets. I hope you don't find the two plus-marks overdramatic. They of course mark the spots where the

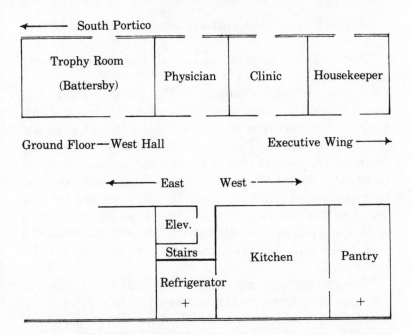

South Portico

| Trophy Room (Battersby) | Physician | Clinic | Housekeeper |

Ground Floor—West Hall   Executive Wing ⟶

East   West ⟶

Elev.		
Stairs	Kitchen	Pantry
Refrigerator		
+		+

bodies were found. I had it drawn for our convenience in sorting out some of the elements of the mystery. Already, I believe, it has helped Sir Alan to raise a point."

"And what is that, Sir Alan?" asked Deconcini.

"Well, I did want to inquire," said Sir Alan Burton, "of the door between the center hall and the Executive Wing. Is it locked at night, or guarded, or both?"

"Sir Alan," said Mrs. Roosevelt, "has been reviewing with me the question of *access* to the kitchen and pantry. Until now, we have focused on *who* might have killed those two young men; let us think for a bit about *how* the killer gained access to where they were killed. You have assumed, Mr. Deconcini, that the killer entered the White House through a window, probably the window by Miss Battersby's desk; but really access could have been by other means."

"Actually, I haven't entirely assumed it," said Deconcini.

"Anyway, my question is logical, isn't it?" asked Sir Alan.

"Certainly," said Deconcini. "The answer is that the door between the west end of the west hall and the passage to the Executive Wing is normally locked after the principal executive officers leave the wing. As to its being guarded, the answer is that at least half a dozen men are constantly on duty in the Executive Wing—of whom one or more would normally have the door we are talking about within his view. I'm talking about Secret Service agents and uniformed policemen. Furthermore, since the war broke out, we have a company of soldiers on the premises."

"Are you saying," asked Sir Alan, "that it is impossible for anyone to have passed between the Executive Wing and the west hall at the time when the two killings took place?"

" 'Impossible' is a hard word, Sir Alan."

"So it could have happened?"

Deconcini shrugged. "It could have happened."

"I am compelled to remind you, Dom," said Leach, "that Wednesday night you and I entered the west corridor, the pantry, and the kitchen, wholly unobserved."

"Which raises a point, I suppose," said Deconcini.

"It does indeed," said Mrs. Roosevelt. "We have focused our attention on the west hall, on the office of the housekeeper, and on the trophy room temporarily appropriated by Mr. Hopkins as an office for his secretary Miss Battersby. Suppose the whole Executive Wing were open to the intruder?"

"Only someone quite knowledgeable of our security procedures could—"

"Precisely," she said. "Which suggests—"

"That someone in the Secret Service—"

"Yes," said Mrs. Roosevelt, nodding emphatically. "Of course, we've already thought of that. But it does not include Miss Battersby, does it? *She* is not privy to—"

"But could have learned, by observation," said Deconcini.

"I suggest," said Mrs. Roosevelt, "that we have given too much attention to Miss Battersby, perhaps at the cost of reviewing other alternatives. I will never seek to divert an official investigation, but I *do* think our attention should be more . . . How shall we say? More catholic?"

"Uh . . . Well—"

"I've a bit of information that may have some significance," said Sir Alan Burton. "With the excellent cooperation of all concerned, I have been able to wire to London facsimile photographs and the fingerprints of the two men found dead in the White House. As to the first, Scotland Yard and our military intelligence agencies are as mystified as we are here. As to the second, there is a possibility. I received this wire today."

Sir Alan handed a yellow radiogram to Deconcini.

"From—" Deconcini began.

"You will understand that it was decoded by our staff here in the White House," said Sir Alan. He nodded at Leach. "I'm sorry it wasn't brought to you, Lieutenant-Commander. It is my standing instruction that everything of this nature is to be given to you."

The decoded message read:

NO INFORMATION ABOUT FIRST CHAP STOP HE IS UN-
KNOWN HERE STOP AS TO SECOND SUBJECT HE BEARS
STRONG RESEMBLANCE TO HASSO VON KEYSERLING
AGENT OF SICHERHEITSDIENST OR ABWEHR MORE
LIKELY SICHERHEITSDIENST STOP FINGERPRINT VERIFI-
CATION IMPOSSIBLE STOP VON KEYSERLING KNOWN TO

SPEAK FLAWLESS ENGLISH STOP VON KEYSERLING PRE-
SENT WHEREABOUTS UNKNOWN STOP ADVISE SOONEST
IF DEAD MAN PROVES TO BE VON KEYSERLING STOP

" 'Sicherheitsdienst,' " Deconcini muttered, shaking his head.

"It means 'security service,' " explained Sir Alan. "Technically speaking, it is the internal security service of the Nazi party, under the command of Reinhard Heydrich. In fact, the SD, as it is called in Germany, has long ago extended its jurisdiction to foreign intelligence, to give Heydrich and Himmler more power. The Abwehr is military intelligence, under the command of Admiral Canaris. If this man was in fact Hasso von Keyserling, and if he was in fact associated with either of those agencies, he was a dangerous Nazi spy and assassin.

"Motive," Sir Alan continued solemnly. "We know why the second man was killed: he was discovered armed in the White House and fired a shot at Agent Baines. But why was the first man killed?"

"Is it possible," asked Leach, "that the second man killed the first one? I mean, could there have been some rivalry or breach of discipline—"

"Speculative," Sir Alan interrupted. "Of course it's possible, but it is too highly speculative to explain anything."

"I am perhaps naïve," said Mrs. Roosevelt, "but the motive seems abundantly clear to me. The first man was killed to prevent his disclosing something. And that something almost certainly was the identity of a traitor and spy in the White House. This, too, is speculation, Sir Alan, but I suspect that Lieutenant-Commander Leach has struck the right chord in suggesting some kind of rivalry or breach of discipline. The killer, who is also a dangerous spy, remains in the White House. The situation is most distressing."

"We must not think in terms of only one traitor and spy," said Deconcini. "There has been more than one at work."

"We—"

Tommy Thompson, Mrs. Roosevelt's secretary, entered the room. "Sorry," she said. "Sorry to interrupt. But there's a District of Columbia police officer downstairs, who says he has some information you want."

"About what?" asked Mrs. Roosevelt.

"He doesn't say, but he says you know him. Captain Edward Kennelly."

"Oh, of course," said Mrs. Roosevelt. "Bring him up, Tommy." She turned to Sir Alan and laughed. "He's the detective who worked with us on the Garber murder two years ago."

Shortly the tall, florid, white-haired Irish detective entered the room, grinning broadly, conspicuously delighted to be once more in the White House and in the presence of the First Lady.

"Captain Kennelly," said Mrs. Roosevelt, "let me introduce the *real* Sir Alan Burton."

"Ho! Sir Burton! You don't look a thing like the man that fooled us into thinking he was you, two years ago."

"The late Archibald Adkins," said Sir Alan. "I believe you stretched his neck, did you not?"

"Actually we electrocuted him," said Kennelly with a nod of satisfaction. "And good riddance it was, too."

Mrs. Roosevelt introduced Kennelly to the others in the room, then asked him to have a seat. "What information do you have for us, Captain?" she asked.

"Well," said Kennelly brusquely. "The Secret Service office sent us some pictures of a corpse and asked us to show them around, to see if anyone could identify the subject. Which we've done. I can't say we can identify the man, but we've learned something about him."

"Anything will help," said Deconcini.

"Well, then," said Kennelly. "One of my boys works a beat up Connecticut Avenue: Dupont Circle and up and down there. He took off some time for Christmas and just came back yesterday. When he saw the picture of the corpse, he said it looked like a young fellow he sees on the street up there, sometimes carrying a bit more of a load than was good for him, if you follow my meaning. Anyway, my man took the picture with him last evening and showed it around in some bars. Sure enough, in one bar they remember him well and were wondering where he'd been the last few days. We didn't go any farther with the matter, not knowin' for sure what you wanted. But I think you could find out something about the boy if you—"

"Can you take me to the place, Captain?" asked Deconcini.

"Well . . . I can tomorrow. It'd be closed today. Tomorrow afternoon is when the regulars would be in the bar and—"

"Fine," said DeConcini. "Tomorrow afternoon."

Mrs. Roosevelt accompanied Captain Kennelly downstairs, to the door of the White House. Sir Alan, Deconcini, and Leach remained in the sitting hall, chatting.

"Dupont Circle," Deconcini mused. "Why couldn't he have said Georgetown?"

"Humh?" asked Sir Alan.

"If the bar where the man was found had been in Bonny Battersby's neighborhood I'd feel a little closer to a solution," Deconcini explained.

"Where, incidentally, is Mr. Baines today?" asked Sir Alan. "I should have thought he would be a part of this meeting."

"Taking the rest of the day off, I suppose," said Deconcini. "It's Sunday, you know."

"Will you be going with the Prime Minister to Ottawa?" Leach asked Sir Alan.

"No. Since he will be returning for another week or so in the White House, I am assigned to the matter that is at the moment before us," said Sir Alan. "The Prime Minister should like to return to find that we have solved the mystery and cleared the White House of all possibility of his being murdered in his bed. The same applies to you, Lieutenant-Commander."

"Marvelous." Leach grunted. "Solve the mystery by Wednesday. Can it be done, Sir Alan?"

"If Winston says it can, it can," said Sir Alan. He pulled a paper from his pocket. "He sent me a little note: 'What progress is being made toward apprehending the perpetrator of the murder of Monday night last? Pray offer every assistance to the President's security staff, that our safety on these premises may not be in question on our return from Ottawa.'"

Mrs. Roosevelt returned, smiling with enthusiasm. "Miss Battersby is in her office," she said. "I've deprived Harry Hopkins of her services for half an hour, so she may respond to some of the questions you have raised, Mr. Deconcini."

"I'm not sure that a confrontation is the best investigative technique," said Deconcini. "It may be premature."

"I've ordered tea and coffee brought up," said Mrs. Roosevelt.

Bonny Battersby arrived shortly. Her face was flushed and she seemed a little breathless. She was wearing a tight black skirt and a well-filled white sweater.

"Mr. Deconcini wants to ask you a few questions, Miss Battersby," said Mrs. Roosevelt.

"I'm sure he does," said the young woman. She fixed an unfriendly stare on Deconcini. "He thinks I opened my window and let a murderer into the White House."

"He's only doing his duty," said Mrs. Roosevelt, "and I feel confident you can erase his suspicions."

Deconcini glanced sternly at each of the others. "There is only one point I would like to clear up with Miss Battersby at this time," he said, "and I would be grateful if you would let me confine my inquiry to the one point."

Sir Alan was mystified by that statement, probably, but Mrs. Roosevelt knew what Deconcini meant: that he did not want the young woman to know he had entered and searched her home. The experienced old Scotland Yard investigator could conceal his thoughts at will; he withdrew as though he suddenly felt sleepy. Leach nodded wisely and folded his hands contentedly in his lap.

"There is really just one thing, Miss Battersby," said Deconcini. "On your employment record you have listed your place of birth and hometown as Bangor, Maine. As recently as last evening you assured Lieutenant-Commander Leach that mail could be addressed to you in Bangor, by sending it in care of your father, General Delivery. In fact, the police department in Bangor has been unable to identify anyone named Battersby living in the town or even in the county, and the postmaster has no address for a Willard Battersby or any record of mail being picked up by Willard Battersby."

The young woman's lips stiffened and twitched, her cheeks reddened, and she put a knuckle to her eye and squeezed out a tear. "Well . . ." she whispered. "So?"

"Well, what is the answer, my dear?" asked Mrs. Roosevelt gently. "Is Bangor, Maine, your family home, or isn't it?"

"Is your name in fact Bonny Battersby?" asked Deconcini.

She shook her head. "No. It isn't." She began to sob. "No. I lied about it."

"But *why?*"

The young woman covered her face with her hands and wept.

Ned arrived with the tea and coffee. Mrs. Roosevelt poured; guessing that the young woman would take coffee, she poured a cup for her, black and strong. Deconcini, now grim-visaged, took coffee, too, while Mrs. Roosevelt joined the two Englishmen in having afternoon tea.

"Ah, now," said Mrs. Roosevelt brightly. "I think now, Miss Battersby, or whatever your name is, we should hear your explanation."

"There's no point in asking me who my father is," the young woman said. "I don't know. I'm from Boston. My mother called herself Fisher sometimes and sometimes Ryan. She picked up names from . . . men who moved in and lived with us. She drank a lot. She sold illegal liquor during Prohibition. She was arrested twice that I know of." She stopped and sighed. "You can imagine how I grew up."

"Indeed," said Mrs. Roosevelt sympathetically.

"Well . . . If you want to work, if you want to get any kind of decent job, you haven't got much chance if you come out of a background like that. So I invented a different background for myself: small-town girl, poor but honest parents, the works. I've never even been in Bangor, Maine. But I've got a phone book from there, and some old newspapers, and a street map. If somebody tries to talk to me about Bangor, I can fake it pretty well. I know what they call the high school basketball team. I know the names of some of the stores. I—"

"Where did you live in Boston?" asked Deconcini.

"You'll check that, too," she said. "All right. We lived in South Boston. Suffolk Avenue part of the time."

"Where did you graduate from high school?"

"I never did. I've shown a Bangor High School diploma,

but it's a fake, made in a print shop in South Boston by
a friend of mine."

"What's your real name?"

She shrugged. "Why not Bonny Battersby? I've been
Bonny Battersby since 1933. My Social Security card says
I'm Bonny Battersby. My personnel file, that you looked
into . . . You found recommendations in there for me,
didn't you? For Bonny Battersby. From the time I got my
first job . . . Bonny Battersby."

"Even so, what was your name before?" asked Deconcini.

"Emmy Ryan."

"Have you ever been arrested?"

"No. You want my fingerprints?"

"As a matter of fact, yes."

"Oh, Mr. Deconcini," murmured Mrs. Roosevelt.

"Now, you worked at the Department of Justice," said
Deconcini. "Before that—"

"In New York. I came to Washington from New York
in 1939. I was highly recommended by my former boss,
Mr. Elihu Weinberg of Goldman, Sachs. His letter is in
my file. I worked as a typist in a brokerage office. I studied
shorthand nights, so I could be a stenographer and secretary, instead of just a typist."

"Could we telephone Mr. Weinberg?"

"Why not?"

"And where did you work before you went with Goldman, Sachs?"

"I was with Goldman, Sachs two years, and before that
I worked in a Woolworth store on Lexington Avenue for
a year. That takes me back to 1936. Before that I was still
in Boston, clerking in dime stores, waiting table . . . And
sometimes I was just unemployed and on relief."

"You've come a long way, to be a secretary to Mr.
Harry Hopkins," said Deconcini.

"Yes, and I suppose you're going to take it away from me," she said defiantly. "And send me back to being Emmy Ryan, maybe hustling blue-plate specials in a diner."

"Oh, no!" exclaimed Mrs. Roosevelt. "Not if—"

"Not if we can clear up one or two other little points," said Deconcini. "I *do* want your fingerprints, and I *will* call Mr. Weinberg. Otherwise, if all we have against you is that you changed your name eight years ago . . ." He shrugged. "Well. It will be up to Mr. Hopkins. If it doesn't bother him, it doesn't bother me."

"I think that's quite fair," said Mrs. Roosevelt. "So, you see? Much can be settled by facing our problems forthrightly."

Mrs. Roosevelt accompanied Bonny Battersby to the elevator.

"She's lying through her teeth," Deconcini growled to Sir Alan Burton and George Leach.

"Be prepared to prove it, Mr. Deconcini," said Sir Alan as he stirred sugar into his second cup of tea.

10

"I don't suppose it makes any difference to you that this is humiliating," said Bonny Battersby.

"It makes a difference," said Deconcini. "I am sorry, Miss Battersby. I really am."

They were at D.C. police headquarters, where a uniformed technician was taking the young woman's fingerprints. A few minutes earlier she had stood under bright lights with an identification board hung around her neck and had been photographed: mug shots. It was only a little after eight on Monday morning; she had shown up sullen and angry, dressed in the black skirt and white sweater she had worn Sunday afternoon; and she chewed at her lips as she submitted to the process of making the fingerprint record Deconcini meant to send to the FBI master file as quickly as possible.

She winced as the technician pressed her inked fingers on the printed spaces on the fingerprint card. "What about my handsome British naval officer?" she asked bitterly. "Did he volunteer what I told him about sending mail to me in Maine, or did you give him the third-degree?"

"I gave him the third-degree," said Deconcini dryly. "In fact, his superior, Sir Alan Burton, ordered him to cooperate with me."

"So you turned him into a weasel," she said.

"I have to acknowledge to you that I am going to be most definitely embarrassed if you turn out to be innocent," said Deconcini. "That's one of the hazards of being in the business of security or law enforcement."

She held her inky fingers at arm's length, away from her white sweater, as the technician firmly pressed the fingers of her left hand onto the ink pad, then onto the card. "Oh, my *entire* sympathy," she said.

"National security, you know," said Deconcini. "The war—"

"Is ample justification for anything," she interrupted.

The technician handed her a damp gray towel, and she began to scrub at her fingertips, trying unsuccessfully to remove every trace of the black ink. She frowned as she saw that some stain would persist.

"I'll drive you on over to the White House," said Deconcini.

"I'd rather walk," said Bonny Battersby.

Deconcini delivered the fingerprint card to FBI headquarters and received assurance that a check would be made in the master files and that he would receive a report before the day was over. The mug shots would be ready before noon, and he would send them to the police departments of Boston and New York.

Returning to the Secret Service office, he found a message from Gerald Baines. The senior agent was down with a bad cold or the flu, the message said, and would not be in today and maybe not tomorrow. Deconcini was left in command of the investigation and was authorized to assign as many agents to it as he needed.

He telephoned Major Bentz and met him in the housekeeper's office.

"I'm just about ready to say that the White House is clean of unauthorized telephone and radio equipment," said the army officer. "I'm sorry to hear Jerry Baines won't be in today. I swear, the man has an *instinct* for where stuff can be hidden in the building."

"Well, he's worked here a long time," said Deconcini.

"We've pulled a lot of it," said Major Bentz. "Elaborate equipment, ingeniously installed. If it had all gone into operation, a lot of important secrets would have gotten into the hands of the Nazis. I shudder to think what damage might have been done."

"I'm more concerned about weapons," said Deconcini. "The second man, the one who may have been Hasso von Keyserling, had a Luger. If he didn't slip it past the guards—which I am convinced he didn't—then how did he get it into the White House?"

"They stashed a cache of weapons somewhere, you think?"

"What's the alternative? If he didn't bring the Luger into the White House himself, then either one of two things happened: he went to a hiding place he knew about and picked it up, or he met someone in the White House and that someone handed it to him."

"Everything," said Major Bentz, "seems to have happened within the west corridor and adjoining rooms on the ground floor. We've been over every room."

"With a metal detector?"

"With a metal detector," said the major. "Concentrating, as you suggested, on the trophy room and Miss Battersby's desk and files. There are no weapons in there, Dom; that I can definitely promise you. So where do we go from here?"

"Hell, how do I know?" asked Deconcini irritably. "The Secret Service is supposed to guard the President, not play Sherlock Holmes. I'll leave the latter up to Mrs. Roosevelt; that's *her* specialty."

*   *   *

"Tell me something, Captain," Deconcini said to Kennelly as Kennelly drove him up Connecticut Avenue in a marked police car. "You've got a lot of experience with murder, but it's a little out of my line. What I'd like to know is, would an autopsy show if a man had been smoking a cigarette within a few minutes of his death? I mean, would there be evidence of it in the lungs?"

"There would," said Kennelly. "They'd have to section a lung to find out, but it could be done, I think."

Deconcini nodded thoughtfully. "We haven't told you much about what's going on, have we?"

"I don't have to know," said Kennelly.

"You worked with Mrs. Roosevelt two years ago, I understand. What kind of experience was it?"

"She's a dear lady," said Kennelly solemnly, his Irish brogue manifesting itself in his emphasized words. "But stubborn. The worst part of her stubbornness was that she was *right* all along. Her instinct for the innocence of young Pamela Rush-Hodgeborne was unreasonable, but it was *right*. Don't underestimate her, Mr. Deconcini. Her damned instincts—"

"For the underdog," said Deconcini.

Kennelly nodded. "A fine lady," he said.

The bar, just around a corner off Connecticut Avenue, was a neighborhood establishment. It was dark inside, and the atmosphere smelled of beer. A few men, obviously afternoon regulars, sat on the bar stools, quietly philosophizing over mugs of beer.

The bartender was the owner, a stout man named Reilly. "On the house," he said as he pushed mugs of beer in front of Kennelly and Deconcini. "Stanley was telling me you gentlemen would be by. I'm not sure what I can tell you about the man in the picture he showed me, but—"

"Whatever it is," said Kennelly. "Anything at all."

"Well, then . . ." mused Reilly. "I never heard his name. He would stop in here in the afternoon, like now, not very often in the evening. Didn't have much to say. He listened, mostly. And he drank. He was a two-fisted drinker." -

"What'd he drink?" asked Deconcini.

"Whiskey," said Reilly. "Rye whiskey, with beer chasers. Two or three, he'd have. Two or three. Then he'd sit and nurse his last beer for an hour, listening to the talk, almost never saying anything. Finally, just before he was ready to leave, he'd have another one or two."

"Where did he live?" asked Deconcini.

Reilly shrugged. "I haven't the remotest notion. I work behind the bar here; I don't go out on the street to see where customers come from or where they go. I suppose he lived somewhere in the neighborhood. All my customers do."

"Apartments, little houses . . ." said Kennelly. "That kind of neighborhood."

Reilly nodded. "A lot of people moving in and out. Not like the old days, when people stayed put."

"You never heard a name?"

"No. He ordered his drinks. He might say something about it being a nice day. Glum kind of fellow. He'd sit there hunched on the stool. When he'd get in a conversation, it was like he was only half in it, and half out; he'd listen, nod, sometimes kind of smile at what somebody said; but he never got what you'd call animated."

"Accent?" asked Deconcini.

"Oh, yeah. Boston. Definitely a New England kind of guy. He'd ask for 'bee-uh,' not 'beer,' like anybody else would say. Bostoner."

"Always alone?"

"Always. He made acquaintances around here, but no friends."

Deconcini handed across the bar a copy of the morning's mug shots of Bonny Battersby. They were grim, ugly pictures, showing her standing before a painted scale that indicated her height, a black name board hung around her neck, her face taut and angry.

Reilly shook his head. "Never saw her," he said. "Sorry, too. Pretty little thing. You got her in the pokey?"

"No."

"Say, I tell you something," said Reilly. "You ought to talk to Lan there: the fellow down at the end of the bar. Ask him."

Deconcini and Kennelly moved to the end of the bar, to talk to the man called Lan.

"Ahh, look at him," the man said when Deconcini showed him the morgue photo. "Poor fellow. I guess that's all of us sometime. Huh? All of us sometime. Right?"

"Know anything about the man, Mr. . . . ?"

"Landsittle," said the man. "Jacob Landsittle. Carpenter and joiner, retired. At your service."

"We're trying to identify this man," said Deconcini.

Landsittle nodded. "He was not a friend. Just an acquaintance. You know how they come and go. Last six months or so, he came in often. He got very drunk, pouring down rye with beer chasers; but he never got obnoxious. A quiet fellow. Easy to get along with. Never much to say. More of a listener."

"Do you have any idea where he lived?"

"Well, he came often here by bus," said Landsittle. "I'd see him get off at the corner, and then he'd come in for his drinks. When he left . . . I don't know. He'd go out and wander away, sort of unsteady from drinking so much. Young fellow, he was, to have the time to sit around here and drink. Retired, like me . . . But he was too young for that. I think he was out of work. Maybe fired by somebody."

"How did he dress?"

"Nice. Suits. White shirts. Neckties. Yes. Neat."

"But you don't know who he was or where he lived?"

"Well, he wasn't from around here," said Landsittle. "He wasn't a foreigner. He spoke good English. But he didn't talk like us—that is, what little he talked."

"What more can I do for you, Dom?" Kennelly asked.

"You've done a lot already, Ed, and I appreciate it," said Deconcini. He heaved a loud sigh. "I don't know where to start. A thousand people live within easy walking distance of Reilly's. There must be hundreds of apartments and little houses in the neighborhood. I would appreciate it if your officers showed the morgue picture around. Plus, I guess, the mug shot of Bonny Battersby. Do whatever you can."

"It's a matter of more than just a little importance, isn't it?" asked Kennelly.

"I'm sorry we're so secretive," said Deconcini. "But, yes, it is important."

"Well, the D.C. department will do what it can, my boy. And let you know."

"I'm grateful," said Deconcini.

"Sit down, Dominic," said the President. "They tell me you're working day and night."

"Well, I suppose all of us are, Mr. President," said Deconcini.

The President nodded. "Yes. No question about it. Day and night." He sighed. "But all of us need an hour's respite now and then. Have you acquired the taste?"

It was the cocktail hour, and the President was mixing his martinis. He was alone, sitting in his wheelchair, wearing a wrinkled gray suit with the black armband of mourning for his mother on his sleeve. Deconcini had come to the second floor to report to Mrs. Roosevelt, and when the President saw him he had jovially summoned him to come in, have a seat, have a drink.

It was an honor Deconcini would not have missed for the world, something he would take away from the White House someday, to tell his grandchildren—as he told himself now. Duty could wait.

"Indeed I have, Mr. President," said Deconcini. "My choice of cocktails any time."

"Ross McIntyre will be in shortly. Damn shame when a man has to drink with his doctor, don't you think? Anyway, Churchill has gone to Ottawa, thank God. Harry's imbibing with his wife's friends somewhere. Missy's not feeling up to it tonight. Pa Watson is off inspecting latrines in some army camp, as I understand it." The President shook his head. "What am I supposed to do, run the war twenty-four hours a day?"

Deconcini was uneasy, uncertain of the proportions in which the President was mixing, not the martinis, but a dash of bitterness with his humor. "And Mrs. Roosevelt?" he asked.

"Probably somewhere rebuilding the world—before I even get it torn down." The President laughed. "Relax, Dominic. No one's going to assassinate me in the next thirty minutes. Anyway, maybe the would-be assassins have gone to Ottawa. Perhaps all they really wanted was to do in the Prime Minister."

Deconcini smiled. "Yes. Maybe so. The British seem to have brought the bad news with them."

"Maybe the isolationists were right all along." The President chuckled. He poured two martinis into stem glasses. "Taste that," he said. "Seven to one. Getting pretty strong when you mix them seven to one, hey?"

Deconcini sipped the icy gin and vermouth. "Excellent,

Mr. President," he said. "Everything their reputation makes of them."

"Fill me in very briefly," said the President. "Is there any news from the criminal investigation front?"

"We have a little something about the first man," said Deconcini. "He seems to have hung out in a bar out on Connecticut Avenue, just off Dupont Circle. A heavy drinker, apparently. Two witnesses identify him there. The D.C. police are circulating his picture in the neighborhood, to see if we can find out where he lived."

"What about Harry's secretary? What's her name, Battersby? My wife says you are too hard on the young lady."

"Maybe I have been," said Deconcini as he took another sip of his martini. "We took her fingerprints this morning and handed them over to the FBI to be checked against the national files. Nothing. She has no criminal record."

"Not persuasive," said the President. "Neither did John Wilkes Booth."

Deconcini smiled. "Neither did Judas," he said.

The President laughed heartily. He put a cigarette in his holder and touched it with the flame from a lighter. "I mentioned the matter to Harry. He swears by her. He says she's a hard worker."

"I've no doubt she is," said Deconcini.

The President leaned back, blew a cloud of smoke, and seemed to focus his attention on it as it spread toward the ceiling. He sipped from his glass. "You've got them on the run now, I'd think," he said, "but we have to suppose there are still some baddies in the White House. Be good if we could smoke 'em out. I'm not willing to offer myself as a decoy duck, so to speak, but—" He grinned. "Wonder if we could set up . . . oh, let's say, John L. Lewis. Wonder if we could get our in-house Nazis to take a shot at *him.*"

As they laughed, Mrs. Roosevelt entered. "What word, Mr. Deconcini?" she asked. "Has the FBI—"

"A clean bill of health," said Deconcini. "No police department has sent her fingerprints to Washington."

"Ah. Well, I hope I am right. I hope I haven't interfered with your performance of your duties. Knowing you were with the President up here, your office switched a call to me. So, I have a message for you. Captain Kennelly wants you to call him as soon as possible."

Kennelly met Deconcini in Reilly's bar.

"Let me introduce Stan Hupp," said Kennelly, nodding toward a big uniformed policeman who sat next to him at the bar, sipping sparingly from a small glass of beer. "Officer Stanley Hupp, Agent Dom Deconcini."

Hupp slipped off the stool and stuck out his hand. He was a heavy, broad-shouldered man of perhaps forty, with a crop of liver spots on his shiny bald head. "Good to meet ya, Dom," he said.

Deconcini noted the policeman's habit of calling everyone immediately by his first name. It was a small psychological trick, useful in interrogation. He responded in kind. "Glad to meet *you*, Stan."

"We've got somethin' for you," said Kennelly. He glanced around. "Not to talk about in here, I think. In the car outside."

They went out. An unmarked black Ford sat in a no-parking zone on the street, and they climbed in: Hupp in the backseat, Kennelly and Deconcini in the front. It was cold, and Kennelly started the car and switched on the heater.

"Tell him, Stan."

"Took the photo of the subject around," said Hupp. "He's known in the neighborhood. Even so, nobody seems to know where he lived. Which means we just haven't asked the right guy yet. Anyway, I took the photo around.

There's some places in this neighborhood that aren't so
. . . Well—"

"Don't beat around the bush, Stan," Kennelly growled.

"Well, you know how it is, Dom," said Hupp. "This is
a nice neighborhood mostly, but like any other neighborhood it's got it's places."

"What are you talking about?"

"Well, on up the avenue there's a little bar and restaurant owned by a woman we call Kay. I don't know what
her name is, really; everybody just calls her Kay. Well,
she's got four rooms upstairs where . . . Uh. You know?"

"Are you telling me she runs a whorehouse?"

"No, no. Nothin' like that. We wouldn't allow that
on *Connecticut Avenue.* But, I mean, she's got these
rooms where, uh, couples who want their privacy can go
and—"

"A hot-sheet operation," said Deconcini.

"Yeah. Like that. In a small way. Anyhow, I showed
Kay the picture of the stiff, and she recognized him just
like Reilly did. Said he'd been in a couple of times with
a girl. Just a couple of times."

"And took the girl upstairs?"

Hupp nodded. "Yeah. Took her upstairs."

Deconcini shrugged. "So our boy got around."

"Kay's got a snapshot of the girl," said Hupp.

Impressed by his identification as a Secret Service
agent, Kay Burling had left her cash register, led Deconcini to a candlelit table in her bar, and ordered a bottle
of champagne put before them.

She had six pictures of the girl: six badly focused snapshots of a blond maybe eighteen years old, maybe twenty-
two or twenty-three. Stiffly posed and conspicuously
shamed, the girl in the photographs was wearing only a
brassiere and a pair of snug-fitting white panties.

"How come?" asked Deconcini.

"How come I got 'em?" Kay Burling was a coarse-faced, over-made-up, hard-voiced landlady. "Because he asked me to keep 'em. He took 'em one night. Had 'em developed down the street. He didn't want to take 'em home." She grinned. "You can figure; he wouldn't want his wife to find *those*. So he left 'em here, with me. Say, the guy's dead! You don't figure the girl . . . Or his wife?"

"What I want to know is, who was he? And who's *she*?" said Deconcini firmly.

"Now, *that* I don't know," said Kay Burling. "You can see the name on the envelope from the camera store. Gil Jones. But who figures that's his name? And the address on the envelope is *my* address, here. And as far as the girl's concerned, I never saw her but the two times. I got no idea where he picked her up."

"How many times was he a customer of yours?" asked Deconcini.

"Two, three other times. Had another girl with him once: a brunette, a hooker, I think; I think I recognized her. I wouldn't have let her in here if I'd been sure, but—"

"And he called himself Gil Jones?"

She nodded. "When he called himself anything at all."

"Let's start over from the beginning, Mrs. Burling," said Deconcini. "You must have known the man pretty well, or he wouldn't have asked you to stash his snapshots. So, why don't you ponder the matter a little and see what else you can remember about Gil Jones."

"He came in sometimes for a sandwich," she said. "For a sandwich and a beer. He'd act like he was mad about something, like maybe he'd had an argument with his old lady at home and had walked out on her and come in here to eat rather than have to sit at the table with her."

"He have money?"

"Enough to pay what he owed."

"How did he talk? With an accent of any kind?"

She shook her head. "No accent. But he did talk funny, sort of. What I mean is, he never used any what you call popular words, like slang words. To give you an example, when he handed me those snapshots to keep, I winked at him and asked him if the girl gave him a good time. And, you know, most guys would have said something like, 'She's okay' or 'She's swell' or something; but he says, 'She is a very pleasant companion.' I mean, his English was *too* good."

"You've talked about his wife. Did he say he had one?"

The woman shrugged. "I assumed . . ."

"Did he talk about his work? Did you get any idea of how he made a living?"

"No."

"So, where did he live?"

She shook her head. "He didn't say. And I got no idea. Which is the truth. The guy's dead, and there's no percentage for me in keeping any secrets for him. Take his pictures with you, will ya? I don't want 'em."

"One more thing," said Deconcini. "Did he smoke? If so, what brand?"

"Sure he smoked. I sold him cigarettes a couple of times. Luckies."

"Not Chesterfields?"

She shook her head firmly. "Luckies."

11

"One more day," said Lieutenant-Commander George Leach to Dominic Deconcini as they sat over coffee with Mrs. Roosevelt early on Tuesday morning. "The Prime Minister will be back Wednesday. If we are to meet the President's deadline—"

"Don't let yourself worry too much about the President's deadline," said Mrs. Roosevelt. "What is important is that you solve the mystery and restore the security of the White House. I don't think you should be rushed. I don't think you should have to work against arbitrary deadlines."

"Anyway," said Deconcini, "with Jerry Baines out sick, I've got more to worry about than meeting a deadline, even one set by the President."

"Ah. Well, I wish *I* had," said Leach. "I feel excluded, as if I'd failed in my assignment. After all, it was *you*, old chap, who told the bonny Bonny that I tattled to you about her conversations with me. If you hadn't done that, I could still be enjoying her company and learning God knows what. As 'tis, she won't speak to me."

"If you could find *this* girl, maybe you could use your charms to learn something from her," said Deconcini, handing Leach the snapshots he had taken from Kay Burling. "This one seems to have been a very good friend

137

of the man we found a week ago. He took those pictures of her."

"Indeed?" said Leach. "Pretty little thing."

"We know where the man lived; the neighborhood, I mean. We've talked to people who knew him. He spoke English oddly. It's a guess, but I'd say he was speaking what was not natural to him, a carefully learned second language."

Leach offered the snapshots to Mrs. Roosevelt, saying, "I'm sorry. P'raps you shouldn't—"

"Oh, but I shall," she said, taking the pictures. "This— Oh, *dear!* Just what are these pictures, Mr. Deconcini? Where did you get them?"

"The man killed Monday night," said Deconcini. "We still haven't been able to identify him, but we've traced him to a neighborhood on Connecticut Avenue, just above Dupont Circle. According to our witness, he took this girl to a room above a little bar and restaurant, where the proprietress rents rooms to couples for, uh, well . . . You understand. He took those pictures of her and left them with the proprietress, for her to keep for him—so his wife wouldn't find them, the woman supposes."

"The first man killed," said Mrs. Roosevelt.

"Yes, the one killed with the ice pick."

"May I offer a suggestion?" Leach asked. "It's awkward calling these people by terms like 'Monday's corpse' and 'Friday's corpse,' or 'Man Number One' and 'Man Number Two.' Do you mind assigning them code names? Hans and Fritz. And—" he put a finger on the snapshots— "Lena."

Deconcini laughed. "Okay. Hans and Fritz."

"The names imply an assumption that the two men were Germans," said Mrs. Roosevelt.

"In the absence of Sir Alan, we can assume what we wish," said Leach with a grin.

"What are you doing to identify Lena, Mr. Deconcini?" asked Mrs. Roosevelt.

"The D.C. police lab copied the snapshots last night," he said. "The copies are being shown around the area where they were taken."

"The girl's identity may well be an important key," she said.

"I wouldn't be surprised."

"Keep me informed of this element of the investigation, will you please?"

"It's my intention to keep you informed of every element," said Deconcini dryly. "Right now, for instance, I have a supplement to the autopsy report on Fritz. It is the doctors' best judgment that Fritz had smoked a cigarette within a few minutes of the time when Jerry Baines shot him."

"The butt I found in Bonny's desk drawer," said Leach.

Deconcini smiled at Mrs. Roosevelt. "Well, we mustn't draw that conclusion."

"Draw any that are helpful, Mr. Deconcini," she said with a nod and a sly smile. "Incidentally, have you spoken with Mr. Elihu Weinberg at Goldman, Sachs?"

"He returned my call yesterday afternoon while I was out," said Deconcini. "Agent Joe Scott took the call. Mr. Weinberg confirmed Miss Battersby's story that she worked for him. I've sent her photograph to him, to be sure we are talking about the same young woman."

"You take no chances, do you, Mr. Deconcini?"

"None with the President's safety—or with yours," he said.

Mrs. Roosevelt noted that Dominic Deconcini was showing the strain of a week without a solution to the death of "Hans" in the White House. He was, she thought, a handsome young man: of Italian origins, dark-eyed, olive-skinned, with sharp features and a hard, piercing glance. She knew that Gerald Baines put much faith in him. Lieutenant-Commander Leach, on the other hand, while immeasurably handsome in his well-tailored Royal Navy uniform, had not the depth of intellect Deconcini was constantly showing. He was, she reflected, characteristically English: good-looking, suave, with an accent suggestive of immense erudition he did not have.

"What news of Mr. Baines?" she asked. "Is his illness anything more than a cold or flu?"

"Probably not," said Deconcini. "His wife called this morning and said he hopes to be in tomorrow."

The telephone rang. It was Agent Ted Norton, asking Deconcini to hurry down to the West Wing.

The Oval Office is on the southeast corner of the West Wing. Adjoining are a private study and bathroom for the President and offices for his secretaries. The Cabinet Room is on the northeast corner. The rest of the first floor of the West Wing is given over to offices for the President's personal staff and closest advisers. In December 1941, the principal offices in the West Wing were assigned to Harry Hopkins, Edwin "Pa" Watson, and Steve Early: two special assistants and the press secretary. Missy Le-Hand was still the President's secretary and had an office, but during Missy's long illness Grace Tully had been given many of her duties.

When Deconcini arrived in the wing on that Tuesday morning, December 30, the President had not yet come down from the second floor. Neither had Harry Hopkins. Watson was away from the White House. Steve Early and Grace Tully were in their offices. It was 9:25.

Ted Norton was with Major Bentz, the two of them talking in hushed but urgent tones in the corridor between the Oval Office and Hopkins's office.

"Jerry said to call you if anything came up," Norton
said to Deconcini.

"Jerry will be in tomorrow, I think," said Deconcini.

Norton was a long-time agent of the Secret Service: an
emaciated, chain-smoking, pallid man who wore rimless
spectacles that magnified his bloodshot blue eyes. He
wore an ash-smeared brown suit. Major Bentz, standing
beside him, was dapper as always in his uniform with
Sam Browne belt.

"What's up?" asked Deconcini.

"Found a pistol," said Norton.

"Where?"

"You're not gonna believe it," said Norton. He cast a
glance toward the far end of the hall. "In Harry Hopkins's office."

"Another Luger?"

Major Bentz shook his head. "Strictly American. A .32
Colt automatic. Little fellow. Loaded, too."

"Where was it? I mean, where in the office?"

"In his chair," said Norton. "Up under the springs.
Tucked in and fastened down with a piece of adhesive
tape."

Deconcini shook his head. "Could be Hopkins's own.
Could have been under there for years, too."

"I don't think it's been there long," said Norton. "The
tape is still white and sticky."

"Where is it now?" asked Deconcini.

"Still in place. We haven't taken it out."

Deconcini walked along the corridor and into Hopkins's office. His regular secretary, the one who handled
his calls and appointments, was in the office, worriedly
staring at his overturned chair and the two soldiers
kneeling beside it.

The thin fabric that covered the underside of the bottom of the big, leather-covered chair had been slit. The little pistol was wedged between one of the coil springs and the wooden frame of the seat and secured there with a strip of heavy, wide adhesive tape.

"Damned convenient," muttered Norton, "for someone who wanted to—"

"The Oval Office," said Major Bentz.

"Too damned close," said Norton. *"God,* I'd like to know how it got in here."

"A week ago you could have brought a tank into the White House—before we closed that storm sewer," said Deconcini. "Once it was inside . . ." He shrugged. "Security has been tight *around* the house, not inside it."

"We're remedying that," said Major Bentz.

Deconcini knelt beside the two soldiers and looked at the Colt automatic. It was a wicked little thing: pocket size, capable of loosing eight shots in quick succession. Too light and short to be accurate, it had only one purpose: to kill a man at short range.

"Are you fellows shooting craps, or did you lose something?"

It was Harry Hopkins. He stood in the doorway of his office, arms akimbo, looking down with scorn and impatience at the three men kneeling behind his desk.

"Have a look for yourself, Mr. Hopkins," said Deconcini, pointing at the Colt.

Hopkins bent over and peered into the underside of his chair. "Right. My new cigarette lighter," he said. "Sure, don't you keep yours handy like that, Deconcini? What the hell's going on here?"

"We wish we knew," said Norton. "Thought you might know something about it."

"I know it damned well doesn't belong there," said Hopkins acerbically. "I know it's damned well frightening to see a pistol—and I suppose it's loaded—this close to the

President's office. I mean, hell, man, there's nobody to stop anybody between here and the door to the Oval Office. I know somebody had damned well better get this place secure and pretty damned soon. That wasn't brought in here to shoot Churchill, you know."

"Absolutely right," said Deconcini. "I'm putting armed guards in the corridors of the West Wing, as of now—frankly, whether the President likes it or not. And there will be others on the second floor. I—"

Abruptly and in unison, they turned toward the door, through which they could see the President, arriving at the Oval Office, wheeling himself briskly as usual, with Arthur Prettyman and Grace Tully striding after him.

"Ho, Harry! What's going on?"

Hopkins started toward the door. He paused for a brief moment, frowning hard at Deconcini, Bentz, and Norton. "I'll have to tell him," he said. "I suggest you guys get this all under control. And damned fast."

Deconcini watched Hopkins hurry along the hall toward the President. "Have you searched the Oval Office itself?" he asked Norton.

"For about three hours," said Norton. "The Boss is going to be madder 'n hell when he finds out. He has a strong sense of privacy, and we had to go through everything in there."

"He'll growl maybe," said Deconcini, "but he knows it's necessary. Anyway, we do what we have to do, even if it does make him mad."

Mrs. Roosevelt met during the morning with a committee of women who sought her support for their project of converting the clubhouses and other facilities of three Washington-area country clubs into convalescent centers for wounded soldiers. Some of them wanted to define the clubs as convalescent centers for officers only, but she advised them firmly that she could not lend her name and support to their effort if they imposed that limitation. A few of the women asked for assurances that Negro soldiers, whether officers or not, would not be accepted at the centers. Mrs. Roosevelt said—(though she was not certain she could make it stick)—that the Department of the Army would not release patients from hospitals to racially segregated convalescent centers.

At noon she left the White House to attend a civil-defense luncheon meeting, where she was the principal speaker. In a text that had been prepared for her from which she deviated little, she urged that every woman and school-age child be introduced to such wartime unpleasantries as the proper techniques for extinguishing incendiary bombs—that is, by pouring sand on them, never water, which would make them explode. Residential neighborhoods in London, she reminded her audience, had been subjected to indiscriminate incendiary bombing. Keeping buckets of sand about, particularly in attics, could save many homes.

Back at the White House in the afternoon, she returned half a dozen telephone calls, then began a search through a score of old expansion folders stored in her breakfront desk and in a nearby bookcase.

"Is this something I can help you with?" Tommy Thompson asked.

Mrs. Roosevelt sighed. "Tommy, do you remember the picnic we had for the children of the White House staff? I mean, the one we held in the summer of 1940? We took a lot of snapshots. And we filed them away somewhere."

"Oh, Lord," said Tommy Thompson. "They're not in those folders, I can tell you. Let me check the storeroom upstairs."

"I'm sorry to bother you," said Mrs. Roosevelt, "but it is rather important."

A quarter of an hour later Tommy Thompson returned, bearing a big yellow envelope. It was stuffed with little pictures, two dozen of them. Mrs. Roosevelt began to shuffle through them.

"Oh!" she exclaimed suddenly. She reached for a little magnifying glass and peered intently at one of the snapshots. She shook her head and began to flip quickly through the rest of them. She found another and examined it under the glass. "Oh, Tommy," she said in a thin, stressed voice. "Did we keep a list of those who came?"

"I'm sure we don't have a list. Not anymore."

"I don't see Mr. Deconcini in any of these pictures. Would you know his wife if you saw her in one of the snapshots?"

"I can answer that," said Tommy Thompson. "Dom wasn't able to be here. He was on assignment somewhere. I don't remember where or why. He asked if his wife could bring their child anyway, and of course we said yes. So, she was here, with their little girl. But Dom was not."

Mrs. Roosevelt sighed. "I see." She put two of the snapshots side by side and stared hard at them through the magnifying glass. She shook her head. "Oh, this is most disturbing."

"May I ask what is so disturbing?"

"Please don't. I really can't possibly talk about it unless it proves to be *true*. And I am going to pray it is not true, that I am mistaken. If it is . . . Well, it is the most awful thing I have encountered in a very long time."

"Can I help in any way?"

"Yes. Whatever you do, do not mention any of this to anyone, not even that I looked at these pictures. *Not anyone.*"

Sir Alan Burton ran his hand over his yellow-gray hair, anxious apparently that not a strand should stray. "Lon-

don has signaled at length about Herr von Keyserling,"
he said. "If our Fritz actually was von Keyserling, Mr.
Baines has performed an important service in shooting
him dead."

"But have they said anything that would aid in the
identification?" asked Deconcini.

"The fellow is somewhat mysterious, I'm afraid," said
Sir Alan. "Facts are hard to come by. It is believed—
notice I say 'believed,' not known—that he spent some
considerable time in England before the war: polishing
up his English p'raps, photographing defense installa-
tions, most likely. Our intelligence chaps fear he may be
at large in England yet and are most anxious to know if
we are in possession of his corpse."

"Identification—"

"Well. A fact or two that might help. His SS rank is
believed to be *Standartenführer,* which is a pretty high
rank. He would have been giving orders in any operation
he was part of. Another fact: he is known to be something
of a ladies' man. Most important, though, I'm sure, is this
element of the signal," said Sir Alan, handing the entire
radiogram to Deconcini but pointing to a particular para-
graph. "See."

MAINTAINING SURVEILLANCE OF VON KEYSERLING HAS
BEEN ALL BUT IMPOSSIBLE STOP DURING BRIEF PERIODS
WHEN IT WAS POSSIBLE, HE WAS OBSERVED IN COMPANY
OF A FEW IDENTIFIABLE PEOPLE STOP OF INTEREST IN
WASHINGTON MIGHT BE U.S. ARMY COLONEL ROBERT
LITTLEFIELD, SEEN SHARING TABLE, BEVERAGES, COM-
PANY OF FEMALES IN BRUSSELS, AUGUST 10, 1939 STOP
COLONEL LITTLEFIELD IDENTIFIED TO US AS INTELLI-
GENCE OFFICER COMMANDING UNIT INVOLVED IN
COUNTER-ESPIONAGE, SECURITY U.S. WAR FACILITIES
STOP

"Is the name familiar to you?" asked Sir Alan. "Colonel Littlefield, I mean."

"It is," said Deconcini curtly. "He is Major Bentz's commanding officer. He is in command of the army units securing important public buildings in Washington."

The senior detective from Scotland Yard folded the deciphered radiogram and stuffed it in his jacket pocket. "I hope," he said solemnly, "this information is entirely irrelevant."

Lieutenant-Commander George Leach was on the streets around Dupont Circle, walking, looking, stepping inside every neighborhood tavern, playing the innocent English tourist with all his might, hoping to spot, maybe even to be approached by, "Lena." A plainclothes detective assigned by Captain Kennelly followed him at a distance.

The sun had set. The air was biting cold and damp. Wartime Washington was trying to achieve a blackout, but anyone who had ever fallen off a curb in blacked-out London understood that the effort was so far ineffective. The monuments were dark, but light still shone from windows and automobile headlights. He was warm in his Royal Navy greatcoat—tailored, in fact, like the rest of his uniform, by his usual bespoke tailors in Saville Row —and he was curious about the Americans he saw hurrying along, skimpily dressed in coats and jackets that seemed to afford them little protection from the penetrating damp. Washington, he remembered, was a sub-tropical city, by definition of the Foreign Office, which allowed personnel dispatched here a pay supplement for duty in an inclement climate. He wondered how British diplomats, sent here expecting heat and sweat and flies, coped with nights like this. Was this week's cold perhaps most unusual?

He spotted her! He was sure he was right. There she was, Lena, hurrying along the sidewalk, her shoulders hunched, a light scarf failing to keep the cold from invading through her coat collar. Her blond hair spilled from under her little maroon hat, falling in curls around her cheeks. She was the girl photographed in her underwear by Hans; he was sure of it.

Leach glanced back, spotted the detective, pointed. The man nodded, and the two of them strode after Lena.

She was young. He had guessed from her pictures that she was between eighteen and twenty-two or three. And she was pretty: prettier than the snapshots had suggested. She walked fast, determined maybe to get in out of the cold. She seemed wholly absorbed in herself, as though she were unaware of the night and the street and the people around her.

The detective caught up with Leach. "Are you sure?" he panted.

"Nothing's ever certain," said Leach. "But—"

"Whoops. Where's she going?"

The girl had boarded a bus that had stopped at the corner. As Leach and the detective trotted toward it, the bus pulled away. They could see the girl working her way back along the aisle, looking for a seat.

12

Missy LeHand sat on the foot of his bed as the President took dinner from his tray on Tuesday evening, December 30. It was their ritual of many years: he spending a lonely evening in the White House after everyone had gone and Babs was away on some errand, Missy come to have dinner with him, sitting on his bed in a nightgown, nibbling something brought up to her, a record on the player to fill the room with quiet music, the two of them discussing lightly the day they had just spent. All that was different tonight was that the nation was fighting the war he had struggled so hard to avoid, and Missy was weak and wan and compelled to expend an effort to mimic the evenings they used to share. That was all. That was all that had changed.

Missy was terribly sick. The world had been unkind to her, the President thought. And in being unkind to Missy it had been unkind to him. She had been for him a source of sympathy and companionship, a relief from the unrelenting *seriousness* of the presidency. He liked to laugh. He liked to engage in warm-hearted amusing banter. He liked women: he liked to be comforted by them, to relax in their company, to trade jokes with them, to touch them affectionately and be touched by them, sometimes implying intimacy he didn't even wish for, that he did not require to find joy with them.

Babs . . . she was a good woman. He was proud of her. He could not have chosen a finer woman for his wife, the mother of his children, his lifelong partner in the marvelous adventure their lives had become. But Babs was *serious*. Dedicated. Organized. Persuasive. Shrewd. Effective. But, oh so damned *serious*.

"They found a loaded pistol in Harry's office today," he said. "Some people are suggesting I move out of the White House until the Secret Service can assure me the place is absolutely secure."

"You couldn't," said Missy. "It would cause a panic, all across the nation."

"Exactly," he said. "So I'll just sit here and wait to be shot."

Missy drew a breath and was ready to protest—until she saw the little smile spreading over his face and understood he had not been seized by a moment of self-pity but was instead bringing to a difficult situation one of the sources of his strength: his indomitable sense of perspective and humor.

"Boss," she said. "I'd put my body in front of yours if someone tried to shoot you. There's not much left of it anyway."

"Oh, Missy." The President touched the corners of his eyes, catching the abrupt tears on his fingertips. "Missy . . ."

In the sitting hall just outside, Mrs. Roosevelt was in a dramatic conversation with Agent Ted Norton, who was on duty that night—Deconcini having taken a couple of hours to go home to dinner with his wife and child. Mrs. Roosevelt had dined with a committee of Polish-Americans; and, facing Norton, she was still wearing her black silk dinner dress, indeed even her fur coat and feathered hat, which she had not yet had time to put aside. The

White House, she had found the moment she returned, was in confused shock. She had been escorted up the stairs to the second floor by a Secret Service agent she did not recognize and a rifle-carrying soldier, neither of whom could or would tell her why the elevator was out of order. She was listening now to a report from Norton, who had run up the stairs after her.

"We haven't told the President," he said.

"I shall tell him," she said decisively. "After I speak to the President I shall telephone Mrs. Baines."

"You may want to see Jerry first, ma'am," said Norton.

She nodded. "Yes. I shall come downstairs as soon as I speak to the President."

She turned to the door that opened on the short hall to his bedroom, knocked, then opened it and entered the little hall. His bathroom was to her left, the door into his bedroom proper was ajar.

"Franklin."

"Come on in, Babs."

She entered the bedroom. "Hello, Missy," she said. "I'm . . . I'm sorry to bring upsetting news at this hour, but there has been another shooting downstairs. It's worse this time. It's Mr. Baines. It appears he's been shot defending us."

"Oh, my God!" cried Missy.

The President's face lost color. "Is the man dead?" he asked.

"No," said Mrs. Roosevelt. "Wounded. He's been taken to the clinic. I'm going down there in a moment. Mr. Norton says the wound may not be too terribly serious. Apparently there was an exchange of shots."

"Where?"

"In the elevator and the elevator lobby, on the first floor."

"And the man who shot Mr. Baines?" asked Missy weakly. "Did they—"

"At large," said Mrs. Roosevelt. "I need hardly tell you, the house is *full* of police and soldiers."

"Not outside police?" the President asked, shaking his head. "We must keep this whole thing a closely guarded secret. We cannot let the country know that we are besieged in the White House by would-be assassins that seem constantly to outsmart and overpower our security officers."

"Everyone has been circumspect," said Mrs. Roosevelt. "Harry has taken charge. There are no District police in the house. On the other hand, you may be surprised to see soldiers on guard outside your bedroom door. In fact, if the man who shot Mr. Baines was on his way up in the elevator, he had a nasty surprise coming when he emerged from the elevator. We are *not* unprotected."

"Ah," said the President. "But recall Juvenal: *'Sed quis custodiet ipsos Custodes?'*—'Who is to guard the guards themselves?' I fear the culprit is a Judas."

"Soldiers who could not have been involved in the events of the past week are guarding the second floor," said Mrs. Roosevelt. "Their orders are to let *no one* pass. No one."

"We are besieged," said the President.

"I'll come back and tell you what's going on, as soon as possible," said the First Lady.

The elevator was not running, and as Mrs. Roosevelt hurried down the stairs, she found the White House was indeed taking on the aspect of a besieged fortress. Helmeted soldiers with bayoneted rifles stood in the halls. Damage from an exchange of gunfire was painfully evident in the elevator lobby on the first floor. The west hall on the ground floor was guarded by soldiers and by Secret Service agents with pistols showing.

Agent Gerald Baines lay on the table in the clinic on the ground floor. Harry Hopkins stood nearby, watching. Admiral Ross McIntyre, the President's physician, was working over Baines, whose jacket and shirt had been cut away and his wound exposed. His face was pale. His forehead glistened with perspiration.

Bonny Battersby sat in a corner, pressing an ice bag to her face. She was sobbing quietly.

"Damned lucky, this fellow," said McIntyre. "You don't have to look at it, Mrs. Roosevelt. It's ugly but not fatal. The bullet missed everything. Just ploughed a furrow, as you might say."

She did look. The bullet had struck a rib at a shallow angle and glanced off, tearing away flesh and exposing the rib, leaving a long, narrow, ragged wound that had bled profusely.

"And what's happened to Miss Battersby?" Mrs. Roosevelt quietly asked Hopkins.

"The man who shot Baines escaped through the window in the room we're using as her temporary office," said Hopkins. "Slugged her, smashed the window, and jumped out onto the lawn."

Mrs. Roosevelt nodded sympathetically at the young woman, then bent over Baines. "Has your wife been called, Mr. Baines?" she asked solicitously.

"No," murmured Baines. "I want to do that myself. I want her to hear my voice."

"Suppose I telephone her," suggested Mrs. Roosevelt. "I shall begin by saying, 'Mr. Baines asked me to call.' That way, before she hears the word she will know you are able to talk. Then I will tell her you have been wounded but are in no danger."

"That would be very kind," said Baines.

"We hadn't expected you in the White House until tomorrow at the earliest," she said.

"I came in to check a few things," he said feebly.

"How fortunate that you did."

She used the telephone in the housekeeper's office to call Mrs. Baines and break the news to her. The woman seemed to hear it listlessly, as if it were only her latest misfortune.

"I think we shall probably keep Mr. Baines in the clinic here overnight," said Mrs. Roosevelt. "Would you like to come to see him?"

"No," the woman said uncertainly. "I should be here when Cecile comes home. That's my daughter. She works nights."

"Well," said Mrs. Roosevelt, "if you change your mind, or if you want to come in the morning, just telephone me. I will receive you myself. Your husband is a hero tonight."

"Jerry is a good man."

"Yes. I concur in that. Oh, please understand, Mrs. Baines, that what has happened this evening is a secret. Word must not get out. It's a matter of national security."

"Jerry has always known many things that are secret," said Mrs. Baines. "That's his work. You can count on us to keep quiet."

When she ended the call to Mrs. Baines, Mrs. Roosevelt called upstairs to report to the President. He asked her to express his sympathy and appreciation to Gerald Baines.

Dominic Deconcini had arrived by the time Mrs. Roosevelt returned to the clinic. A small conference seemed to have assembled around the table where Baines lay, his wound now covered by a large bandage. Hopkins and

Deconcini were talking with Baines as he sipped Coca-Cola or something of the like through a bent straw. Bonny Battersby still sat in the corner, rocking on her chair and holding the ice bag to her right cheek.

Mrs. Roosevelt stepped over to the table. "Well . . . ?"

"We've been reconstructing the events," said Hopkins. "Let's leave Jerry to some rest for a bit. Dom and I can fill you in."

They left the clinic and went into Admiral McIntyre's adjoining office, where Deconcini suggested to Mrs. Roosevelt that she take the armchair. He stood, and Hopkins sat down behind the admiral's desk.

"Things get odder and odder and odder," remarked Hopkins. He lit a cigarette, frowning hard over the flame. "There must be an arsenal in the White House. We know that no one is bringing pistols in. Did they search even *you*, Eleanor? They did me. Still, another pistol was used tonight—and abandoned. Where the hell did it come from?"

"I understand one was even found in your office, Harry," said Mrs. Roosevelt.

Hopkins turned to Deconcini. "I think you and Major Bentz had better start all over," he said. "Top to bottom, east to west, however you want to do it, I think you've got to search this building like no building was ever searched before. Let Bentz—"

"Excuse me," said Deconcini. "What I'm about to say has to be one hundred percent confidential. I'm going to ask you, Mr. Hopkins, and you, Mrs. Roosevelt, to prevail on the President to relieve and replace the White House guard battalion with a unit drawn from somewhere else."

"You'd better have a good reason for that one," said Hopkins coldly.

"I probably don't," said Deconcini. "But British intelligence has come up with something that, in the circumstances, we can't ignore. The battalion commander is Colonel Littlefield. The man we're calling Fritz has been tentatively identified as a top Nazi agent named Hasso von Keyserling. On one of the rare occasions when British intelligence was able to keep a shadow on von Keyserling, he was seen with Colonel Littlefield. That was, of course, before the war broke out in Europe, but this von Keyserling is described as having never been anything but a Nazi fanatic; and why an American intelligence officer was having drinks and—"

"You're accusing *Littlefield?*" Hopkins asked sharply.

"I'm not accusing anybody," said Deconcini. "But there can be little doubt that somebody who knows the White House extremely well and has access to places as securely guarded as the President's study and your office—"

"Sed quis custodiet ipsos Custodes?" interrupted Mrs. Roosevelt. "Someone in the Secret Service, someone in the battalion, or someone very highly placed in the White House is betraying us all. I can understand your interest in replacing the army batallion. I will speak to the President about it."

"And what of the Secret Service?" asked Hopkins.

Deconcini shrugged. "We keep checking. At least Jerry Baines is aquitted."

Mrs. Roosevelt frowned hard. "I have not heard an account of what happened to Mr. Baines," she said.

"He came to his office this evening," said Hopkins. "He says he went over some reports there and talked for a while with the duty officer, getting filled in. Then he came on into the house here and made a sort of inspection tour of the stations, checking to see that everybody was alert and everything was quiet. He stepped into the pantry and asked Henry for a cup of coffee. He drank coffee and chatted with Henry for a few minutes, then left the pantry and started east along the hall. Suddenly he heard the elevator door close. Well, with Henry in the pantry and all the security men at their posts, who could be going up in the elevator? He ran to the elevator, yelling to whoever it was to wait a minute. He banged on the door and he yelled, 'This is Baines. Stop!' The elevator hadn't started up, but it started then, in spite of his yelling and banging. That's when he decided something was really wrong."

"So he ran up the stairs to get ahead of it," said Deconcini.

"Right," Hopkins continued. "He knew the elevator is not so fast, so he ran up to the first floor and began banging on the door there. He knew if it went on past he could still run to the second floor before it got there and intercept anybody coming up to where the President was."

"Whoever it was would have faced at least four armed, trained men between the second-floor elevator hall and the door to the President's bedroom," said Deconcini.

"Well, anyway," said Hopkins, "Jerry was banging on the door—actually kicking at it, he says—and yelling that he was Baines, Secret Service, when suddenly whoever was in the elevator started shooting. Right through the doors. The first shot got him and knocked him back, which saved his life because three more shots were fired. He got off two shots himself. But apparently he didn't hit whoever was inside."

"Or so we assume," said Mrs. Roosevelt.

"So we assume," Hopkins agreed wryly. "A misfortune. Anyway, everybody came running to where the shooting was: the elevator lobby, first floor. Meanwhile, the elevator went back to the ground floor, the gunman ran across the hall, slugged Bonny, who was just coming out to see what was going on, heaved her chair through the window, and jumped out."

"And are we to suppose he escaped from the grounds, through all our soldiers?" asked Mrs. Roosevelt.

"Or maybe he *is* one of our soldiers," said Deconcini.

"To conclude," said Hopkins, "he dropped the pistol. It was on the elevator floor."

"A German pistol?"

"Is it, Deconcini? I never saw anything like it."

"It's a Walther. The very latest and very best officers' sidearm, carried by German officers lucky enough to get one."

"How badly is Miss Battersby hurt?" asked Mrs. Roosevelt.

"She took a hell of a chop on the jaw," said Hopkins. "She was scared half to death, poor kid."

"Is she required to work *every* evening?" asked Deconcini.

"The truth of the matter is, she's a little slow," said Hopkins. "Another girl would finish earlier. But I've never seen anyone so devoted, so good-natured about being worked long hours. She's a treasure."

"You know of course that her name is not Battersby."

"I got the report," said Hopkins. "I'd have to hear something worse than anything I've heard, to be moved to get rid of her. If that's what you're suggesting."

"I'm not suggesting—"

"I think we can return to that subject later," said Mrs. Roosevelt. "For now, we have more troubling problems. Uh . . . Mr. Deconcini, has any progress been made toward identifying 'Lena'?"

"Definitely," said Deconcini. "Leach saw her this evening. He called me at home, all excited. All he has to do is be at the bus stop where he saw her board a bus. I mean, tomorrow evening. And, if he's right, we'll have our Lena."

"I know you had pictures of Hans shown in Sears, Roebuck stores," said the First Lady. "And I know you didn't find out where he had bought the clothes he was wearing when he was found in the refrigerator. But have you thought to show the personnel in those stores the pictures of Lena?"

"As a matter of fact, no," said Deconcini. "We've had her picture shown in Reilly's bar and in some other places, to no avail."

"Well, why not try it? If the girl in the pictures is not a prostitute or a girl of generally loose morals, it is possible, is it not, that she was a participant in his effort to make himself anonymous?"

"I'll have copies of the Lena pictures shown at the Sears stores in the morning," said Deconcini.

Mrs. Roosevelt nodded. "I feel so *sorry* for Mrs. Baines," she said. "Do you know her, Mr. Deconcini?"

"I've never met any of Jerry's family," said Deconcini. "Jerry's all business, doesn't speak much of personal things."

"I sense that you are following a line of reasoning all your own, that you're not telling us," said Hopkins.

She nodded. "So painful a line of reasoning that I will not even admit it ever occurred to me, unless it proves to have truth at the end."

"Then we will go on without the benefit of it," said Deconcini with a small, ironic smile.

"And I shall go upstairs and report to the President," she said. "I will of course be available all night."

When she returned to the President's bedroom, he was talking on the telephone. Missy LeHand sat in a chair by his bedside and, although dressed in a light blue nightgown, had her shorthand pad on her lap and was taking notes. The President's conversation seemed grim.

"You know of course," he said glumly when he put down the telephone and looked up at Mrs. Roosevelt, "that they declared Manila an open city to prevent civil-

ian casualties among its population. Well, MacArthur
has lost it. He's withdrawing into the Bataan Peninsula,
leaving Manila defenseless. In a day or so, it will be a
captive city. And after that . . ." He shook his head. "And
they're pleading with me to send army divisions out
there! Even Doug has the brains to understand it would
take three months for a convoy to be assembled and deliver reinforcements to the Philippines. In three months
there'll be no Philippines to defend!"

13

At ten A.M. the President received a few members of his official family in the Oval Office. He sat behind the desk covered by the famous Rooseveltian clutter: Democratic donkey figurines, mementos, pictures, flags, books, letter knives, pens, an ashtray, a wire basket, a carafe, a telephone, a lamp, a green desk blotter, scattered notes and other papers . . . He leaned back in his chair, cigarette holder atilt, beaming, nodding and murmuring personal greetings. He wore a gray, chalk-striped suit, with the black crepe mourning band still in place on his left sleeve. His pince-nez sat astride his nose.

"Well," he said. "Some of you would like to get out of here early today. That's why I called you in early. And the purpose is just to say a word, just to express my gratitude to all of you, and to wish you all something good for the new year."

Harry Hopkins was there, and Steve Early. Missy had managed to come down and sat beside Grace Tully on the couch to the right of the President's desk. Pa Watson had returned to the White House and stood near the door. Dominic Deconcini was there, standing beside Admiral McIntyre. Secretaries stood back shyly. There were maybe twenty people in the office, in all.

"When some of you signed up for this," the President

161

went on, "you probably expected about what I did: four years of it, eight at most, with some tough problems to work on but nothing that would keep us at work on Christmas Day. But here we all are, facing 1942, which is going to be the toughest year that any of us has ever known. I expect most of us will be here at work on Christmas Day, 1942, also."

He paused and glanced around, into solemn faces. His extemporaneous little greeting had taken on a grim air he had not intended. He picked his pince-nez off his nose and put it on his desk blotter, and he smiled.

"I couldn't ask for a better group of people to join with me in shouldering the heavy burdens we face this year. I have every confidence in you. And, with God's help, when we meet like this on this day in 1942 we'll know the worst is behind us and that we're on our way to victory. God bless you all. Take good care of yourselves. And thank you."

As the little crowd pressed through the doors and returned to work, Hopkins edged forward and touched Deconcini on the shoulder. With a toss of his head he summoned Deconcini to remain.

The President had replaced his pince-nez, and he looked up at Deconcini, his face grave. He put his cigarette aside. "The Prime Minister will be back in the White House this evening," he said. "Should we maybe put him up instead at Blair House or somewhere else?"

"Security is tight . . ." said Deconcini tentatively.

"Well, that's another point," said the President. "He returns to a White House with halls filled with armed soldiers." The President shook his head.

"We're learning a bitter lesson, Mr. President."

"That gentlemen do indeed read each other's mail," said the President somewhat derisively. "Yes, and try to kill each other, too. But will Churchill be safe in the White House tonight?"

"There may be a break in the case today, Mr. President," said Deconcini. "In fact . . . Well, Mrs. Roosevelt has a theory. I wish I knew what it is. I—"

"She hasn't told you?"

"No.

"I must say, I hope she is not playing games," said the President. "She's a shrewd analyst of the clues in matters of crime. Several times she has offered valuable help to the police in solving mysteries—never before in the White House, thank the Lord. But, uh, she does have her own ways; I mean, her sympathies and instincts, and you may have to press her to take you into her confidence, Dom."

Deconcini smiled. "I can't imagine myself pressing Mrs. Roosevelt," he said.

"Well, try," said the President. "And, incidentally, we can't replace the military guard *today;* but if this thing isn't cleared up in the next forty-eight hours or so, then we'll have to do it."

"And replace the Secret Service with federal marshals," said Hopkins.

"Yes," said Deconcini. "I could hardly blame you."

Special Agent Gerald Baines had not remained in the White House clinic overnight, as Mrs. Roosevelt had thought he might, but had been taken home about two A.M. He telephoned in mid-morning, asking that a car be sent for him early in the afternoon. The situation in the White House was too critical, he said, for him to remain away; and anyway he insisted he was only a little weak and sore and quite capable of returning to take command of the search for the man who had shot him.

Although Hopkins had insisted Bonny Battersby need not report for work on Wednesday, December 31, or on New Year's Day, she was at the White House before noon; and the clatter of her typewriter sounded through the west hall. Her cheek and jaw were swollen and bruised, and she had a sullen air about her; but she worked doggedly, rolling sheets of paper interleaved with carbons into her typewriter and pounding the keys as if she were punishing the machine.

Captain Kennelly arrived. Mrs. Roosevelt had asked to be called when he checked in at the gate, and as soon as he was in the White House he was ushered up to her little office, to which Deconcini had been summoned. Sir Alan Burton had been called also, and when he arrived there was not enough room for them to sit, so Mrs. Roosevelt moved the meeting out to the sitting hall.

"Well, we've done what you asked," said Kennelly. "We took the pictures of Lena in her underwear to the Sears, Roebuck stores." He nodded. "Bingo! They recognized her. At the main store."

"Well, then," said Mrs. Roosevelt. "Who is she?"

"Ah, that they don't know," said Kennelly. "But they remember her well. She came in and bought a man's suit. She had the exact measurements, and she ordered the suit altered to fit. Then she bought a shirt and tie, and underwear, and shoes and socks—all to sizes she had written on a little notepad. Whoever the man was, he never showed up to try the suit on."

"How did they describe the girl?" asked Mrs. Roosevelt.

"Well, they were surprised at the kind of pictures I showed them of her," said Kennelly. "She hadn't impressed them as the kind likely to pose for pictures with most of her clothes off, they said. They took her for about nineteen years old, twenty at most. Said she didn't seem to like much what she was doing. Kind of pitiful it all was, they said."

Mrs. Roosevelt sighed. "Yes."

"You know who she is," said Deconcini bluntly.

"Well, I have a very strong suspicion," said Mrs. Roosevelt.

"You must tell us."

"The matter must be handled very carefully, Mr. Deconcini. With the greatest circumspection. If I am wrong, it will do a grave injustice. Even the fact that the suspicion is raised will be devastating to a fine person I would not harm for the world. I am most anxious to pursue my line of reasoning without anyone learning of it. Then, if I am wrong, no one will ever know."

"The danger in the White House is so great, Mrs. Roosevelt, that we have to place protection of the President and Prime Minister ahead of all other considerations," said Deconcini. "If you know—"

"I *don't* know. That's the point," she said. "But we must find out. As I say, it must be done most circumspectly."

"Maybe I should leave," said Captain Kennelly. "This is a little out of my line."

"We have worked together before," she said. "I know I can trust you, Captain. And we'll need your help."

"Well, where do we start?" asked Deconcini.

"The girl," said Mrs. Roosevelt. "Lena. We must find her as quickly as possible, not waiting for the chance she will catch a certain bus this evening. Surely, Captain Kennelly, since we have pictures of her and know the neighborhood she frequents—"

"I'm ahead of you, ma'am," said Kennelly. "I've got extra men working the area right now."

"Then let me ask your complete cooperation," said Mrs.

Roosevelt. "When the girl is found, please arrange to have her taken to some private place where I can confront her. Let it not be police headquarters. Treat her very gently, Captain. Just hold her until Sir Alan, Mr. Deconcini, and I can get there."

"If I can use a phone—"

"Certainly. My secretary will show you one you can use."

When Tommy Thompson had taken Kennelly to the President's study, where he would use the telephone, Sir Alan rose and stepped to the window. Clasping his hands behind his back, he grumbled, "I hope this does not turn out to be a wasted effort, ma'am."

"Oh, I almost hope it *does*, Sir Alan," said Mrs. Roosevelt.

Baines arrived as he said he would, not long after noon. He went to the elevator lobby on the first floor to look at the bullet-shattered elevator doors and at the bullet holes in the door of the private dining room. Ted Norton accompanied him.

"You were damned lucky, Jerry," said Norton, looking at the damage. "If that first shot hadn't grazed you and knocked you over—"

"What I'd like to know," said Baines, running a hand across his liver-spotted bald head, "is how I could have missed the guy inside that elevator. All I can figure is, he dropped to the floor and my shots went over him."

"We've made no progress in identifying him," said Norton. "He managed to slip through everything and everybody outside."

"Not necessarily," said Baines. "Maybe after he smashed his way out of the trophy room he climbed back in another window and reentered the White House."

"All the windows were locked."

"Except maybe the one he unlocked for the purpose—and locked again after he was back inside."

"He'd have to be an agent, then," said Norton.

"Or a soldier," said Baines.

"Well, Miss Battersby says the man who slugged her was in civilian clothes. She didn't get a good look at him, really; but on that point she's adamant: that he was wearing a civilian suit."

"Big fellow, little fellow . . . ?"

"You ought to talk to her. We questioned her last night, of course, but she was in shock. She might remember more now."

"All right. I'll haul my achin' body down there."

"The elevator is running," said Norton. "The President went down in it this morning. Made some little joke about the new ventilating holes making it less stuffy inside."

Baines shook his head. "What a man!"

As they descended in the bullet-scarred elevator, Norton snapped his finger and said, "Oh, incidentally, Jerry, we found no fingerprints on the pistol. None. Inside or out. It had been wiped thoroughly. So had the cartridges. One little clue, though, for what it's worth, which I figure is not much. The gun was probably wiped with Kleenexes. We found a little shred of what looks like Kleenex tissue stuck in the slide. We're sending that little shred to the manufacturer to see if they can identify it as Kleenex."

"Couldn't be more than a hundred people in the White House use Kleenex," sneered Baines.

"Yeah, but suppose it's some other special kind of tissue, something not so common," said Norton. He shrugged. "Anyway, it's a line of investigation."

They reached the trophy room, where for the moment Bonny Battersby had stopped typing and was staring glumly out the window.

She all but shrieked when she saw Baines. "*Mr. Baines!* You should be at home in bed!"

"True." Baines sighed as he lowered himself painfully into a chair. "But I need to review our joint experience of last evening. Whoever shot me and slugged you is at large and probably in the White House."

"I know," she said. "It's scary."

"So, what happened? You heard the shots?"

"Yes. It sounded like . . . well . . . shots." She smiled wanly. "At first I was just petrified. Then I got up and went to the door. It was open. You know, I'd left it open so it wouldn't be so bleak and lonely in here. Henry says hello when he goes by with a tray for upstairs. And some of the agents do. Anyway, I got up and went to the door and looked up and down the hall. I heard the elevator door open. Then suddenly this man runs across the hall as fast as he can come. He—"

"Can you remember *anything* more about what he looked like?"

"Pretty much just what I said. He was wearing a suit. He had on a hat—gray, I think. You understand, I just got a quick glance at him before he . . . Well, he came running toward me, and before I could say anything or do anything, up came his fist and he hit me as hard as he could. After that, I don't know much about what happened. It hurt, and I fell down. I was lying on the floor, all confused and—"

"All right," said Baines gently. "He was a white man, with a suit on and a hat—"

"White man? You don't think Henry—?"

"No. Just the basics of a description."

"All right. He was a white man, with a suit on, and a hat."

"If you saw him again—"

"I wouldn't know him," she said definitely.

* * *

A few minutes after Baines and Norton left the trophy room, Lieutenant-Commander George Leach arrived.

"I came to tell you how sorry I am that you were injured last night," he said. "I should rather it had been almost anyone else."

"Did Deconcini send you to say that?"

"Please. When it was learned that you use an assumed name, it was only natural that suspicions would arise. I . . . I came to ask if you would take dinner with me this evening. And maybe find somewhere to celebrate the advent of the new year afterward. I don't know anyone else whose company I would enjoy as much."

"Are you about to sail away, George?"

"I am not privy to the Prime Minister's plans," he said soberly. "I have to assume *Duke of York* will return to sea shortly."

"And you'd like to have a memory."

"I have one already, Bonny."

"I can't chew," she said. "You'll have to feed me soup."

"And champagne," he said.

She smiled. "I think I could manage that."

"Corporal William Thompson reporting as ordered, sir," said the man in khaki to Major Bentz.

"At ease, Corporal," said Bentz casually.

They were in the housekeeper's office, where Deconcini had met the major and asked him to summon, one by one, all the soldiers who had been on duty on the White House grounds during the previous night. Deconcini sat at Mrs. Nesbitt's desk, with Major Bentz on a wooden straight chair to one side. The corporal stood stiffly, his flat World War I–vintage helmet still planted solidly on his head and secured by a heavy leather strap just under his chin. He was a big man, with cheeks ruddy from the close scraping of his razor yet blue from the oncoming whiskers, heavy black brows, a strong, cleft chin.

"A few simple questions," said Deconcini. "To start with, where was your duty post last evening?"

"South grounds, sir. West of the South Portico, sir."

"A window was smashed out in the trophy room," said Deconcini. "First window west of the portico. Did you hear that? If so, where were you when it happened?"

"I did hear it, sir. I was at that point around the corner of the building, sir, toward the West Wing. My orders are to patrol the walls from the Oval Office to the South Portico."

"Do you pace that area like a sentry?"

"Not like a sentry, sir. I move back and forth at will, along the south walls, checking against lurkers in the shrubbery, checking the windows, and so on."

"When you heard the window break, what did you do?"

"I blew my whistle, sir, to call for help. Then I ran toward the portico. When I reached the broken window, I looked inside and saw the young woman lying on the floor. I considered climbing in, to help her, but men ran into the room at that point; and I took charge of a detail that was assembling outside and began to search for whoever broke the window."

"When you ran from the West Wing toward the South Portico, you saw—?"

"No one, sir."

"How long did it take you to run from where you were to the broken window?"

"I'd have to guess, sir. Ten seconds. Probably a little more. Fifteen."

"And were other soldiers running toward the same window?"

"Yes, sir. A little confused. None of us knew which

window it had been until we reached the one that was broken."

"But none of you saw anyone?"

"None of us saw anyone, sir."

Deconcini thought for a moment. "How difficult would it be for someone to escape from the White House grounds?"

"I'd think it would be very difficult, sir."

"Well, then, how do we explain this, Corporal? A man smashed out the window in the trophy room and jumped down. If he ran west, he had to climb in another window, maybe one left open earlier—"

"I don't think a south window was open, sir. I keep an eye out for that."

"Say unlocked then. Anyway, if he ran west and climbed in another window, he had to get past you running toward the trophy room. If he ran east, he would have run right into the guards at the portico entrance. If he ran south, he was out in the grounds, among your sound detectors, gun emplacements, and personnel. And I guess the fence is closely guarded all around. Where'd he go, Corporal?"

"I have an idea, sir."

"Good. What is it?"

"That he never came out that window, sir. He knocked Miss Battersby unconscious, smashed out the window to make it look like he jumped out, then turned around and ran back into the White House."

Deconcini nodded. "Right. You're not the only one with that idea."

"There is one more possibility, sir."

"Which is?"

"Well, the other possibility, sir, is that one of us out there *let* the man through. Begging your pardon, Major, but we have an assortment of men out there, some new recruits, sir, and it's not impossible that—"

"We follow your line of thinking, Corporal," said Major Bentz coldly.

"Yes, sir. Thank you, sir."

"Thank *you*, Corporal," said Deconcini. "This has been helpful."

14

"The game's afoot, Mrs. Holmes," said Deconcini with boyish enthusiasm about four that afternoon. He had encountered Mrs. Roosevelt in the hall on his way to her office. "Kennelly has called. He has Lena."

"And is holding her according to our instructions, I trust," said Mrs. Roosevelt.

"So he says. We're to meet him at an apartment on L Street. Do we take Sir Alan with us?"

"Unless you object," she said. "He is an experienced investigator, skilled at interrogating witnesses."

Sir Alan accompanied them, dressed in a gray overcoat with black velvet collar and a black derby. The apartment, they found, was in a modest red-brick building; and, on entering, they saw that it was the home of one of Captain Kennelly's subordinate officers. His wife, flustered to have the First Lady in her home, had made tea that was too strong and coffee that was too weak; but Mrs. Roosevelt went out to the kitchen to thank her for them and to apologize for the intrusion into her home. The woman asked her for an autograph and then, at a loss for a piece of paper on which Mrs. Roosevelt could sign, asked her to write her name on a Bisquick box. Mrs. Roosevelt made a mental note to send her a letter on White House letterhead.

The girl they had called Lena was in the living room, in the custody of a policewoman and Captain Kennelly. She was the girl in the snapshots beyond any question: young, blond, pretty, and desperately frightened. Her eyes were wet with tears. Her cheeks were red. She sobbed, and when she looked up and saw Mrs. Roosevelt she covered her face with her hands and wept.

"One of the boys picked her up in a grocery store," explained Kennelly. "She says it's all a mistake, that we have no reason to arrest her; and we haven't told her why. It's all up to you, ma'am."

"Show her the pictures, Mr. Deconcini," said Mrs. Roosevelt sadly.

Deconcini took the snapshots from his pocket and handed them to the girl. She glanced at them, then slumped in tears, shaking with sobs.

"Let her cry it out," said Mrs. Roosevelt. She reached for the cup of tea Sir Alan had poured for her. "Give her a little time."

The girl took five minutes, and when she looked up finally and faced them, she was slack-shouldered, defeated, and weak.

"I believe I know your name, child," said Mrs. Roosevelt. "We've met."

The girl shook her head.

"Your name is Cecile, isn't it?" Mrs. Roosevelt asked gently.

The girl coughed out a deep, painful sob, but she nodded.

"Cecile Baines," said Mrs. Roosevelt.

Deconcini gasped. "Baines," he whispered hoarsely. "Jerry . . . ?"

Mrs. Roosevelt nodded. "Mr. Baines's daughter. When I saw the snapshots, I thought I recognized her. I hoped I didn't, but I was afraid I did." She turned to the girl.

"You were at the picnic we had for the families of the White House staff in the summer of 1940. We took many snapshots that day. I still have them." She turned to Deconcini. "You wouldn't remember. Your wife and child were at the picnic, but you weren't."

Cecile Baines reached for the snapshots. "Where did you get these?" she asked.

"From the woman who runs the place where they were taken," said Deconcini. "The man who took them left with her to keep for him."

The girl rocked back and forth on her chair, sobbing. Mrs. Roosevelt rose, stepped to her side, and put her hand on her shoulder.

"Maybe it's not as bad as it seems, Cecile."

The girl looked up into her eyes. "Worse than you can possibly imagine." She wept. "My life is over."

"You can help yourself if you tell us the truth, Cecile. We must know who the man was who took these pictures. What was his name? Who was he?"

The girl exhaled so long a sigh that she seemed to deflate. "My father . . . I want to talk with my father."

"You will, very soon," said Mrs. Roosevelt. "But it is most important that we find out who that man was. You know what happened to him, don't you?"

Cecile shook her head. "He's gone. He's missing."

"He's dead," said Mrs. Roosevelt.

Cecile lifted her chin. "Dead?" she asked. "He's dead? *Good!* Thank God!"

Deconcini intervened. "What was his name, Cecile?" he asked firmly.

She drew breath, straightened her shoulders. "His name was Kurt Kluber," she said. "A *Nazi!* An animal!"

"Where and how did you meet him, Cecile?" asked Mrs. Roosevelt. She returned to her chair and picked up her tea. "And when?"

"Six months ago," said Cecile Baines. "Eight. Last summer, anyway. He came to our house, and he moved in. He just moved in. My mother and father were scared to death of him. He took over. He just took over the house, like it was his. And he turned us into his servants."

"Your father?" asked Sir Alan. "Your father impresses me as a strong man, unlikely to be turned into anyone's servant."

"My father . . . He had something on my father. Something awful."

"Not exactly," said Mrs. Roosevelt. She opened the small leather zip-top case she had carried from the White House. "I believe I can guess what it was that enabled this man to exert influence over your father."

She took a manila file folder from the case. "This is Mr. Baines's personnel file," she said. "Mr. Morgenthau was good enough to send it over from the Treasury Department. I've reviewed it since it arrived just after noon. Let me see here— Uh, here is some information . . ."

Deconcini was all but silenced by the appalling implications of what Cecile had revealed. "It fits," he muttered. "Jerry . . ."

Squinting at the file, Mrs. Roosevelt ran her finger over the topmost paper there. "Let me see. Your grandfather's name was Henri Jacques de Bainville, wasn't it, Cecile? He came to this country from Belgium in 1888 and changed his name to Baines. Your father was born three years later. He has a sister, somewhat younger than he, whose name is . . . What is her name, Cecile?"

"Marie. Aunt Marie," the girl mumbled.

"Marie Duclos," said Mrs. Roosevelt. "Married to Louis Duclos. Right?"

"Yes. Uncle Louis."

"And where are your aunt and uncle, child?" asked Mrs. Roosevelt gently.

"In Antwerp," whispered Cecile.

"Yes. In Nazi-occupied Belgium."

Cecile nodded.

"And you have cousins?"

"Daddy wanted them to leave Belgium before the blitz-krieg," whispered Cecile disconsolately. "He called them. He tried everything to get them to come to the States, at least to go to England. But Uncle Louis wouldn't move. His home and business are in Antwerp, and he wouldn't consider leaving them. So, when the German army over-ran the country, they were trapped. It's been a nightmare since April of 1940. Aunt Marie, Uncle Louis, my cousins Charles and Brigitte and Jeanne . . . all still in Antwerp."

"And this man Kluber—"

"I don't know what he told Daddy the Germans would do to his sister's family, but it put Daddy in shock. He told us we had to tolerate this man, to take him into our house, to feed him, to take orders from him."

"And above all, keep his presence secret," said Sir Alan.

Cecile nodded. "Even my brother, who lives in Florida, didn't know this awful man was living with us."

"Did you know what Kluber was doing in Washington?" asked Deconcini.

"I didn't know exactly what he'd gotten my father involved in," the girl said quietly, "but I knew it was something very wrong and that it would get my father in terrible trouble. Kluber said he could arrange it so nobody would ever know my father was involved; and he would arrange it that way if I . . . if I made him like me. He'd do that for me, he said."

"And he abused you," suggested Mrs. Roosevelt gently.

Cecile nodded. "Every way you could think of," she whispered. She lowered her head and for a moment hesitated. "He talked sometimes about how he would go away and leave us alone, if we did everything he ordered us to. He . . ." The girl raised her eyes and spoke directly to Mrs. Roosevelt. "He said if I was good to him and he liked me . . . I mean, he said I—"

"I think we understand," said Mrs. Roosevelt. "You need not embarrass yourself further."

"Are you telling us you *believed* what this man said?" asked Deconcini skeptically.

She shook her head scornfully. "I didn't believe anything he said. But what could I do? I thought of killing him. I'm glad he's dead."

"Tell me something, Cecile," said Deconcini. "Did your father know that Kluber was abusing you?"

The girl shook her head doubtfully. "I don't . . . I don't know," she said. "I mean, he knew something of what was going on. The whole thing was so confusing."

"Do you know how Kluber died?" asked Sir Alan.

Cecile shook her head.

"He was murdered," said Sir Alan.

"You're telling me this because you think my father did it," she said, her voice breaking.

"He could have," said Deconcini.

The girl nodded. "He could have. I could have myself. I wish I had."

"We can understand that," said Deconcini, "but unfortunately a great deal more is involved than whether or not the death of Kurt Kluber was justifiable homicide. I'm sorry, Cecile, but we're going to have to hold you for a while."

Cecile's eyes widened. "I'm going to jail?" she asked in a thin whisper.

"No," said Deconcini. "We'll find somewhere else where you can be held in custody." He spoke to Mrs. Roosevelt. "The army has a secure guest house at Fort McNair, where she'll be comfortable but can't get out. We can put her there for a day or two, with a woman to keep her company and watch over her."

Crushed, the girl only shook her head and did not protest.

"In fact," said Deconcini, "I imagine Mrs. Baines knows something about what's been happening. We'll let her keep her daughter company."

"It seems cruel," said Mrs. Roosevelt sorrowfully.

"There is too much at stake to take any chances," said Deconcini.

"I am compelled to agree," said Mrs. Roosevelt. She rose and stepped to Cecile's side, to put a hand on her shoulder. "Be brave, child," she said. "We can hope this thing will work out without . . . too much pain."

"You are going to arrest my father," said Cecile fearfully.

"We're going to ask him a lot of questions," said Deconcini.

Harry Hopkins insisted on being present at the confrontation with Gerald Baines and officiously herded everyone into the Cabinet Room in the West Wing. It was just after seven when they were all seated around the cabinet table and were ready to meet Baines.

The cast of characters was: Mrs. Roosevelt, Hopkins, Sir Alan Burton, and Dominic Deconcini. Hopkins was at the head of the table, where the President sat during cabinet meetings. Mrs. Roosevelt sat to his right, with Deconcini beside her. Sir Alan sat opposite Mrs. Roosevelt, to Hopkin's left. Lieutenant-Commander Leach, Deconcini explained, was carrying out an investigation assignment.

Agent Ted Norton brought Gerald Baines into the room.

"Please take the chair at the other end of the table," said Hopkins.

Baines sat down stiffly, showing some pain. Norton sat beside him, to his right.

"Would you be so good, Jerry, as to hand over your pistol to Ted Norton?" said Hopkins.

Baines nodded. "So," he said quietly. "Fat's in the fire, is it?"

"It would seem to be," said Hopkins. "Of course, you may have some explanation for the facts we know, but—"

"I haven't," said Baines. He slowly withdrew his revolver from the holster under his jacket and handed it to Norton. "That is, I have none but what the facts imply."

"Well, we have a lot of questions to ask you," said Hopkins.

"I can well imagine."

"I'll let Dom ask most of them."

Deconcini sighed. "Jerry, we—"

Mrs. Roosevelt interrupted. "Mr. Baines," she said. "We will remain mindful of your long and devoted service —indeed that apparently you risked your life for us only last evening. We have some understanding also of the circumstances in which you have found yourself. I don't want you to think you are without friends here, or without sympathy."

Baines folded his hands on the table before him. His lips were stiff and white, and he nodded curtly. "Thank you, ma'am," he said.

"Jerry, we know about Kurt Kluber," said Deconcini. "We know who he was and what he was and where he had been living."

"How did you find out?" asked Baines.

"In a rather unfortunate way," said Deconcini. "I wish

it had been some other way. Through your daughter, Jerry."

Baines's face darkened. "What do you mean? How—"

"Mr. Baines," said Mrs. Roosevelt. "The German took some snapshots of Cecile. They fell into our hands. When I saw them, I recognized her. I remembered her from the family picnic we held a year and a half ago."

"Bad pictures?" Baines asked.

Mrs. Roosevelt shook her head and smiled kindly at Baines. "Oh, not so bad," she said. "Just embarrassing, I would call them."

"You've questioned Cecile?"

"We've taken her and her mother down to Fort McNair, Jerry," said Deconcini. "To the secure guest house. For their protection, mostly. But we did question Cecile for about half an hour. We know what Kluber did to you—and to her."

Baines drew in a deep breath and straightened his back and shoulders. "I killed him," he said. "And I killed the other one, too. His name was—"

"Von Keyserling," said Sir Alan Burton.

"Yes. Yes, of course."

"Uh . . . if I may," Hopkins interrupted. "We're going about this illogically. Couldn't we take things up in sequence, putting the facts together so they make some sense? Would you be willing to give us a statement, Jerry? I mean, would you be willing to let us bring in a stenographer and dictate a formal statement?"

Baines shrugged. "I might as well. You can put it all together whether I do or don't."

"I'm not sure we can, Jerry," said Deconcini. "Frankly, I'm not sure we can. You can be very helpful. And I suspect you want to be."

"Yes," said Baines dejectedly. "I'm in terrible trouble,

but it's nothing to what I've *been* in. My family . . . You understand my family is innocent. My wife and daughter. You understand, I . . ."

"We'll do everything we can to shield your wife and daughter," said Hopkins.

"I assure you of it," said Mrs. Roosevelt.

"All right. I'll give you a formal statement."

"My secretary has gone home for her New Year's Eve," said Hopkins. "But I think Miss Battersby—"

"Please," said Deconcini. "Is it quite appropriate that *she—*"

"Isn't the question of Miss Battersby settled?" asked Hopkins.

"I gather that Mr. Baines would know," said Mrs. Roosevelt. "So tell us, Mr. Baines: Has Miss Battersby been in any way involved in any of the things you are going to tell us about?"

Baines shook his head. "No," he said firmly. "No. Not at all."

"Then there is no reason why she cannot take his statement," said Hopkins. "Her shorthand is not as fast as we might like, but on New Year's Eve . . ." He reached for the telephone.

Bonny Battersby arrived a few minutes later, carrying a stack of little green shorthand pads and a fistful of pencils. At the suggestion of Hopkins she sat down at a small side table and spread her materials out before her. She was tense; her face was flushed, and her eyes flitted from one face to another, all around the table. She wore what was characteristic for her: a white sweater, tight across her full bust, and a black skirt. Hopkins asked her if she was ready, and she nodded. She bent low over her pad and began to scribble hurriedly as the dialogue continued.

"All right, Jerry," said Hopkins. "Why don't you just tell us the story from the beginning, in your own words?"

"To begin with," said Baines despondently, "you understand my family was Belgian. My father came over from Belgium in 1888. His name was de Bainville, which he changed to Baines. He used to go back as often as he could, to visit his family and friends. And as soon as any of us were old enough, he took me and my brothers and sister with him. He wanted to show us off, I guess. Anyway, my sister Marie is the baby of the family. I'm fifty years old, but she's only thirty-six. She went over with him every summer during the twenties. She was—to be perfectly frank—not very attractive or marriageable; so when she received a proposal from a well-off Antwerp businessman, we were all glad for her. She was married in 1930. They have three children. They visited the States in 1935 and 1937, and I got to go over and visited their home in 1936.

"When the war broke out," he went on, "I figured Belgium would bear the brunt of it, just as it did in 1914–1918; and I urged my brother-in-law to bring Marie and the kids and come live in the States until it's over. He wouldn't do it. He stayed. They all stayed. And when the German army broke through in April 1940—"

"Your family were trapped in a Nazi-occupied country," said Mrs. Roosevelt.

"Worse than that. The Germans knew who my sister was. They knew I was a senior agent of the Secret Service. They arrested the whole family and put them in a Gestapo prison. When Kluber came to my door, he showed me pictures of my sister behind the bars of a prison cell. He had a letter she had written me, begging me to do whatever I could to get her and her husband and children out. He showed me other pictures: the children in another cell; Louis, my brother-in-law, in prison uniform, digging with a shovel."

"Who *was* Kurt Kluber and where did he come from?" asked Deconcini.

"He was really a secondary sort of fellow. He worked for von Keyserling. I didn't meet von Keyserling until Kluber had been here several months."

"When did Kluber first appear?"

"Last summer. It was in June."

"And he began to blackmail you."

"Yes. He wanted me to help him to install spy equipment in the White House. Radios. Telephone taps. The sort of thing we've been taking out."

"It wasn't too difficult for you to find, was it, Jerry? You knew where it was."

"I knew where it was," Baines agreed. "I knew what you knew, Dom: that the South Lawn is crisscrossed with tunnels that carry off the rainwater from the White House roof and grounds and that you could crawl into that tunnel system from several points on the streets, including the one you used on East Executive Avenue. Once down in there, you could come up several places, all inside the fence, inside White House security, even inside the tighter security we set up after December 7. Kluber was in the White House twenty times between the middle of June and the night I killed him. I helped him bring in radio equipment and—"

"Weapons and explosives," interrupted Deconcini.

"No. Absolutely not," said Baines emphatically. "It was when I saw that he'd brought in a pistol and grenades and intended to attempt to assassinate the President—"

"That you decided to kill him," said Mrs. Roosevelt. "To protect the president. Is that right, Mr. Baines?"

"That's right."

"You'll forgive my cynicism," said Hopkins.

"I expected it, and I forgive it," said Baines blandly.

"We're just getting started here," said Deconcini. "Are you keeping up with us, Miss Battersby?"

"I am so far," she said, flipping over a page.

"It still doesn't make sense, Jerry. Let's keep going," said Deconcini. "There are still a thousand questions."

15

The little motorcade sped through the cold, dark streets of Washington to the northwest gate of the White House, then in and up to the entrance. The Prime Minister had returned from Ottawa.

A few minutes later, Winston Churchill was with the President at cocktails: he and Lord Beaverbrook, Lord Halifax, Field Marshal Dill, Admiral Pound, and Sir Charles Wilson; with Americans General George Marshall, Secretary of State Cordell Hull, Secretary of War Henry Stimson, and General Edwin "Pa" Watson. The President shook martinis as usual, but most of his guests let Arthur Prettyman pour them Scotch or brandy or wine.

The Prime Minister offered a toast to the new year, 1942: "Let us hope and pray that, through the toils and perils of this year, we will emerge united and firm and well set on our road to victory."

The President raised his glass to: "The new year, a year in which the cordiality and unity of this meeting will be sustained. Let us recall the famous words of Benjamin Franklin: 'We must indeed all hang together, or, most assuredly, we shall all hang separately.' "

The Prime Minister sat down beside the President. "I have come to feel at home here, almost," he said. "But do tell me: where is your charming lady, and where is the redoubtable Harry Hopkins?"

The President allowed a long moment to pass before answering. "Do you know, Winston," he said then, "I do believe they are on the verge of a solution to our terrible mystery. They are hard at it belowstairs, interrogating the man who may hold the key. In any event, I believe I can promise you a sound night's sleep, without fears of assassination."

"Tomorrow," rumbled Churchill, "if I read our agenda rightly, we are to assemble on the first day of the new year to affix our signatures to the Declaration of the United Nations. You and I and—what? twenty-five other nations?—pledging ourselves to the cause, not just of victory over fascism, but to the cause of humanity everywhere and always. It would be a shame, would it not, if you or I were murdered in his bed tonight?"

The President chuckled. "Do you ever wish, Winston, that it could happen—*at the hands of a jealous husband?*"

In the Cabinet Room, the meeting went on: Mrs. Roosevelt, now sipping coffee, a little tired but very much alert, dressed in a gray wool suit; the chronically rumpled Hopkins, smoking almost as heavily as Louis Howe had done, smearing his lapels with ash and coughing painfully; Sir Alan Burton, rigidly erect, self-consciously playing the tweedy upper-class Englishman, occasionally touching his wispy yellow-gray hair; Dominic Deconcini, impeccably dressed in a dark blue pin-striped suit with every crease sharp but his keen Italian features softened by fatigue; Bonny Battersby, blond head down, shoulders hunched over her work, tensely working to record all the conversation around the table; the gaunt, chain-smoking

Ted Norton; and, finally, Gerald Baines, bald, liver-spotted, bland-faced, sober, and accused.

Deconcini continued to lead the interrogation. "All right, Jerry. You helped Kluber to install spy equipment in the White House. And so on. Now, you say you did not help him bring in arms and explosives."

"That is exactly so," said Baines, "I never saw him bring in a gun. I certainly did not see him bring in the grenades. I wouldn't have allowed it."

"But they did come in," said Deconcini. "Or at least they got as far as the tunnel, where Lieutenant-Commander Leach and I found them."

"Simple answer," said Baines. His broad, wrinkled, liver-spotted forehead gleamed with perspiration. He had achieved a degree of self-control that was remarkable in the circumstances, but this he could not control. "Once he had learned the way, he came in alone."

"And hid weapons where he could find them later," said Deconcini.

"Well. I never saw any weapons until the night when—"

"When you killed him."

Baines nodded. "When I killed him."

"Let's talk about that night," said Deconcini.

Baines glanced at Norton, as if he saw in him alone someone who was not an accuser. "The whole deal," he said, "had been to put spy equipment in the White House, to tap the President's telephone, and yours, Mr. Hopkins, so the Nazis could hear our war plans. So long as there wasn't a war—I mean, as long as the United States wasn't in the war—it seemed like a price I could pay for my sister's life, for her family's. It was peacetime, so far as the United States was concerned. I . . . I knew it was wrong. I . . ."

"Go on, Jerry," said Deconcini sternly.

"Kluber never spoke about murder," said Baines firmly. "I swear it. I never saw a weapon. He never suggested he would try to kill the President. If he had—"

"I think," said Mrs. Roosevelt, "that none of us have any doubt on that score, Mr. Baines. If you had suspected he meant to try to kill the President, you would have—"

"Killed him first," said Baines.

"Brought him to American justice, I would hope," she said.

"The same thing," muttered Hopkins.

Baines went on, his voice becoming strained and throaty. "The evening of the twenty-second of December, I went off duty about ten o'clock," he said. "I got home, expecting to see Kluber sitting in my living room as usual: half drunk, swaggering, making obscene jokes to my wife and daughter. But he wasn't there. He was out, and my wife and daughter didn't know where. He'd gone out without a word. I . . . I was afraid he'd gone to the White House. I don't know: I just had an instinct that maybe he had gone through the storm sewer. So I decided to go back to see."

"The evening when the Prime Minister arrived," said Sir Alan.

"Yes. I came back to the White House, came in through the storm sewer. I suppose I got here around midnight. Maybe a little after. I climbed in the window of the housekeeper's office. I'd kept that window unlocked for months, so we could open it and climb in after we got out of the storm sewer."

"Not the trophy-room window?" Bonny Battersby interrupted, looking up and allowing herself a triumphant grin.

Baines shook his head. "No. The window in Mrs. Nesbitt's office. I locked it later. I was as surprised as you were, Miss Battersby, to find the window unlocked in the trophy room. We never came in or went out through that window."

"My apologies, Miss Battersby," said Deconcini.

"Accepted, Mr. Deconcini," she said with a warm smile.

"Anyway," Baines continued, "Kluber was there, in the housekeeper's office, sitting at Mrs. Nesbitt's work table, a little drunk. That was what made him a second-rate agent: that he drank too much. He grinned at me, sort of foolishly. 'Ah, Baines,' he said. 'You have come to help me?'

" 'Help you do what?' I asked.

" 'Strike a memorable blow for our cause,' he said. 'If this night's work is well done, your sister and her family will be sent into Switzerland.' "

"Did you believe that, Jerry?" asked Deconcini.

"Not a word of it," growled Baines. "But I wasn't thinking of that. The grenades were lying on Mrs. Nesbitt's work table."

"I listened to your speech on the radio," said the President to the Prime Minister. " 'Some chicken! Some neck!' A memorable line, Winston. History will remember it."

"I thank you," said Churchill. "I fear, my dear friend, that most everything you and I say will be remembered by history, not so much for our force and wit in saying it, but because of the unhappy circumstances in which we spoke. I wish I could believe my words are remembered for my brilliance of speech. I am afraid, in truth, Neville Chamberlain's words would be remembered if he were speaking them in these troubled days."

"By that token," said the President, "everyone would remember the words of, say, Randolph Hearst or Bertie McCormack, who speak out with all their might in these troubled days—but I don't think posterity will be able to recall a single word ever written or spoken by either of them. History does justice better than ever we could imagine, my friend. Randy and Bertie prick at me today, but another generation, hearing their names, will wonder who they might have been."

Churchill glanced across the room. "Do you suppose that will happen to Beaverbrook?" he asked slyly.

"I wondered why he was wearing a new suit," said Baines. "I could see it was new. I questioned him as to why he had come to the White House that night, and he only grinned. He picked up one of the grenades and made some comment about how it would do a job of work. Then he pulled the Colt revolver out of his jacket. 'What do you think of this?' he asked."

"What *did* you think of it?" asked Hopkins.

"I thought he meant to kill the President with it," said Baines grimly. "Worse. The grenades. He meant to attempt to kill the President and the Prime Minister as well."

"And you . . ."

Baines shuddered. "I couldn't let that happen. Even if—"

"Even if it meant the murder of your sister and her family," said Mrs. Roosevelt quietly.

Baines nodded. "Even if it meant that," he said.

"So, what did you do?" asked Deconcini.

Tension around the cabinet table was palpable as Baines continued his narrative. Bonny Battersby frowned over her shorthand pad and scribbled determinedly. Mrs. Roosevelt stared at her hands in her lap. Deconcini stared at Baines.

"Kluber," said Baines, "told me he was waiting for Henry Taylor, the night butler, to receive a buzz to go upstairs. Henry, you know, could see the door of the housekeeper's office from his table in the pantry; and

Kluber and I had often waited for Henry to get a call before we slipped out of Mrs. Nesbitt's office and went about our business in the White House. Many times we had waited for Henry to go upstairs before we could return to the housekeeper's office. Sometimes, when we were upstairs, I would slip into a room and push the button to call Henry up, so we could hurry back and out the window while he was off answering a false buzz. Sometimes, though, Henry would sleep, late at night. Sometimes we could hear him snoring, and we would slip past him."

"And that night?" asked Deconcini.

"I'd heard the buzzer," said Baines. "I knew Henry had gone upstairs. Kluber hadn't heard it. I said I'd go over and see if Henry were asleep. I could do that, of course. It wouldn't have alarmed Henry to see *me* in the White House in the middle of the night. So I went over to the pantry. And, over there, I did two things—"

"You tampered with the buzzer box and you picked up the ice pick," said Deconcini.

"Exactly, Dom," said Baines. "All the rest of you people would be wise to notice how good this guy is."

"Noted," said Hopkins. "Go on."

"I opened the drawer in the kitchen and pulled out an ice pick," said Baines. "I didn't know it was anybody's special ice pick. To me, it was just an ice pick. Then I climbed on a chair, opened the little glass door on the buzzer box, and pushed up one of the little arrows, to indicate that someone on the third floor had buzzed for service. I knew the first thing Henry did when he returned would be to look at that box, to see if he had any more calls. The little arrow broke loose under my fingers. It was stuck in the 'call' position permanently."

"Which Mrs. Nesbitt would soon notice," said Mrs. Roosevelt.

"Mrs. Nesbitt," said Baines ruefully, "is a determinedly methodical woman. Nothing escapes her attention long."

"So Henry—"

"Henry returned, saw the button up, and hurried off to the third floor. So far as I knew, that vacated the west end of the ground floor. I didn't know Miss Battersby was still typing in the trophy room."

"But with the door closed that night," said Bonny Battersby. "I didn't—"

"Hear a sound," said Baines. "I intended to kill Kluber with the ice pick the first chance I got—in any case before he tried to go upstairs. Okay, at this point Kluber decided he wanted a drink. Typical Kluber. He asked me where the White House liquor was kept. 'One drink of good brandy,' he said. He said it two or three times: 'One drink, good brandy.' He wanted to toast the *Führer,* thought I'd join him in that. He went across the hall to the pantry. I pointed out the liquor cabinet. To tell you the truth, I didn't know it was locked. I'd never had occasion to take a drink of the White House liquor. But I knew where it was kept, and I showed Kluber the cabinet. I thought maybe he'd get drunk and make things easier for me."

Baines sighed and shook his head. Everyone else waited, staring at him.

"He tried the door of the liquor cabinet," Baines said in a lowered voice. "It wouldn't open, of course; and he kind of muttered and tried to force it. His back was to me, and he was angry and concentrating on that little lock; and that was my opportunity. I pulled out the ice pick and . . . Well, you know what happened from there."

Deconcini nodded. "Jerry," he said. "Miss Battersby is taking an official record. A confession, I guess we could call it. So—"

"I stabbed him in the base of the skull with the ice

pick," said Baines. "I knew it would kill him: quick and quiet. And it did. He just slumped to the floor. There wasn't much blood. What little there was, I stopped with my handkerchief."

"His pockets were empty," said Deconcini quietly.

"He had meant to frustrate an investigation after he had killed the President and possibly the Prime Minister," said Baines. "He expected to be killed himself. He had worn a new suit, with absolutely nothing in the pockets. New clothes from the skin out. Nothing that would identify him. What was more, he knew we didn't have a fingerprint record of him. The only fingerprint record of Kurt Kluber was with German agencies, his employers. I went through his pockets in the little time I had. I took the pistol off him. Other than for that, I found nothing. When you searched him in the morning, you found him clean of identification, just as I had."

"The refrigerator . . . ?" asked Mrs. Roosevelt.

"I knew Henry would be back shortly. I didn't want the hue and cry raised until I'd had my chance to get out of the White House and go home. So I dragged the body into the refrigerator and left it there."

"You took the time to return the ice pick to the drawer," said Deconcini.

"I had time for that. Only three or four minutes had passed. I went back to Mrs. Nesbitt's office, picked up the grenades, climbed out the window, went down into the storm sewer, and left the White House grounds."

"And dropped the pistol and grenades in the sewer tunnel," said Deconcini.

Baines nodded. "I expected to arrange to have the manholes welded shut the next day, on my authority as a senior agent. There was so much excitement around here on Tuesday that I didn't get around to making the arrangements." He shrugged. "It never occurred to me that you and Leach would go exploring in the storm sewers before I could get it done—or that Major Bentz would send a platoon through with mine detectors. Even so, what difference did that make? Even when you found the Colt and the grenades, you didn't know where they came from."

"And the next morning," said Deconcini, "you went to Mrs. Nesbitt's office and locked the window."

"Exactly," said Baines. "When you found the trophy-room window unlocked, it was a surprise to me."

"You made a great show," said Hopkins, "of helping find and remove the telephone taps and radio transmitters—to divert suspicion."

Baines smiled sadly and shook his head. "With all due respect, Mr. Hopkins, I didn't need to do anything to divert suspicion."

"Because none of us suspected him," said Mrs. Roosevelt.

"Yes," said Baines. "I helped locate and remove the equipment because I had decided to try to undo what I'd done."

A small group assembled for dinner: the group that had assembled for the cocktail hour, joined by Admiral King. Conversation had turned somber, as the President and the Prime Minister, with their generals and admirals, reviewed once more the deteriorating situation in the Pacific.

"You can't move men and equipment all the way from your west coast to the Philippines in time to relieve MacArthur," said the Prime Minister. "And similarly we can't move anything much to the relief of Singapore. We may have to accept its fall. I am reminded of a bit of poetry by Alexander Pope:

Ye gods, annihilate but space and time
And make two lovers happy."

"We sent out a fleet to relieve Wake Island," said the President. "Before it was halfway there, the admiral turned it around and came back. Wake Island fell to the Japanese, of course. What would you do, Mr. Prime Minister, with an admiral who did something like that?"

Churchill withdrew his cigar from his mouth. "I've learnt never to dispute with admirals, Mr. President. They can always confound you with data about weather, want of fuel, broken propeller shafts, and the like. There is nothing to be gained by arguing with them."

"Or generals, I suppose," said the President.

"Oh, for generals we have no sympathy," rumbled Churchill, casting a sly glance at Field Marshal Dill and General Marshall. "If they don't take orders, we sack 'em. Learnt the technique from Herr Hitler, who sacks his regularly."

"For which we may all be grateful," Marshall commented dryly.

"My government are most concerned about Hasso von Keyserling," said Sir Alan Burton. "They wish to be assured absolutely that the man killed in the White House on the night of December 26 was he."

Gerald Baines had accepted a small glass of Scotch and ice, brought in from the pantry. The glass was before his face as he nodded. "You may assure your government, Sir Alan, that von Keyserling is dead."

Hopkins had called for bourbon and half a dozen oysters. He was eating. "Tell us about von Keyserling," he said. "Everything you know about him."

Mrs. Roosevelt had ordered another pot of coffee and some tuna sandwiches, which she was sharing with

Deconcini. Sir Alan was sipping Scotch and nibbling from a bowl of peanuts.

"Von Keyserling," said Baines, "showed up in the fall. It was apparent from the beginning that he was Kluber's superior. His English was perfect. He had a military bearing. He had a most impressive way of expressing himself: just two or three stern words that said everything he meant to say and invariably struck dread into Kluber. He was impatient with what Kluber had accomplished. Nothing was good enough. Kluber was terrified of him."

"But who was he?" asked Hopkins.

"An officer of what the Germans call the *Sicherheitsdienst,*" said Baines. "Security service. Kluber called him *Herr Standartenführer:* meaning that he held an SS rank, roughly equivalent to a colonel in military terms. He wasn't like Kluber. When I saw him, he didn't drink. He never relaxed. He was a fearsome Nazi fanatic. Also, he had spoken directly with my sister in a Gestapo prison in Belgium. He told me things she had said, things he could not possibly have learned except from her."

"What was he doing in the States?" asked Hopkins.

"Installing telephone taps and radio transmitters in the White House was too important to be left to an underling like Kluber," said Baines. "I suppose he was working on other projects, since he certainly did not give full time to this one; but what they were I could not guess."

"Why don't we let you go on telling your story?" said Deconcini.

Baines nodded. "He bullied me. But never like Kluber did. In fact, I even considered appealing to him to call Kluber off, to order him to leave my daughter alone." Baines stopped and sighed. "I judged, though, that a man like him would let one of his subordinates amuse himself in any way that didn't interfere with his duties—and probably be amused by it. Von Keyserling gave me orders the same way he gave them to Kluber: succinctly, stiffly, with never a thought that I wouldn't jump to obey. He had such an aristocratic air!"

"Where was he the night you killed Kluber?" asked Deconcini.

"I don't know. He called me the next night and demanded I come out and meet with him after two A.M. I went to an all-night diner on E Street. We sat and drank coffee, and he ate pie; and he accused me of killing Kluber. He said I must have done it; I was the only one who could have. Then he talked about the dismantling of the equipment in the White House. He knew all about it. He said I had betrayed the anti-Bolshevist cause, as he called it. My sister's life was *forfeit,* he growled at me. If I didn't want her to die in prolonged torture . . . Well. You can imagine."

"Oh, Mr. Baines!" cried Mrs. Roosevelt.

"That's the kind of people they are, ma'am," said Baines somberly.

"How did he get into the White House, and how did he smuggle in the Luger that was on him when you shot him?" asked Deconcini.

"You know how he got in," said Baines. "He came in the guise of a telegraph delivery boy. And I don't think he smuggled the Luger past the gate and door. I think he picked it up after he got inside."

"Meaning," said Deconcini, "that there was—and maybe is—a cache of weapons hidden inside the White House."

"Meaning that exactly," said Baines. "I told you Kluber came in by himself several times. He brought the grenades and . . . Well, I don't know what all he may have brought in."

"Kluber could have told him where to find the Luger," said Deconcini.

"Yes. He could have."

"All right. But how did you know he would be in the White House the night of December 26?"

"I didn't," said Baines. "I was afraid he might try to pick up where Kluber had left off, and I watched for him; I was roaming the halls that night. I came along the west hall, and there he was, dressed as a telegraph boy. I could guess what he was here for. He was a fanatic, and he meant to attempt the assassination of the President, no matter if he had no chance whatever of escaping alive. I suspect he was receiving angry questions from Berlin."

"Go on, Jerry."

"He greeted me. He grinned and said, 'Ah, so. How lucky. You will help me.' He didn't show me his gun, the way Kluber had done; but you can't hide a Luger in a telegraph-delivery-boy's uniform, and I saw it. I pulled my service revolver, poked it into his belly, and marched him down the hall toward the pantry. I—"

"Why the pantry, Jerry?" asked Deconcini.

"I'd just come from there," said Baines, "and I knew Henry was upstairs, carrying bourbon and oysters to the Lincoln suite."

"To *you*, Harry," said Mrs. Roosevelt with a faint smile at Hopkins.

"I was going to kill him in the refrigerator," said Baines. "I thought that would be an interesting touch, confounding the mystery, so to speak. Besides, the shot would be muffled by the insulated walls and doors of the refrigerator. I—"

"You *intended* to kill the man?" asked Mrs. Roosevelt. "You had no other thought?"

"None," said Baines. "I thought killing him might put an end to the threat to the President; and I thought maybe there was a chance I would get away with it. There were two things I was not going to let him do: get away or talk. I guess he knew. I suppose he knew I was about to kill him. Anyway, as we walked through the pantry, he grabbed for the Luger. I hadn't taken it off of him, and he made a grab for it. I shot him in the back."

"Before he could get off a shot?" asked Sir Alan. "What of the nine-millimeter Luger slug dug out of the pantry wall?"

"I wrapped my handkerchief around my hand, picked up the Luger, and fired a shot into the pantry wall," said Baines.

"To make it look as though the fellow had fired at you first," said Sir Alan, nodding. "And the handkerchief accounts for the fact that von Keyserling's fingerprints on the trigger were smudged and indistinct."

"So," said Hopkins. "Two mysteries solved."

"And three or four remaining," said Deconcini. "Who was in the elevator last night, Jerry? Who shot you? Who hid the .32 Colt in Mr. Hopkins's chair?"

Baines turned down the corners of his mouth and shook his head. "I was hoping to find out," he said, "before you identified me as the one who killed Kluber and von Keyserling. I wasn't making any progress, I have to tell you. And it's the most important question in the world right now. There's still somebody dangerous in the White House."

16

"Would you prefer brandy to champagne?" Mrs. Roosevelt asked Winston Churchill.

"I would, my dear lady, if you don't mind."

"Don't you like champagne, Mr. Churchill?"

"I do, very much," said the Prime Minister. "For breakfast."

Mrs. Roosevelt laughed. They were in the President's oval study on the second floor, just the three of them: she, the President, and Churchill, sharing a quiet half hour before they toasted the advent of the new year at midnight.

The others had left—Harry Hopkins to join his wife in the Lincoln suite at the far end of the second floor, where they would greet the new year alone; the generals and admirals and cabinet members to their homes, to be with their families. The White House, though heavily guarded by soldiers and Secret Service agents in the corridors, was quiet.

Mrs. Roosevelt had left Dominic Deconcini, Sir Alan Burton, Lieutenant-Commander Leach—who had returned—Ted Norton, and Gerald Baines in the Cabinet Room, where they remained as midnight approached. Baines was technically in custody, and when he left the White House it would be to jail; but for now he sat at the cabinet table and participated in a review of the evidence and of every possible inference that could be drawn from it. The danger was not past, they understood.

Bonny Battersby was in the trophy room, at her desk. Hopkins and Mrs. Roosevelt had insisted she was not to stay up all night typing the long transcript she had taken on her steno pads; and she had said she would go home as soon as she had glanced over the many pages of shorthand, to fill in a few blanks while her memory was fresh. She sat slumped, tired, the harsh light of a gooseneck desk lamp throwing chiaroscuro shadows over her face. She was so sitting when Lieutenant-Commander George Leach came into the room.

He was wearing civilian clothes: a heavy-wool, double-breasted, black, pin-striped suit.

"Ho," he said. "Working so late again? Is there no limit to conscientiousness?"

"Yes," she said. "Where were you the early part of the evening?"

"Between them, Sir Alan and Dom Deconcini have turned me into a bloody errand boy," he said. "I've spent the time running down false leads."

"Well, it's pretty much over now," she said.

"Yes, but it's not over, actually," said Leach. "Too much is unresolved."

She sighed. "I suppose so." She lifted her pile of steno pads. "Look at how much typing I have to do tomorrow," she said. "New Year's Day."

He glanced at his watch. "We're entitled to take a bit of cheer at midnight. A few minutes from now. Couldn't you—"

"Yes," she said. "Yes, I could."

"Could we get home in time? I mean, to your house? No, I suppose we couldn't. I—"

"George." She looked up at him with a suggestive

smile. "Uh, you *do* have a room of your own on the third floor, don't you? You don't share it with anyone?"

"I do have a modest room to myself, actually," he said tentatively. "Uh . . ." He grinned nervously. "Yes, I . . . I do."

"Well, then," she said. "Since it's a long, cold trip out to Georgetown, and I doubt we could get a cab, and since all is forgiven between you and me . . . I believe we can get a bottle of champagne from Henry."

"Uh . . . *Good!* Let's waste no time."

"Fine," she said. She stood. "Let's see . . . You go to the pantry and tell Henry I asked for a bottle of champagne. I'll tuck the shorthand pads in my desk drawer. And I've got to turn out the lights, lock the door, and—"

"I'll just wait for you."

"No, no. We haven't much time before midnight," she said. "And Henry might get a call and go upstairs. Go on. I'll be with you in two minutes." She pulled a book from a bookcase and stuffed it in her purse. "Hurry, George!"

Laughing merrily, carrying his overcoat and hat, Lieutenant-Commander Leach hurried down the hall toward the pantry.

In the President's study, the President and the First Lady raised their glasses with the Prime Minister, and together they toasted the coming of the year 1942.

"Tomorrow," said Churchill, "we will gather: you and I, Mr. Soong for China, and Mr. Litvinov for Russia, and we will sign the United Nations Declaration. Incidentally, my friend, I am very pleased that you substituted the words 'United Nations' for 'Associated Powers.' It has a far better ring to it."

"I do hope the spirit of the Declaration may endure," said Mrs. Roosevelt.

"I am reminded," said Churchill, "of certain lines of Byron's, from *Childe Harold:*

Here, where the sword United Nations drew,
Our countrymen were warring on that day!
And this is much—and all—which will not pass away."

The President raised his champagne glass and, joined by Mrs. Roosevelt and Churchill, silently toasted the thought.

At the northwest gate Captain Kennelly and Sergeant Jack Crown, a plainclothes technician of the D.C. police department, waited while the guards telephoned the Cabinet Room, then searched through the two large cases of equipment they had brought with them. Shortly they were admitted, and two rifle-carrying soldiers led them up the walk to the door. There the men on duty insisted on searching the cases a second time. They were thorough and were not finished by the time Deconcini arrived at the door to receive the two D.C. policemen.

"This is above and beyond the call of duty, Captain, Sergeant," Deconcini said as he led them—Sergeant Crown gaping—through the brightly lighted first floor of the White House. "New Year's Eve. Midnight. When our job is done, I'll see if we can't break loose some champagne from the presidential wine supply."

"We'd as soon raise a toast in good Irish whiskey, if the White House can provide," said Kennelly.

"Well . . ." said Deconcini doubtfully. "Scotch. I know they keep Scotch on hand."

"Figures," said Kennelly caustically.

They walked down the stairs to the ground floor, then west to the Cabinet Room in the West Wing. There, Baines sat glumly, sipping from another glass of Scotch.

Sir Alan Burton started when they entered the room, having taken advantage of the lull to catch a few winks of sleep.

"You know everyone, Captain," said Deconcini; but he introduced Sergeant Crown around the table.

"Baines," said Kennelly cordially, not knowing that Baines was in custody. "I don't believe I've met Mr. Norton. And Sir Burton. Good to see you again."

"There's our project," said Deconcini. He pointed to two little packages lying on a white linen handkerchief in the center of the table. "If you can lift fingerprints off those and match them to . . . Well, it can be very important."

The gray-faced Sergeant Crown peered at the two items through his rimless, octagonal spectacles: one, a package of Chesterfield cigarettes; the other, a package of Sheik condoms. "Cellophane," he muttered, nodding at the cigarette package. "Get good prints off that. The rubbers . . ." He shrugged. "Maybe."

"We'd appreciate your best effort on it," said Deconcini.

"We can try," said the sergeant.

Deconcini and Norton helped him unpack the two cases and set up his equipment on the cabinet table. He picked up the two packages with a pair of tweezers, laid them on a sheet of white paper, and began to dust them with white powder from a small, pliable brush.

"This will take a while," said Kennelly.

"There're prints on the cellophane, all right," said the sergeant.

"Good night, Franklin," said Mrs. Roosevelt. "Do you need any help? I mean, since you insisted you would not need Arthur anymore tonight . . ."

He had wheeled himself to the door of his bedroom. "I can do it, Babs," he said.

She nodded doubtfully. They were talking about the effort of undressing, using the bathroom, and going to bed: things the President needed help to do. It would be a struggle for him to take off his clothes and his braces, pull on his pajamas, lift himself into bed. He always insisted he could do it easily, but she knew he had to work at it, and she dreaded his falling and being unable to rise. She decided not to insist on helping him, which would humiliate him, but to check on him later.

"Well, then," she said. "A very happy New Year, my dear."

"And a happy New Year to you, Babs. We didn't bargain for what we've got, did we?"

"I haven't heard you complain," she said. "And I know I shan't. And you haven't and won't hear me, either."

He looked up at her and nodded. "I am confident of that," he said.

She closed the door behind him after he had wheeled himself into the short corridor to his bedroom. She had told him she was going to bed, but she meant to go to the Cabinet Room, to learn what progress, if any, was being made.

Sergeant Crown had transferred the fingerprints from the two packages to transparent slides. He was preparing to mount them in a dual projector. With other, known prints projected side-by-side with the newly taken ones, they could compare them. He could also superimpose one print over another to determine if they were identical. It was, as Kennelly had promised, a slow process; and when Mrs. Roosevelt arrived, the sergeant was just ready to set up the screen and projector.

Deconcini introduced Crown and explained what he was doing. He told her it would be a few minutes yet before any comparisons could be made.

"I'm afraid I don't know what fingerprints you are working with, Mr. Deconcini," she said.

"It's something I've withheld from you, Mrs. Roosevelt," he said. "The comparison may prove meaningless. If it *is* meaningless, I had meant not to tell you about it. Since you're here—"

"I won't press you about it," she said.

"I'll be grateful," said Deconcini. "I'd like to avoid the embarrassment."

She nodded toward the door, and Deconcini stepped out into the hall with her. "Mr. Baines?" she asked quietly. "How is he holding up? I feel sorry for the man."

"We all do," said Deconcini.

"Is it possible that he is *still* withholding information?" she asked.

"I don't think so. I think he came back to our side the night he killed Kluber, just as he said he did."

She nodded. "I hope so. I would like to think there is some way he need not suffer the extreme penalties of the law."

"I'm afraid that's not up to me," said Deconcini.

"No. Nor up to me. But I do hope every appropriate factor will be taken into consideration."

"I, too."

Mrs. Roosevelt drew in her lower lip and frowned. "Be frank with me, Mr. Deconcini," she said. "You are not satisfied that Miss Battersby is wholly innocent, are you? Indeed, that is what you are pursuing tonight and didn't want to tell me. The fingerprints—"

"I can't ignore the implications—"

"Of course not," she interrupted. "Please don't think I would want you to."

"In fact," he said, "I have to go over to the trophy room right now, to pick up a possible bit of evidence."

"I shall come with you," said Mrs. Roosevelt. "You may

be surprised to learn that I have developed a suspicion about Miss Battersby. Something has been running through my mind, and I want to settle a small question to my own satisfaction."

They passed through the guard stations and returned to the White House proper, into the long ground-floor corridor. It was quiet, deserted. Henry Taylor dozed at his table in the pantry. Walking east, they came to the door to the trophy room. It was locked, but Deconcini had a key. He opened the door and switched on the lights.

"What are you looking for?" Mrs. Roosevelt asked.

"A package of cigarettes," he said. "The package of cigarettes with the half-smoked butt in it."

"And I want to see the stenographer's pads on which she took the record of Mr. Baines's statement," said Mrs. Roosevelt.

"Good luck to you," said Deconcini wryly. "The cigarette package is gone. I'll look in the trash can. But tell me, why do you want to look at the steno pads?"

Mrs. Roosevelt faintly. "A minor suspicion. I'll keep it to myself until I see if it amounts to anything."

"Well, here you are," he said, pulling the green pads from one of the side drawers of the desk.

Mrs. Roosevelt opened the first pad on the top of the pile. She frowned hard. Then, with abrupt movements, she flipped through a dozen pages. Finished with that pad, she looked through another one, her face turning pink.

"I owe you an apology, Mr. Deconcini," she said gravely. She tossed the pads on the desk. "Look at those. No shorthand. She wrote nothing, took no record of those hours of talk."

Deconcini picked up the pads and stared at the pages. The paper was covered with disordered squiggly lines. He sorted through until he came to the pad she had numbered *1*. On the first page she had written a few notes in hasty abbreviations. After that—nothing. She had sat there hour after hour, pretending to take shorthand notes, writing nothing.

"This makes it more likely," said Deconcini, "that the fingerprints will prove significant. Let's go back to the Cabinet Room."

He locked the door and Mrs. Roosevelt carried the steno pads as they hurried back toward the West Wing. When they arrived again in the Cabinet Room, Sergeant Crown had his projector set up and was displaying two fingerprints side-by-side on the screen.

"I should explain what fingerprints we are looking at," said Deconcini as he pulled back a chair for Mrs. Roosevelt.

"The one on the right is a left index from the body you identified as 'Hans,' " said Sergeant Crown.

"Which was Kurt Kluber," said Deconcini. "Let me explain that while we were hearing Jerry Baines's statement, I sent Lieutenant-Commander Leach out to Georgetown to have another look at Bonny Battersby's house and pick up a couple of items for me if he could find them. I gave him a key that would open her door. I might tell you also that I gave him a pistol to carry."

"So that's where the cigarettes and, uh, other items came from," said Mrs. Roosevelt.

"Yes. When I searched her house Friday I noticed the package of cigarettes in the nightstand by her bed, even though we have observed she doesn't smoke. There was another pack in her desk drawer here in the White House. Also, she had shaving equipment in her bathroom. Finally, there were the . . . uh, prophylactics. We need not care particularly if a man spent nights regularly in her bedroom. That's really none of our business—unless the man was Kurt Kluber or Hasso von Keyserling."

"Well, what have you learned, Sergeant Crown?" asked Mrs. Roosevelt.

"Nothin' much yet," said Sergeant Crown. His voice was thin, piercing, with a twang from the Ohio Valley. "I believe in going at these things methodically. There are two sets of prints on the cigarette cellophane, three sets on the package of rubbers. Okay. I checked them first against the Battersby girl's prints, the ones we took Monday morning. Bingo. She's handled both items. Now I'm looking at the prints off the 'Hans' corpse: the one you now say was a man named . . . what was it?"

"Kluber," said Kennelly.

"Kluber. The prints aren't his. Now we take a look at the prints off the 'Fritz' corpse—"

"Von Keyserling," said Deconcini.

"Von Keyserling," the sergeant repeated. He frowned and nodded. "You realize something. Even if the prints on the package of rubbers are von Keyserling's, since there are three sets and none of them is from Kluber, that means there's a third man involved."

"I think," said Sir Alan Burton dryly, "we may anticipate that the third set of fingerprints are those of Lieutenant-Commander George Leach."

"You mean because he brought the items in," said Sergeant Crown. "Huh-uh. His prints aren't on the Chesterfields. He had enough sense to handle them without getting his prints on them. So, we—"

"They would be on there for another reason," said Sir Alan, grinning. "Let us proceed."

"Oh," said Crown. He used both hands to resettle his glasses on his nose. "Well, then. Let's look at the von Keyserling prints. First against the prints from the cigarette cellophane, which are a lot clearer."

He manipulated his slides and the projector. The prints appeared on the screen.

"They look very like, don't they?" said Sir Alan.

Sergeant Crown moved the two images over each other, until one was superimposed on the other. "Ah-hah!" he said triumphantly. "Is that what you wanted to know?"

Deconcini nodded grimly. "To be perfectly frank, I rather hoped I was wrong."

"It explains a lot," said Baines. He had drunk enough Scotch to slur his voice a little. "The Colt automatic under Harry Hopkins's chair. As a secretary working for him, she had access to his office. And last night. The man who shot me . . . *Christ!*"

"I have just reached the same conclusion," said Mrs. Roosevelt. *"She* shot you. She was in the elevator. She was on her way up to the second floor to make another attempt on the life of the President. After she shot you through the doors of the elevator, she came back down, ran across the hall, threw her chair at the window, struck herself hard in the face with something, and lay down on the floor."

"Well, all that is a bit facile, if I may say so," said Sir Alan. "How could she have supposed she would get past the guards on the second floor: she a woman alone, armed with nothing but a pistol?"

"Maybe she was armed with more than a pistol," said Baines. "You remember, we *did* find grenades in the tunnel."

"But the White House has been searched," said Ted Norton. "Major Bentz has been through the place with metal detectors. He has poked into everything, even in the Oval Office."

"Where is she now?" asked Mrs. Roosevelt.

Deconcini had the telephone in his hand. Putting his hand over the mouthpiece, he said, "I'm checking the gate." He listened for a moment, then put the telephone down. "She has not left the White House," he said ominously.

"Lieutenant-Commander—"

"Right," Deconcini interrupted Sir Alan. "When Leach left here, he was going to the trophy room, to see if she was still in the White House. He wanted to—"

"Ask her a few subtle questions," said Sir Alan, interrupting in turn.

"Where have they gone, he and she?" asked Mrs. Roosevelt, alarmed.

"I think we had better find out," said Deconcini, dialing another number.

Running up the stairs ahead of the elevator, Deconcini and Norton reached the third floor well before Mrs. Roosevelt and Sir Alan Burton. They ran to the door of the room assigned to Leach, and Deconcini threw his shoulder against it and burst into the room.

Leach lay on a blood-soaked bed, barely breathing. They could hear his breath gurgling through a tiny bullet hole in his throat. He had knocked the half-empty bottle of champagne off his nightstand in a futile attempt to make a noise that would bring help. His eyes were open, and he seemed to recognize Deconcini.

The telephone had been ripped from the wall. "Get help," said Deconcini curtly to Norton. "Get to another phone."

Leaving Leach, Deconcini rushed back into the hall and encountered Mrs. Roosevelt and Sir Alan just emerging from the elevator vestibule.

"Are you armed, Sir Alan?" Deconcini asked.

"Why, no."

"Then . . ." He looked around. "Then, in here," he said, opening the door of the linen room and reaching inside to switch on the lights. "You stay in here. Lock the door from inside if you can. Barricade it. She's loose in the White House with a gun, and she'll kill you, Mrs. Roosevelt, if she sees you. If she can't get to the President—"

"Really, Mr. Deconcini, do you think—"

"Absolutely," said Deconcini curtly. "She has shot Leach. She's somewhere on the third floor, or maybe on the second; and the only thing I can figure is that she's a Nazi fanatic."

"Lieutenant-Commander Leach is—?"

"Alive," said Deconcini. "But the woman is at large and armed."

"We will do as you say," said Mrs. Roosevelt, and she closed the door, shutting herself and Sir Alan in the linen room.

When Deconcini stepped back out into the central hall of the third floor, Norton came toward him.

"I called for help and for reinforcements," he said. "Where the hell you suppose she is?"

"I don't know," said Deconcini grimly. He pulled a snub-nosed revolver from his shoulder holster. "But if you see her—"

"Shoot to kill," said Norton, pulling his own pistol. "They're alert down on the second floor. Soldiers are coming up from the first floor to reinforce the guard around the President's bedroom. I think we can stay up here and begin to search the rooms."

An agent and an army corporal came up the stairs. Deconcini put the soldier in front of the door to the linen room, then he and Norton, backed by the other agent, began to open doors.

They opened six doors and did not find her. An army captain came up the stairs to report that a squad armed with Thompson submachine guns had barricaded itself around the door to the President's bedroom; another was barricaded around the door to the Prime Minister's suite.

The President and the Prime Minister had been informed of what was going on, and the President asked only to be assured that Mrs. Roosevelt was safe. Deconcini formed a cordon of men around her and escorted her down the stairs to join the President.

Deconcini returned to the third floor. Sir Alan had come out of the linen room and was conferring with Norton and the army captain in the central corridor.

"A woman," Sir Alan was saying. "And she could not be heavily armed."

"What if she had grenades?" asked Deconcini.

"Is it possible?"

"Everything she's done has been impossible," said Deconcini.

"We start on this floor, I suppose," said the captain. "Every room. If she tried to go down the east stairs, she runs up against my men in the east hall. If she—"

"*The roof!*" cried Deconcini.

"Why the roof?"

"Maybe she retreated out there when we began to arrive in force up here. Or maybe . . . Let's get out there!"

Deconcini ran along the corridor toward the solarium, turned right, and opened the door onto the rooftop promenade. Sir Alan followed him. They stopped out into the cold and dark of night, uncertain and cautious. Deconcini held his revolver in his right hand. Sir Alan had accepted the captain's .45 Colt.

Deconcini pointed to the west and to the balustrade. "Over the edge there is the President's bedroom," he said quietly, decisively edging forward. "She . . . *My God, look!*"

He was pointing at a sheet tied around a post of the balustrade, just beyond the point where the half circle of the portico met the straight line of the southwest facade. He ran to it and leaned over.

She was there, in the light from the President's bedroom window, hanging on a rope of sheets knotted together. She was pushing against the wall with her feet, as if she meant to swing out and smash into the window with both feet, maybe falling inside the President's bedroom. Or she could be lining herself up to fire a shot.

"Hey!" yelled Deconcini. "Stop or I'll shoot!"

She looked up, and he saw on her face a grimace of furious hate. She raised a hand toward him. He did not see the pistol, but he heard the crack, and a bullet whizzed by his head. He leaned out farther and tried to take aim on the figure swinging between light and darkness below. She raised her arm again, and he knew she was going to fire another shot.

Then suddenly she shrieked and fell out of sight in the darkness below. He heard the thud when she hit the ground, and he heard her scream.

"Convenient thing sometimes, a pocketknife," said Sir Alan Burton coolly. He was refolding his knife. He had knelt behind the balustrade and cut the sheet.

17

Mrs. Roosevelt opened the door between the President's bedroom and his oval study, and the President wheeled himself briskly into the room. It was after one A.M., and he was dressed in his pajamas and a silk monogrammed robe. Winston Churchill, in one of his famous siren suits —a pair of zip-up coveralls tailored in maroon velvet— came in at just about the same time, accompanied by Sir Alan Burton.

"I've word from the surgeons," growled Churchill, his lip out, his mouth twisted with anger. "Lieutenant-Commander Leach will survive. He will be in hospital some weeks and will not be able to rejoin *Duke of York* when she steams to Bermuda; but he will not die of the wound so treacherously inflicted." He scowled at the young woman they had known until now as Bonny Battersby. "Which is well for you, young woman," he growled. "Otherwise, I should have seen you hang if I had to make it a condition of continuing the alliance."

"She will hang anyway," said Harry Hopkins.

The young woman sat in an armchair by the President's desk, her wrists fastened to its arms by two pairs of handcuffs. Her right leg was wrapped in bandages from the knee down, and a trace of blood had soaked through the layers of gauze and made a faint reddish-brown stain.

Her left ankle was tightly bound with tape. Her clothes were torn, and her arms and face were bruised and scraped; but she had not been seriously injured in her fall through the limbs of a small tree and to the ground just outside the trophy-room window: the window she had smashed the night before. She held her chin high, ground her teeth, and stared hard into the face of anyone whose eyes met hers.

"You can interrogate her here if you want," said the President. "All I wanted was a look at the traitor or spy or whatever she is who has caused us so much trouble. I am going back to bed. The Prime Minister and I have more important things to occupy us than the machinations of one squalid little gang of Nazi spies."

"That is exactly so," rumbled Churchill. "So I shall not remain, either. I do, though, wish to express my gratitude to all who have worked to save us from this threat, at great labor and at some risk to life."

"I join in that," said the President. "My very great thanks, particularly to you, Dom. And . . ." He looked up into the face of Mrs. Roosevelt and smiled. "And also to my own special private detective."

"We may all be grateful to her, Mr. President," said Deconcini earnestly. "Without some shrewd instincts she brought to the investigation, we might not have—"

"Actually," Mrs. Roosevelt interrupted with a warm smile, "it was I who have been consistently wrong and Mr. Deconcini who has been consistently correct."

"I shall have a medal struck for each of you," said the President. "And for now, good night." He cast a final glance at the young woman chained to a chair. He shook his head. "Find out what she is, traitor or—"

"I'll tell you, before you go to bed, old man," hissed the young woman. "I am a soldier of the Third Reich, a servant of my *Führer!*" She grinned grotesquely, shifting her eyes to Hopkins, then to Churchill, then back to President Roosevelt. "Your cowardly, stupid little henchman talks of hanging. So does the fat old lackey of Zionism. And I may hang. But you will too, at the end, *from your wheelchair!*"

The President scratched his cheek. He shrugged. "We shall see," he said, and he spun his wheelchair and propelled himself out of the room.

Churchill snorted, turned on his heels, and walked out through the other door.

Mrs. Roosevelt sat down behind the President's desk. She was on the verge of exhaustion, from a long day and from the emotional burden of all that had happened. But she straightened her back and shoulders and spoke to Deconcini as she picked up the telephone, "See if she will answer a few questions, Mr. Deconcini. I will see if a pot of coffee is available."

Deconcini pulled a chair into position so he could sit and face the Nazi woman. Hopkins also sat down, wearily. He still wore his rumpled gray suit, but he had not put on a necktie, and his limp shirt collar hung open. Sir Alan Burton, still erect and alert, took a chair.

The study was dimly lighted. The President's naval prints and ship models were the chief decoration. Usually a restful room, it was now tense. Deconcini leaned forward.

"Are you going to answer any questions?" he asked. "For example, are you going to tell us your name?"

The young woman shrugged. "My name is Eva Ritter," she said.

"How long have you been in this country?"

She sighed. "Since 1934. I volunteered. I had worked as an office girl for an American businessman who maintained a home and business in Dusseldorf, and I had been required by him to learn American-accented English. It was easy enough to come, to establish an identity, to become employed. I was brought into New York Harbor on the liner *Bremen*, came through immigration with a perfectly legitimate passport in the name Eva Ritter, and simply disappeared in this big country."

"And we had no fingerprints on record for you because—"

"Why should you have? I never committed a crime."

"Who do you work for? Who is your chief in Germany?"

She shook her head. "That I will never tell you."

"Von Keyserling was your lover," said Deconcini.

"A wonderful man," she said. "The very ideal of the new Aryan man."

"And Kluber?"

"A soldier. He took his orders from Hasso von Keyserling—and from me."

"Baines?"

She shrugged. "Poor old fool."

"You, uh, cannot write shorthand, can you, Miss Ritter?" asked Mrs. Roosevelt.

Eva Ritter glanced over at Mrs. Roosevelt behind the desk. She shook her head. "Did you notice?"

"Or type very well, either," said Hopkins.

She laughed at him. "Far better than you could imagine, you ignorant fool. By pretending I couldn't, I made myself a reason to remain in the White House during evening hours, when it was easier to do what I was there to do."

"Where had you hidden the pistol?" Deconcini asked. He turned to Mrs. Roosevelt and explained, "The pistol she used to shoot George Leach, and to fire a shot at me, is called a Baby Browning. It is tiny, a purse or pocket pistol. Which is lucky for George Leach; a bigger bullet would have killed him." He faced Eva Ritter again. "Anyway, where was it?"

She laughed. "Under my typewriter at night when your soldiers searched. A metal detector doesn't discover a steel pistol under a steel typewriter. In the day it was inside my clothes. I am full-breasted, as you have noticed, Deconcini; you stared often. The little pistol fit right down between . . ." She tried to gesture, but the handcuffs caught her short. "Well. You can picture the hiding place. No one asked to look."

"And the two small bombs you had?"

"Sooner or later you will find in Leach's room a copy of a 1937 report of the House Agriculture Committee. I doubted anyone would want to read it, so I cut it out and hid my two little packages of TNT inside. The metal detector would have found grenades, but it didn't find my little bombs."

"How did you intend to use them?"

"I didn't intend to use them. Until Baines betrayed us, it seemed unlikely I would ever have to do anything but keep my job, service the telephone taps and radios as needed, and keep my eyes and ears open for useful information. But . . . Well, when Baines deserted us and murdered Kluber, then everything changed."

"Where did Kluber get the grenades and revolver he was carrying the night when Baines killed him?"

"As you have guessed, we brought into the White House as many weapons as we dared: whatever we could obtain, a variety of weapons. Von Keyserling smuggled in the good weapons, the Luger and the Walther. The little Colt you found in Mr. Hopkins's chair—that I bought in a second-hand shop in Virginia. Kluber bought the Baby Browning—a foolish little popgun but easily hidden and deadly at short range. The grenades and the TNT . . . I don't know where the two of them got those."

Someone knocked discreetly. Deconcini let in Henry Taylor, who placed a tray on the President's desk bearing a pot of coffee, cups and saucers, some small sandwiches, and some cookies.

When he noticed Eva Ritter chained to the chair, his mouth fell open. "Oh, Miss—"

"Miss Ritter, Henry," said Deconcini. "Not Miss Battersby. A German. A Nazi. She shot Lieutenant-Commander Leach tonight and tried to assassinate the President."

Eva Ritter had taken the interruption as a moment to flex her shoulders, tug at her handcuffs, stretch her legs. "I'm sorry, Henry," she said. "I couldn't tell you. You *schwartzers* should be on our side. We'll take care of you. What will the Jews ever do for you?"

Stricken, Henry Taylor backed toward the door.

"Thank you, Henry," said Mrs. Roosevelt. "There will be no more calls tonight, I promise. It's New Year's. Find yourself a place to sleep. The cot in the clinic would be a good idea."

The old black man looked down ruefully at Eva Ritter. "What the Jews will do for us, if nothing else," he said, "is not suppose we are ignorant enough to fall for the Hitler line."

"Thanks for the bottle of champagne, Henry," she said to him with a sneer.

"I wish I'd put poison in it," said Henry Taylor as he backed out the door and quietly closed it.

"Where were the weapons and explosives hidden?" asked Deconcini.

"Unhook one hand so I can have some coffee, and I'll tell you," she said.

With a small key he unlocked the cuff on her left wrist. Mrs. Roosevelt pushed a cup of coffee across the desk for Deconcini to hand her. The girl glanced at the sandwiches, and Mrs. Roosevelt put three of those on a napkin and pushed them to where she could reach them on the corner of the desk.

Eva Ritter sipped coffee, then sighed wearily. "Here and there," she said. "It was easy enough until Baines killed Kluber. Baines thought Kluber wanted nothing but a drink of *schnapps* from the liquor cabinet in the pantry. Actually, there was a bottle of nitroglycerine in there— and still is. No one in the Roosevelt White House drinks white *crème de menthe* apparently, and the bottle had been pushed to the back of the cabinet and was dusty and apparently forgotten. Whoever tries to pour a drink from it has a surprise coming. Since there is no one left to use it, you may as well know."

"Mr. Baines didn't know," said Mrs. Roosevelt hopefully.

"Baines knew as little as possible," she said contemptuously. "He had no idea Kluber took orders from me."

"All right," said Deconcini. "Your original purpose was to install telephone taps, transmitters, and—"

"And to transmit or carry out of the White House as much information as possible," said Eva Ritter. "This fool"—glancing toward Hopkins—"let me read and type the most secret of documents. When we learned that the Zionist warmonger Churchill was coming to the White House—which of course I learned from reading the secret papers of Harry Hopkins—my superiors in Berlin decided we had a marvelous opportunity to strike a blow for humanity: eliminate the Jews' two most influential friends at one blow."

"It was a suicide mission," said Sir Alan Burton.

"Of course," she sneered. "Kurt Kluber expected to die. Throwing grenades to clear the way, firing his pistol, he expected to use the nitroglycerine to eliminate both Roosevelt and Churchill—in an explosion he could hardly have escaped himself. In any event, he could not have made his way out of the White House."

"Where were you and what was your role in the Kluber operation?" asked Deconcini.

"I had no role in it, none directly anyway. We still hoped I might not be identified and would be able to continue to carry useful information out of the White House. I knew when he came in. I expected to hear the explosions above."

"Your unlocked window?" asked Deconcini.

"An absurdity," she said. "No one *ever* entered through my window, and if we had known it was unlocked we would certainly have locked it. An accident. One of those little accidents that ruins the best of plans. Baines let Kluber in through Mrs. Nesbitt's window. We would not have risked exposing me by allowing Kluber to climb in through my window."

"But it *was* unlocked and—"

"And that *Gottverdammt* Baines took the precaution of locking Mrs. Nesbitt's window to cover himself," she muttered as she sipped strong black coffee.

"When did you put the pistol in my office chair?" asked Hopkins.

She turned toward him and grinned scornfully. "Oh, in October, I think it was. Just as a backup, as we might say: in case the need for it might arise. I could go to your office pretty much any time I wished. I could retrieve a pistol there and walk down the hall toward the Oval Office." She shrugged. "It might have proved useful sometime."

"Are there others hidden?" asked Deconcini.

She shook her head. "Not anymore."

"All right," said Deconcini. "Now Kluber is dead. What happened next?"

"Hasso . . ." she said quietly, showing human emotion

for the first time. "Hasso and I discussed it. Our orders were to kill Roosevelt and Churchill, and we understood the great importance of that assignment. Once we had been betrayed by the pig Baines, it was much more difficult. Our suicide-soldier had died in futility, and security was much tighter. Baines was at work tearing out all our equipment. Our weapons would be found. We had little time and no choice but to repeat the attempt as soon as possible."

"Friday night," said Hopkins quietly.

"A telegram for you, Mr. Hopkins," she said. "Of course, Hasso could not come through the gate carrying a weapon, so he came without one. I had retrieved the Luger from one of our hiding places: the table on which I was held down tonight while the army doctor worked on my leg. A steel examining table: once again, proof against the metal detectors they were using all through the White House."

"You anticipated the use of mine detectors," said Mrs. Roosevelt.

"Of course. It would have been gross negligence not to have used them."

"So you had the Luger in your desk?" asked Deconcini.

"From about seven o'clock Friday evening I did," she said. "And Hasso arrived. He came to the trophy room, my office."

"And started to smoke a cigarette," said Deconcini.

She started. "Uh . . . Yes. You are an observant snooper, Dom," she said.

"But—"

"But I was urging him to move, to get on with it. He did not have time to indulge in tobacco. Everything was right. All he had to do was go to the pantry. And this time, if Henry Taylor was there, in the way, he was to smash his skull with the butt of the Luger, break open the liquor cabinet, and get out the bottle of nitroglycerine. There were guards at the entrance to the private quarters, but he could heave the explosive at them and eliminate them, then he could rush in and dispatch Roosevelt and maybe Churchill with a few shots. But—"

"But he ran into Baines in the hall," said Deconcini.

"And Baines murdered him!" she shrieked furiously. "As you heard him say in the Cabinet Room. He had no idea of bringing him to trial under so-called American justice. All he meant to do was kill him! He was worth any four of you Jew-mongrel American pigs! Any *six!"*

"Leaving you alone to attempt the assassination," said Sir Alan.

"Yes. Everything was deteriorating so rapidly that I couldn't wait for the return of the fat Englishman. I decided to go for the President alone."

"And Mr. Baines frustrated you once again," said Mrs. Roosevelt.

"Yes. Baines still didn't know who I was, but he must have understood that, whoever I was, I wouldn't give up. I took my two little TNT bombs from the volume of agriculture reports and started up in the elevator. If only I could have reached the second floor, I could have tossed a bomb in the middle of the hall, then come across shooting, with still another bomb in my hands." She shook her head. "Baines was prowling the White House. He fired at me through the elevator doors. I dropped to the floor and returned his fire. Unfortunately, I only wounded him."

"With the Walther you had hidden . . . ?"

Eva Ritter grinned. "I shouldn't tell you. Your Major Bentz will be a better snoop next time. It was in the electrical switch box in the elevator vestibule—the one with the switches and fuses for the elevator machinery—in the paper carton that once contained extra fuses, those big cylindrical fuses that go in that kind of equipment.

Again, a steel pistol inside a steel box. If Major Bentz were a member of *our* security forces, he would be *shot* for his inefficiency."

"And when you came back down—"

"Everything had gone wrong," she said. "I couldn't believe I would escape. But I ran back to the trophy room, replaced my TNT in the agriculture reports, smashed out the window, and—"

"And struck yourself in the face," said Mrs. Roosevelt.

"Banged my face on the edge of my desk," said Eva Ritter.

"It took a certain amount of courage," said Mrs. Roosevelt quietly.

"Which all of us have in superior measure," said the young German woman. "Which is what will defeat you in the end."

"And tonight, then?"

"It was beyond winning, I supposed. I thought I'd had my last chance. When you"—she glanced at Hopkins—"called on me to take notes of the meeting with Baines, I was astonished. But I came. Of course I couldn't take shorthand, but I thought I might brazen it out and learn how much you knew and what chance I had to make still another attempt. I had, after all, one more pistol, and I still had my TNT bombs."

"L'ftenant-Commahnder Leach . . . ?" asked Sir Alan.

She sighed. "Oh, let me scratch my nose first." She had finished her coffee and sandwiches, and Deconcini was reaching to reattach her left wrist to the arm of the chair. "I thought I could use him to get some inside information about security arrangements and the course of the investigation," she said as he snapped the cuff once more around her wrist. "Also, Hasso had ordered me to learn anything I could about the radar equipment aboard *Duke of York*. Tonight George was just a convenient way to stay in the White House and to get to another floor. All our attempts to get to the second floor from the ground floor had come to naught. I thought maybe I could get down from the third floor. That's why I offered to spend the night with Leach in his room."

"And you shot him."

"He knew too much. I thought I could slip out after he was asleep, especially after he drank most of a bottle of champagne. But he was suspicious of me. I think his suspicion must have been nearly accurate."

"What made you think you could get down from the roof to—"

"Desperation," she said. "It was my duty to make a last attempt, any way I could, so long as I was alive. I had shot Leach and was on my way to the stairs when I heard you running up. I ducked inside the nearest door, which happened to be the linen room. I grabbed some sheets and ran for the door to the roof, not sure if I would try to lower myself to the ground or might find one more chance to get to the second floor. I got out on the promenade and . . . Well. I found myself right above the window to the President's bedroom."

"Two more minutes . . ." murmured Deconcini.

She grinned brightly. "That close," she said. "After everything else had failed, after our carefully laid plans had resulted in nothing but the death of two fine young Germans; after all that, I came within two minutes of succeeding by an impromptu effort that I was driven to by desperation. Could any of you have done it, Deconcini? Mrs. Roosevelt? Could any of you? We of the Third Reich are trained for things like that! You escaped tonight, but you will not always have luck on your side. Another time will come! Then—"

"Then you will learn again," Mrs. Roosevelt interrupted, "that people you call 'Jew-mongrels' and 'schwartzers' and the like are *at least* as strong, *at least* as brave and intelligent as you think you are. And it will be your Mr. Hitler, and not my husband, who will come to a shameful end."

Epilogue

Eva Ritter was tried for espionage and attempted murder before a closed military court. Convicted, she was sentenced to death. Mrs. Roosevelt suggested to the President that he should exercise executive clemency, but the attorney general, who had other spies to contend with, did not recommend it; and on Saturday, April 18, 1942, Eva Ritter was hanged on a gallows temporarily erected inside a warehouse in the Navy Yard.

Gerald Baines, tried before the same court, was convicted of espionage; but, in view of all the circumstances, including his testimony for the prosecution, he was sentenced to just two years' imprisonment, against which was credited the months he had spent in jail pending the trial. He was discharged from the Secret Service, forfeiting his accumulated retirement benefits.

His wife and daughter were held in custody only three days. While Baines was in prison his wife took employment as a waitress in a Connecticut Avenue restaurant. His daughter, Cecile, continued to work as a night clerk in a pharmacy. So they were able to retain their home, to which Baines returned when he was released from the federal penitentiary in Atlanta in January 1944. He took a job in an A&P market, stamping prices on packages and boxes. When he retired in August 1955 he was an assistant manager of the supermarket.

Baines's sister and her family survived their ordeal at the hands of the Gestapo. Reestablished in their Antwerp home, they urged Baines to bring his family to Belgium. Cecile Baines accepted their invitation and went there in 1948. She married a Brussels physician.

Lieutenant-Commander George Leach recovered from his wound but never rejoined the *Duke of York*. He was assigned to the British staff of the Combined Chiefs of Staff Committee. In June 1944 he married the daughter of a vice president of Morgan Guaranty Trust; and after the war he remained in the United States, establishing residence in Greenwich, Connecticut.

In May 1942 Dominic Deconcini requested his release from the Secret Service so that his United States Marine Corps reserve commission might be activated. He served as a Marine lieutenant, then captain, in the Pacific. He was awarded the Distinguished Service Cross for gallantry under fire on Iwo Jima. Wounded, he was discharged. He returned to the Secret Service and duty in the White House. In the 1950s he and his wife were occasional guests of Mrs. Roosevelt at her New York apartment and at Val-Kill, where twice they spent Christmas with her.

In January of 1959 Mrs. Roosevelt received a letter from a woman who signed herself Irma Ritter. She was, she said, the sister of Eva Ritter and asked Mrs. Roosevelt to intervene with President Eisenhower to secure the release of the body of Eva Ritter, that it might be exhumed and returned to Germany for burial. Mrs. Roosevelt forwarded the request to Attorney General William P. Rogers, but an assistant attorney general replied for him that the Justice Department had no record of how the body had been disposed of and could not meet the request. Mrs. Roosevelt so advised Irma Ritter in a sympathetic letter.